NORAH BENNETT

EVERNIGHT PUBLISHING ®

www.evernightpublishing.com

Copyright© 2016

Norah Bennett

Editor: Katelyn Uplinger

Cover Artist: Jay Aheer

ISBN: 978-1-77339-079-6

NORAH BENNETT

DEDICATION

To Laura, Samantha, Mina, and my sweet husband, Samy, who encouraged me every step of the way. You never even blinked when I said I was going to write fiction. You rolled up your sleeves, helped me create a new identity as a romance writer, and answered my social media pleas for help at all hours of the day and night. I thank God for you.

To Carl Carruba, the first person I trusted to read what I wrote. Although this isn't the story of Max and Nina, your support and thoughtful critique of my work encouraged me to keep writing. You never doubted I would get published and because you believed, I did too. Don't worry, Max and Nina will make their debut shortly.

To Jules Dixon who innocently answered my plea for a critique partner two and a half years ago and got saddled with a needy, newbie for life. Few give of their time, experience and energy as you do. Thanks for talking me off ledge, giving me a reality check, and frankly telling me to stop whining and write. I needed every one of those written and verbal counselling sessions. Your unwavering belief in me propelled me forward. I cannot thank-you enough for all your mentorship.

NORAH BENNETT

R.I.L.Y. FOREVER

Norah Bennett

Copyright © 2016

Chapter One

Julia stood outside Lexi's front door trying not to vomit on the wriggling child in her arms or the cream colored pumps torturing her feet. Her stomach churned and although a cool breeze carrying the scent of freshly cut grass and spring blooms brushed against her cheeks and ran its fingers through hcher long, blonde hair, sweat trickled down her back and between her breasts. After twenty-two years of monopolizing her dreams, Ethan Sullivan had somehow stepped through the veil separating fantasy and reality and found her. Logically speaking, Ethan was a common name with hundreds, possibly thousands of men named Ethan, any of which could be in Lexi's house. But Julia knew with all certainty, her Ethan, the man who stole her heart when she was sixteen and whose heart she shredded in return, found his way back to her. He was the only man in all of her forty years to love her, really love her. She never knew a love like that, not before him and not since losing him. She had no choice but to let him go all those years ago, but he didn't know that.

Should I knock or run?

Julia was paralyzed and petrified, unable to make a decision. Five minutes into this exercise, Lilly reached her two-year-old limit. She squirmed in Julia's arms and reached for the doorbell, her new favorite toy in any house.

"Down, down, down!"

"Okay, Lilly, just a minute."

"No, Mama. Stop. Down."

Lilly was a persistent ball of energy who recently mastered the word "no" and peppered her vocabulary with it. Despite her angelic features—chubby cheeks, blonde ringlets, and big green eyes—Lilly could go from angelic to possessed in seconds. Over the last three months, when she didn't get her way, she shrieked and held her breath until her lips turned blue, her eyes rolled to the back of her head, and she lost consciousness. Each time Lilly acted out in this fashion, she sucked the will to live right out of Julia.

Julia had two choices: harness her nerves and deal, or continue wrestling with a restless toddler whose piercing screams would bring the entire house, if not the entire neighborhood, out to see what massacre was taking place on Lexi's front lawn. Either way, the night was sure to be life altering.

"Okay, Lils. Go ahead and ring the doorbell. Mama's going to stop being a chicken-shit now. Oh darn it, that's going to cost me another dollar in the potty mouth jar."

Lilly giggled and jabbed her tiny finger over the doorbell repeatedly. The incessant ringing brought Lexi to the door and Julia's pulse ratcheted. She was sure the galloping of her heart could be heard by anyone within a five-mile radius.

"Well, well, look who finally decided to show. Come on in, we're starved. Hello sweetness. How's the world's most beautiful baby today?"

Julia put Lilly down, straightening the child's

fuchsia party dress. Lilly squealed in delight and pulled at Lexi's skirt, insisting to be picked up. She got her wish while Julia lingered behind.

Julia was used to being ignored when Lilly was in the room and today Lilly was a fantastic diversion, giving her a few extra moments to pull herself together. Julia flapped her slick palms in front of her, trying to dry them then tugged at the skirt of her simple silk, coral shift dress. Lord, she was a wrinkled mess. She tucked her hair behind her ear, took a deep, steadying breath, and followed them in. Dropping Lilly's bag and her purse in the entryway, she followed the sound of laughter and conversation and the delicious smell of Lexi's famous lasagna wafting from the kitchen.

Julia stood out of eyesight and listened as Lilly and Lexi made their grand entrance and everyone oohed and ahhed over her baby girl. Like a coward, she hid in the hallway and identified the owner of each voice: Lexi, Todd, Aimee, Adam, Christine, and … Ethan. Two decades had flown by, but she could recognize his husky voice and sexy laugh anywhere. She sagged into the nearest wall as an electric current, raced through every nerve and into each muscle group of her limbs, rendering them useless. This was the moment she dreamed of and the moment she feared. Although her limbs were paralyzed, her brain was a runaway train speeding through images of the past so fast, everything was a blur until it came to the last day she laid eyes on Ethan. There the train came to a screeching halt, then proceeded in slow motion.

Julia closed her eyes and gripped the silver, heart-shaped locket hanging around her neck and hovered between her breasts. Although decades had elapsed, she clearly saw the two young people standing by the creek, behind the high school, still dressed in their graduation attire—so innocent, so in love.

"Here are your wings and my heart, baby. Go ahead and fly. I won't hold you back. Remember I love you, forever," young Ethan said, his voice breaking, his eyes filling with tears.

"RILY, forever." Those words were inscribed on the inside of the locket he'd given her, the one Julia wore every day since. The front was uniquely designed as two angel wings folded side by side with marcasite gemstones embedded throughout. The wings separated and opened from the center to reveal the hidden inscription. It was a beautiful, one-of-a-kind treasure that reminded her no matter what life bombarded her with, she was one of the lucky ones. She knew what it was to be loved. Ethan had loved her with a passion and ferocity few experienced. He'd loved her enough to let her go.

Julia held no illusions of rekindling that all-consuming, life-altering young love they once shared. The time for that had long past and she no longer believed in or wanted to drown in that crippling emotion. Perhaps if Ethan was willing to let the past stay buried, they could start fresh and renew the precious friendship they once shared. Because before they were lovers, they were friends. Ethan promised they'd always have one another. That promise, however, was made when they were young and naïve, swayed by the power of their own emotions and convinced their love could conquer anything life threw at them.

Julia wiped her sweaty palms down her dress, this time not caring about the streaks she left on the silk. She pasted on a smile and entered the room on teetering legs. She scanned the room, searching for her baby and was relieved to find Christine and Lexi entertaining Lilly, while Todd, Lexi's current boyfriend, stood close by looking bored. Perusing the rest of the room, her eyes landed on Adam, Lexi's brother, uncorking a bottle of wine at the kitchen island while Aimee, her best friend, stood chatting with Ethan.

Julia stopped walking, thinking, breathing! Her world narrowed to him—his tousled, thick, brown hair, his mesmerizing gray-blue eyes that changed with his every mood, and his long, thick lashes that were the envy of every girl in high school. Julia devoured Ethan with her eyes. She couldn't help herself. She was starved. He was taller and more built than she recalled, but his handsome face with its square chin, slightly crooked nose from years of playing football, and full, sensuous lips, was the same image that visited her dreams nightly.

Julia knew the instant he became aware of her. He stopped answering Aimee as his gaze shifted and centered on her. His pupils widened and his eyes darkened to a smoky gray. Aimee followed his gaze. Her brows furrowed and she took a step toward Julia. But Ethan grasped her elbow and shook his head.

Julia's eyes never left Ethan's tall, muscular frame as he walked toward her. The room and all its inhabitants fell away until there was only him. The soft caress of his eyes touched every inch of her. She studied his face, but his expression was neutral. He stood silently examining her and it was left to Julia to break the silence. The problem was she had no idea what to say. No words were adequate to express how she felt. But as her eyes locked with his, she hoped they voiced what her lips couldn't. She missed him. Missed him every second, minute, and hour they were apart. When he was hers, he was her best friend, her lover, her confidant. He was her everything. When she lost him, the ground beneath her feet shook so violently, it brought her to her knees and it took years to learn how to stand on her own, without him.

Tears pooled in Julia's eyes and spilled down her

cheeks. She wrapped her arms around herself. Ethan's assessing gaze tracked her every movement and then his eyes, followed by his mouth, softened.

He remembered.

He was the only person, other than Ella, who understood why she was compelled to hold herself together in this manner. What it meant. She hadn't folded into herself like this in a long time, hadn't allowed her past to bubble up to the present, and hadn't allowed the hurt to bleed to the surface. The understanding and pity she read on Ethan's face was more than she could bear. Old wounds that had scarred over stretched and pulled.

A sharp, tearing pain started in Julia's chest and as she rubbed her breastbone and gasped for air, her fight-or-flight reflex kicked in. She couldn't do this, not here, not now. If she didn't move now, those old scars would rip open and her already traumatized heart would be shredded. Tearing her gaze from his, she shook her head, turned and ran out of the room and out of the house.

Julia slumped against her car, bent at the waist, and sobbed. She wept for all the lost years, all the time she could've spent with him and could've had him in her arms and in her life. She cried for the two young people who loved and lived for each other, but were ripped apart due to the intolerance of one manipulative man. Scenes from the past she'd buried unearthed themselves and assaulted her. She was lost to the first time she saw his face and he smiled shyly at her and lost to the first time he slid her a note in biology class asking her out. She remembered the first time he held her, kissed her, and the first time he made love to her and told her he loved her.

Julia didn't hear Ethan approach until his hands reached for her. He grasped her shoulders, straightened her, and pulled her into his arms. At first she resisted and tried to pull free, but he tightened his arms around her like he did a hundred times before. Ethan slid one hand in her hair and held the back of her head to him, cocooning her in his warm embrace. As she buried her face in the side of his neck, his other arm wrapped around her waist, molding her to his frame.

She gave in. She melted into his familiar yet new embrace. He was no longer a teenager, but a grown man. His powerful arms held her firmly to him. This was how he'd always held her when she hurt. He would wrap his body around hers, protecting her from the world and all its inhabitants and whisper, "I've got you baby. It's okay, let go. I've got you and *I'm* not letting go." She missed this the most—someone to hold her, comfort her, and keep her safe—even if it was for a few minutes. She inhaled Ethan's familiar, spicy scent, her body and mind remembering what it was to be soothed by him, and so she was.

Her crying ceased and she pulled away, raw and exposed. She couldn't believe she unraveled in front of him and a houseful of people. What the hell was she supposed to say to him or to them now? She rarely fell apart, in public or otherwise. Julia hated crying and she didn't allow herself to do it often. Crying was a waste of time and energy and it showed weakness. It solved nothing, left a person vulnerable, and it was damn messy. She was grateful she always carried tissues in her pocket for Lilly because she was certain she looked like a hot mess with mascara streaming down her blotchy, reddened face. She pulled one out and dried her face and nose.

"I—I'm sorry. I don't…" She dropped her head again and closed her eyes. Clenching her fists until her nails bit into her palms, she struggled to lasso her runaway emotions. She took a deep breath and raised her head. The second their eyes met, *poof*, the words escaped and she didn't have the energy to pursue them. Julia

13

opened and closed her mouth having no idea where to start. What used to come easy was impossible now. She longed for the days when they talked about anything and everything for hours, the words sliding from their mouths like warm chocolate syrup over ice-cream, smooth, sleek, and satisfying.

"Hello, Julia."

Julia examined every inch of his face, noting the fine lines around his eyes, a new addition to his handsome features, and the familiar dimple on his right cheek she used to tease him about. To the untrained eye he appeared calm, even welcoming, without a hint of anger or loathing clouding his handsome features. However, she'd made an art of studying his face. In the time they'd spent together she mastered its every expression and nuance. Hell, she could've earned a degree in it. She catalogued his tightly controlled smile that didn't reach his eyes, the almost imperceptible tick in his jaw, and the squaring of his shoulders.

Over the years Julia imagined their reunion a thousand different ways. She ran scenario after scenario in her head and each time his anger and hurt crashed over her like a tidal wave, smothering her and pulling her under. He wasn't one to hide his feelings or play games. In her imagined reunions, he didn't hold back. He lashed out, his words biting, his pain scoring her soul. She deserved no less. But the person standing in front of her had matured, morphing into someone her heart recognized and claimed, while her brain whispered a word of caution. He was tightly wound, his every word and movement controlled. Although he held and comforted her as she cried, sympathy and kindness weren't the only emotions he was experiencing. They were the only ones he was choosing to unleash at this time. This was a new Ethan.

"Hi Eth," she whispered. "It's … it's good to see you again."

"Is it?" he said, as he folded his arms across his chest.

Yup, he was hurt and he was angry. He was all the things she imagined he would be. He was holding it all in. Was it good to see him again? That one question was a tipping point for a hundred more. Julia was astute enough to recognize what he was asking. She read each question in his eyes.

Where the hell have you been all these years?
Why did you go?
After everything we shared, everything we were to each other, how could you walk away?
How could you tear us apart so callously?
Why?
Why?

So many questions, so much pain. She owed him an explanation. She wanted to give him closure. It was the only thing she could offer him, but it came at a high price, one she'd saved for, but still couldn't afford. The simple answer was—God, yes! It was good to see him. She would give him that simple, honest answer now because it was the truth and because she needed to say it and he needed to hear it. He deserved a full explanation, and maybe one day she'd be brave enough to utter the words that would surely tear his world apart, but not here and not now.

Licking her lips, she straightened her spine, cleared her throat, and said in a strong, clear voice that left no doubt to her sincerity, "Yes, Ethan. It *is* good to see you. Really, really good! It's been a long time."

Silence. She waited in silence doing her best to stand still and not squirm under his intense gaze as a variety of emotions passed over his features. After a few minutes he seemed to reach a decision. He unfolded his arms and the storm clouds cleared from his eyes. With a hint of a smile he said, "Yes, it has. Too long I think. I guess you were surprised to see me."

Julia let out the breath she was holding and her shoulders sagged in relief. "Yes and no. Lexi told me she invited a friend to dinner who recently moved to Lakes Crossing and joined the staff at Lakes Community Hospital. Yesterday she mentioned the friend's name was Ethan and for some odd reason my gut told me it was you. I thought my imagination was running away with me. Guess not." Julia looked down at her hands. "I'm sorry about all the drama. Everyone must think I've lost my mind."

She glanced back at the house thinking she better go apologize for her behavior and check on Lilly. Then his words hit her. He said *she* was surprised to see him.

"Wait, you weren't surprised to see me? You knew I'd be here?"

"Yes and no," he teased. "I had no idea you and Aimee would be here. When Aimee arrived, we were both surprised to see each other and we behaved like lunatics hugging and kissing. Aimee told me you were on your way. She wanted to call you, to warn you, I guess. But I convinced her it would be okay. Maybe I should've let her call you, but I was afraid you wouldn't come. I'm sorry you were upset, but I wanted to see you. It's good to see you again. You're even more beautiful than you were twenty-two years ago."

Ethan's smile widened and this time it went all the way to his eyes and all the way to her heart rendering her speechless. Julia's body heated at the compliment and she felt her face burn. She looked down at her hands again, unable to hold his gaze. Now what?

She wasn't ready to deal with the past.

She had no idea of how to proceed in the present.

And, she was both excited and terrified of the future.

Panic set in. Her palms dampened and the tearing pain in her chest made a comeback. This wasn't one of her dreams or one of her many reunion scenarios. This was happening … here, now. She'd never planned for nice. She'd planned for resentment and recriminations. Why did he have to be so damned nice? One minute he was aloof, holding back his hurt and anger, and the next he was charming and genuinely happy to see her. She was spiraling, overwhelmed and confused.

"Jules, look at me," Ethan commanded.

Jules. No one had called her Jules in a long time. She was Julia to everyone, but Ethan. From the very first day he met her, he dubbed her Jules and each time he said her name, she felt precious.

"Take it easy. It's going to be okay. We have a lot of catching up to do, but I guess we'll have plenty of opportunity to do so since we'll be working at the same hospital."

Relieved, Julia took a calming breath. She'd been granted a reprieve for the time being. "Yes, Adam mentioned you're a pediatrician."

"A pediatric oncologist, actually. I'll be starting at Lakes Community Hospital in a week. What do you do?"

"Respiratory therapy. I moved to New York to attend Holy Cross University after graduation. I completed a community-based rotation at Lakes Community Hospital and I loved it. New York never felt like home, but this little New Jersey town did. I fell in love with Lakes Crossing and I was lucky enough to be offered a fulltime position at the hospital. The people are great. They're very welcoming. It's a small town, but there's a lot to do and see. And…"

She was babbling and sounded like a commercial for the town. She had to stop. She cleared her throat. "Uh, what made you come to Lakes Crossing?"

"I've been in Boston since I finished my residency and I needed a change of scene. I've known Adam and Lexi since undergrad and we've kept in touch. Adam told me Lakes was expanding their pediatric services, so here I am. I'm trying to put this all together, though. You obviously know Adam from the hospital, but how do you know Lexi?"

It was a good question with an easy answer, but she hoped she wouldn't have to go there so soon.

"Uh … well. Adam introduced me to her and well … Lexi handled my divorce."

"I'm sorry, Jules. I didn't mean to bring up a painful subject."

"It's okay. It's in the past," she said in a small, sad voice as she reached for the locket nestled between her breasts and fisted it.

His eyes shifted from her face, down her neck and to her chest. She felt the locket come to life, heat, and pulse in her hand.

"Is that…? It can't be. After all these years, after all this time…"

Julia met Ethan's eyes and nodded, cutting him off. She swallowed passed the orange-sized lump in her throat. Her eyes filled with tears and she looked away. She didn't have it in her to continue this conversation, not where it was going. Seeing him after so many years wrung her out. She was as wobbly as an over-cooked noodle. If they delved further into the past right now, she'd lose it. She needed time to adjust to having him in her world again.

Julia released the locket that had imprinted itself on her palm and turned back toward him.

"I have to go in and see to Lilly. She can be a handful when I'm not around."

She was using Lilly to get some distance and after a second of hesitation, he smiled and let her have that play.

"Sure. There's plenty of time to catch up. Let's go see what mini-Julia is up to. Did you know that kid is the spitting image of you? She's sweet, Jules."

"Thanks, but she has her moments. Lately she's been doing her damnedest to try my patience. We'll see if you still think she's sweet when she throws a fit. She specializes in those."

Together they walked back to the house and into the kitchen where Lilly came barreling into Julia. Lilly wrapped her small body around her mother's legs and pulled at Julia's dress. Everyone looked up and then continued what they were doing as if nothing extraordinary had happened. Aimee's troubled eyes met Julia's from across the room. Julia nodded, assuring her friend she hadn't lost her mind.

"Mama, up. Mama, up." Lilly's demanding voice broke through Julia's fog.

"Say please, Lilly."

"No. No."

The hint of willfulness Julia heard in her child's voice warned a tantrum was right around the corner. Julia had to turn things around or the evening was going to come to an early end. Lilly, she learned the very hard way, had a remarkable amount of stamina and stubbornness for a child her age. Once she committed to getting her way, it could be hours before she capitulated. The terrible twos had hit the Walker household like the plague a few weeks back and Julia had yet to discover the magical antidote.

Julia called upon the directory of tricks she

learned from the dozens of *Super Nanny* episodes she watched. She ignored everyone, including Ethan, and took charge of Little Miss Demanding before Lilly took charge of *her*.

Julia bent down to Lilly's eye level. "Lilly, do you want me to pick you up?"

"Yesh. Yesh." Lilly fisted her tiny hands at her waist and stomped her patent leather shoes.

"I'll pick you up as soon as you ask nicely and say please. If you don't say please, you and I are going up to Aunt Lexi's room for a time-out. Do you understand?"

For a few seconds Lilly glared at her mother and thrust out her lower lip in an adorable pout. Lord the child was cute and a weaker woman would have caved. But if she did, it would be a free-for-all for the rest of the night. In a move Julia couldn't have predicted, Lilly turned to Ethan, tugged on his pants, and raised her arms.

"Up, pu-weese."

Julia's mouth hung open as she stared first at her child—who normally was distrustful of strangers, especially men—and then at Ethan. She heard her friends' hushed laughter, but she couldn't tear her gaze away from the surprising scene playing before her.

"Sure, angel face. Up you go." Ethan hoisted Lilly into his strong arms and held her to him as if he'd been doing this her entire life. He smiled at her and the little rat snuck a peek at Julia then gave Ethan her most adorable toothy grin followed by a loud smooch on his cheek.

"Thank-um." Lilly laid her head on his chest and stuck her thumb in her mouth.

"You're very welcome. I haven't been kissed like that in a long time."

Okay, this was too much. In less than five minutes, Ethan had somehow won Lilly's trust, gotten her to say please and thank you, and was granted one of her few precious kisses. Although he'd always been good with children, Julia never knew he was the antidote to the terrible twos.

"Okay Lils, good please and thank you. Come to Mama and leave Ethan alone. You look tired, baby." Julia tried to take Lilly out of Ethan's arms, but her daughter surprised her again. Like a baby ape, she latched on to Ethan's shirt and wrapped her chubby legs around his middle, molding herself to his frame.

"No. No." Lilly protested.

Ethan's arms went around the child and tenderness flooded his face. "She's fine," he murmured as he gazed down at the bundle in his arms. "I don't mind. Besides, I come with experience. Angel here is going to nap on me I think. Why don't you get a drink and relax?"

Ethan rubbed Lilly's back in soothing circles, just the way she liked it. The child settled deeper into him, her eyelids drooping. Julia was riveted by the beautiful picture they made.

"Okay. If you're sure. Let me know when you've had enough and I'll take her."

"No worries. We're perfect as we are, aren't we angel eyes?"

Ethan whispered in Lilly's ear and she smiled and tumbled deeper in sleep. He cradled the child and kissed her forehead. Julia's chest ached, this time in a good way.

Julia envied her child's ability to let go and trust the people in her world to keep her safe. Lilly's life, to this point, was unblemished, pristine—untouched by ugliness, pain and tragedy. Of course, she could surrender to sleep. Her world was filled with goodness and light. Julia had done everything in her power to shelter her. She made damn sure Lilly never knew the darkness and for as long as she could, she would. Julia hadn't been so lucky and she wanted her baby to have the one thing she never had, not until Ethan entered her life … joy and everything that came with it. Love. Acceptance. Peace. Safety. Security.

She had it.

She lost it.

And now Ethan was back. He waltzed right into her life, grabbed her by the heart, and started twirling her around and around. Her world, which had dimmed for twenty-two years, was now flooded with blinding sunshine, warming her as she danced with him under its powerful rays. She had no idea how to execute this dance, the steps were complex and the lunges and twirls that were sure to come were down right terrifying. Yet, she was helpless to resist the hypnotic rhythm of the song that kept her feet moving and her body swaying right along with his.

Years ago, like Lilly Julia let go, trusting him to lead her, to not let her stumble and fall. But he couldn't protect her. Those days were long gone. Now, if she chose to continue this dance, she'd have to sharpen her skills and learn some new moves. Over the years she learned a valuable lesson about the dance called life. At any time, day or night, the smooth, glossy floor you were dancing on could turn to rubble. No matter how flawless or polished your performance was, the end was inevitable … you'd still stumble and you'd still fall.

Chapter Two

Ethan woke up to the sounds of the forest as he did every morning since moving into the farmhouse at the edge of Lakes Crossing. The place was a ramshackle wreck, but he fell in love with it the second he laid eyes on it. Adam thought he was insane to take on a project of this magnitude, but all Ethan saw was potential. According to the realtor, the old colonial-style stone farmhouse was built somewhere around 1900, although no one knew for sure. It sat on twenty-three acres of beautiful, heavily wooded land and had five bedrooms, two baths, and a multitude of nondescript rooms. Every single room was dated and falling apart, and it took the men two weeks of back-breaking labor to get one room habitable enough for Ethan to move in to.

Ethan stretched his aching body and thanked God the place had running water and electricity. He shivered under the down comforter thinking if it was this cool in May, he better make good use of the summer and come up with a plan to prepare the place for winter or he'd freeze to death. Today marked the beginning of his last week of vacation. He planned to spend it meeting with a few contractors he needed to do some of the work on the house and surrounding property. Although he could do much of the repairs on his own, if he didn't hire help, he would be old and gray before the place was done.

Studying the cracked ceiling, peeling walls, and rotting floorboards, Ethan realized he still had a shitload of work to do to in this room alone, but he came into this project with his eyes wide open. It was going to take years to restore the house to its former glory. But that was fine because he had a lot of time on his hands and needed the distraction. Putting all his energy into a massive project like this meant he'd be too tired to think about the last two years of his life and what a fucking waste they were.

He and Alyssa were married for four long, arduous years filled with argument after argument over everything and anything. From the second he put a ring on her finger, to the second she threw it at his head when their divorce was finalized, he had nothing but heartache. It took two full years to get her and her team of lawyers to agree to a reasonable divorce settlement, and when it was all said and done, he wondered what she got out of the hell she'd put them both through. After the divorce was final, he packed everything that meant anything to him, which in hindsight was precious little, and moved to New Jersey.

It took months of covert planning to get this move to happen. If it weren't for Adam and Lexi, he didn't think he'd be here. Had Alyssa gotten wind of his plans to start a new life without her, she would've done everything in her power to sabotage him at every turn, just for the hell of it. That was her way. If she couldn't be happy—and he finally came to terms with the fact she was incapable of being happy—then she wouldn't allow him to be happy either. Adam and Lexi, God love them, appointed themselves his superheroes and waded into the fray to help plan his escape. Lexi handled the legal mess, while Adam helped Ethan manage the relocation of his personal and professional life to New Jersey. He thanked God for their friendship every day.

Ethan sat up, stretched, and grabbed his cell from the moving box that served as his nightstand to check the time. 7:30 already. Time to get up and greet the day. Unlike many people, he was a morning person, waking up with more energy than he knew what to do with. This was a major point of contention with Adam who'd been his college and med school roommate. Adam didn't join the land of the living until 10:00 a.m. and then stayed surly until12:00 p.m.

Ethan met Adam Coulter his freshmen year at Duke University. They were assigned to the same dorm room and unlike most students who wanted to kill their roommates by the end of the first week, they got along great once they learned to safely navigate around each other in the morning hours. Adam strongly believed the phrase "good morning" was a contradiction of terms.

Over the years Ethan and Adam formed a close friendship. The Coulters essentially adopted Ethan and Lexi was like a sister to him, although it wasn't always that way. When Adam brought Ethan home for Thanksgiving that first year, Lexi took one look at him and fell hard. Ethan was still mourning Julia's loss and wasn't interested in starting a relationship with anyone. When he came out of the fog of misery, the only thing he was interested in was school. In time, Lexi got over her crush and they formed a close friendship. Ethan couldn't help but wonder how his life would have unfolded if he'd let Lexi in when she pursued him or if he'd listened to Adam and not married Alyssa.

Alyssa was his biggest mistake and his biggest regret. After years of battling his parents and not giving in to family pressure to marry the right type of girl, Ethan dropped his guard for one lousy family dinner and got saddled with Alyssa for his troubles. In less than six months, under his parent's vigilant eyes and manipulative ways, his relationship with Alyssa advanced at the speed of light, from a few casual dates to wedding plans. It was the first time in his life he had his parent's full attention and approval. Like any child, he reveled in their praise and acceptance not seeing the path he was travelling would lead to disaster, until it was too late.

Adam tried to convince him to reconsider his

engagement, but Ethan felt obligated and pressured to go through with the wedding. By the time it was all said and done, the wedding resembled a three-ring circus. While Alyssa had the time of her life, he was miserable. That pretty much described the next four years of their marriage, followed by two years of separation, reconciliation, unending family arguments, and the ugliest divorce proceedings imaginable.

Ethan pulled on his running gear and laced up his sneakers. It was time to clear his head and the best way to do that was to run. Thanks to Alyssa, he developed a love for this solitary sport that challenged his body and lulled his mind into serenity. While he picked his way to the front of the house, avoiding the piles of power tools, boxes of nails, and wires that snaked out of the walls and hung from the ceilings, he sketched out his day. Exercise, shower, and then breakfast at the diner he discovered during his run the day before.

After breakfast, he'd give in and stop by the massive Food-Feast in town to stock up on groceries. Other than coffee and beer, he didn't have anything in the house. Grocery stores, especially the ones that took up an entire city block, or in this case an entire strip mall, intimidated him. They were too large and offered too many damn choices. While he got lost and wandered from aisle to aisle unable to make a decision, the women he observed there seemed to know exactly what they wanted and where it was located. Those women intimidated him too.

Ethan stepped out into the sunny, but chilly day, filled his lungs with clean forest air, and scanned the small rundown cobblestone courtyard in front of the house. It too was a mess with weeds growing in between each cream-colored brick, and green moss, like primordial ooze, beginning to blanket them. In the center of the courtyard was a large, circular fish pond with a water fountain in its center, also made out of the same cream-colored stones the courtyard and farmhouse were constructed of. The pond was filled with rainwater, dirt, weeds, and God knew what else. Getting it cleaned and working was going to be a hell of a job. But Ethan was determined come July, he'd hear the sound of splashing water along with the birds singing in the trees. At the end of his run he'd stick his head under the running fountain to cool off.

Ethan put his body through a series of stretches that had his muscles tightening and tingling, preparing for their daily challenge. He never listened to music on his runs, preferring the sights and sounds that came from his surroundings—the awakening of nature, the city and all its inhabitants. He learned a lot about Lakes Crossing and its people through his morning runs. This wasn't hard to do since the entire city was a little over three square miles. Each day, he took a new route discovering the small town's historic homes and buildings as well as its lush green parks.

Finished warming up, Ethan found his rhythm on the pavement and let his muscles and joints take over the running, while his brain did double duty, cataloging the scenery for review later and reviewing the previous day's surprising events. He ran down Spring Street, the town's main drag lined with a variety cafés, diners, boutiques, and antique shops on both sides. People recognized him and many waved or called out a greeting. He returned their gestures, warmed by their acceptance of the stranger amongst them. He loved this charming town of 8,000 inhabitants. He couldn't believe how lucky he was to get out of Boston and to land in this well-kept secret, deep in the woods of Northwest Jersey.

He left Boston in hopes of starting fresh,

rebuilding, and finding some peace. So far, his decision to move was the right one. For the last few weeks the farmhouse consumed his time and when he wasn't mired deep in it, he enjoyed reconnecting with his friends. A great new job, new house, loyal friends—what more could a man ask for? He was content and at peace … until last night. Julia. What were the chances he would pick the one small town in America Jules lived in to start fresh? It was absurd.

He was convinced that chapter in his life was done. For years he struggled to put her behind him, to accept he would never see her again and never find the answers to the questions that plagued him. He made his peace with the past long ago and got over his hurt and anger at the way they parted. At least that's what he thought. Dealing with death every day, he learned the value of life. He forgave them both for the mistakes they made as teenagers. But seeing her yesterday triggered all kinds of conflicting emotions and a deluge of memories he had trouble sifting through.

What it came down to was he wasn't a saint. Part of him, the adult reasonable version of himself, was happy to see her. The teenaged, love-struck boy never got over his confusion, hurt, and anger at being thrown away like he was nothing more than safety blanket she outgrew. He harbored no doubt what he'd felt for her was real and her abandonment changed him forever. He became reserved and distant with everyone but his patients, always holding a part of himself back. He never told Alyssa about Jules, but she sensed there had been another. Many times she even accused him of having an affair and nothing he said or did convinced her otherwise. Perhaps she was right. Jules was the third person in their marriage, the third person in their bed, and the only person in his heart.

No matter how angry he was or how hurt he was, he was damn happy he stumbled back into her life. He didn't know what it meant or where it would lead, but for some reason fate brought them back into each other's lives again. At the age of sixteen Jules moved into his heart, becoming a permanent resident. He carried her with him everywhere he went. It was evident by Julia's reaction yesterday she too carried a part of him with her. She didn't stop living her life, but she carried him with her. The evidence was in her eyes and around her neck. The problem was, for him, her memory was not a burden. That clearly wasn't the case for her.

Julia's emotional outburst intrigued and alarmed him. His sudden appearance was unexpected surprise, but why the tears? She was the one who walked away. More importantly, why the fear? He was certain he saw panic and fear on her face and in her eyes. He loved her expressive, big green eyes, which her daughter inherited. When she stopped crying and pulled away from him, for a few seconds, her guard was down. The pain and loneliness that lingered in her eyes nearly brought him to his knees. Every protective instinct he ever felt for her reignited like a flame to a can of gasoline. The years and circumstances separating them disintegrated leaving only her, his girl, standing in his arms crying, trembling, telling him how much she missed him, and how good it was to see him. That was it. She had him again. He couldn't help himself.

There was much to be said and much to uncover, but there was time now she was back in his world. First, he wanted to figure who or what put fear in Julia's eyes. All signs indicated she too had changed and she wasn't going to make this easy. She spent most of the time at Lexi's avoiding any direct conversation with him. Like a mama bear watching over her cub, she observed him closely as he held Lilly. She ate and drank little and when the topic of how they knew each other came up over dinner, she was quick to dismiss it with a brief explanation they dated in high school. No one believed she was telling the full story, but the other women moved in to protect her and changed the topic of conversation. This was how it went all through dinner. The instant dinner was over, Julia scooped Lilly out of his arms and bid them all goodnight.

Lost in his thoughts, Ethan was surprised to find himself standing in front of the farmhouse once more. He was so distracted, he'd finished his morning tour of the town but couldn't remember a single thing he passed or even what streets he took to loop back. He shook his head and got a sense of déjà vu. When Julia was in his life, he often lost time like this. When they weren't physically together or speaking on the phone, he was absorbed in thoughts of her. It used to drive his parents insane not being able to control his thoughts, yet another aspect of his life they wanted full reign over.

Ethan stretched, drank a couple bottles of water, and showered. He drove to Frank's Diner in the center of town and parked his new Ford F-150 in one of the few spaces left on the street. Two weeks ago he traded in his BMW for the pickup, and although he loved it and didn't miss the BMW one bit, he was still learning how to maneuver it around town. Finding a parking space and being able to park the monster was a fantastic way to start the day.

From the street, the delicious scent of coffee, syrup, and bacon filled his nose and his stomach growled in anticipation, begging to be fed. Ethan went inside and scanned the tables for an open seat. He didn't care where he sat as long as he could get food and coffee fast. His eyes landed on the slim figure of a woman with long, straight hair the color of honey that fell down her back in a thick sheet. She sat in a corner booth wrestling the salt and pepper shakers out of the hands of one persistent, curly-headed blonde toddler in a hot-pink sweat suit with the word "Angel" printed on her bottom in white block letters.

As he made his way to their table, he couldn't help the grin that suffused his face. Poor Julia was flushed and frazzled as she grabbed one item after another out of Lilly's hand while lecturing the little girl. Lilly wasn't impressed by what she was hearing because she reached for Julia's partially-full coffee cup just as he made it to the table and scooped her up.

"Angel baby, what are you doing to your poor mama this morning? She looks like she's about to have a coronary."

Lilly squealed and fisted Ethan's shirt in her tiny hand.

"Hi," she said. She flashed a devilish grin at him and favored him with a sloppy kiss on the cheek.

"Hi yourself." Ethan smiled at the squirming bundle in his arms and leaned into her, his eyelashes brushing against her skin as he blinked. He whispered in her ear, "Butterfly kisses for you, angel face."

Lilly giggled and threw her chubby arms around his neck, holding him close as he sat across from Julia.

Sitting Lilly on his lap, he gave her his keys to play with. He glanced up to see Julia gawking at him. Her beautiful face was pink and her eyes flashed. But the thing that completed the scene for him was the message on her t-shirt. "You couldn't handle me, even if I came with instructions." It was hilarious and couldn't be more perfect. Ethan had to exercise a significant amount of control not to burst out laughing because he was certain if he did, she would throw her coffee at him.

It was good to see time hadn't changed Julia's low-maintenance style or her sense of humor. In their time together, she never wore makeup unless she had to for an evening event. Her skin had been flawless and it still was. Julia was comfortable with who she was, and didn't try to hide under makeup or fancy clothes as so many women did, including Alyssa. He wondered if she still preferred shopping at discount retail stores and secondhand shops to big department stores.

"Good morning, sunshine. How are you today? Hope you don't mind me joining you."

"Morning" Julia grumbled. "It doesn't look like I have a choice since you've already made yourself comfortable. What are you doing here and what did you say to my child?"

"My aren't we grumpy this morning. Haven't had your coffee yet? If I remember correctly, you can be a bit temperamental if you don't get your morning dose of caffeine."

"No, I haven't had enough coffee yet. The little monster in your lap has been awake and up to no good since five. If I didn't know better, I'd swear she was out to kill me."

"Hang on. Sit and decompress and let me see what I can do to help you." Waving a waitress over, Ethan ordered coffee for both of them and asked for a menu. He gave the waitress his most engaging smile and asked if she had any crayons and paper for the little angel in his lap.

The harried young waitress froze in the midst of pouring their coffee with her mouth hanging. Then she caught herself and gave him a shy smile. She went out of her way to please him, bringing coffee, crayons, paper, and even a Sippy cup of apple juice for Lilly Julia swore she ordered along with their meal thirty minutes prior.

"Some things never change. I see you're still using that smile to get whatever you want," Julia mumbled as she put cream in her coffee and began drinking it in haste.

Ethan didn't know anyone who could drink scalding hot coffee like that and not burn their mouth raw. "I do what I have to. As for angel, I don't know what you're complaining about. She's behaving beautifully, aren't you sweetness?"

Lilly looked up from her coloring, flashed him a grin and said, "Yesh."

"See, I told you. She's angelic."

"Great, now you've got my kid falling for that grin. Whatever! If I can get a few minutes of quiet and coffee, I'll take it. What are you doing here anyway?"

"Same thing you are, breakfast. I live only a mile from here. I passed this place yesterday on my run and thought I'd try it. You come here often?"

"Lilly and I live a few miles away. We come here at least once a week when I have a late shift and we can get a slower start in the morning. Of course, that usually means sleeping in past 5 a.m., but Lils had different plans for us today. Where in Lakes Crossing do you live?"

"I bought an old colonial farmhouse at the edge of town. It needs some work, but it has great bones. Just needs a good facelift."

"A farmhouse? Oh my God, you don't mean the old Johnson farm on Renner, do you? That place doesn't need a facelift, it needs a wrecking ball. Jesus, Ethan, were you drunk when you looked at that place? I know you like a good challenge, but honestly, that place is about to collapse."

"Well now, that's no way to speak about my humble abode. It has its challenges, but all it needs is some TLC. You and all your doubting friends will eat your words once it's done. It's a diamond in the rough, that's all."

"Ethan, did you get scammed into buying that place? Seriously, it's a health hazard. It should be condemned. You don't actually live there now, do you?"

"Yup, I moved in to one of its many rooms. Adam has been helping me redecorate a bit. You should come by sometime. It's a charmer. I bet it wins your heart when you see what I've done with it."

"Is there running water or electricity in that dump? I bet it's infested with all kinds of animals and bugs."

"Again, I think you have the wrong impression of my castle. It took a couple of weeks, but yes, I have running water. In fact, I have it in abundance, even in places it shouldn't be. I see it as an added bonus, though. I also have electricity, and yes some wildlife I'm still negotiating squatters' rights with."

"Oh Ethan, what have you done? You can't live there."

Seeing the look of horror on her face and hearing the concern in her voice mixed with her unique blend of teasing, Ethan couldn't help himself. He threw back his head and laughed. It was good to let go. It'd been so damn long since he had anything to laugh about and someone to share a smile with. God, he missed her. He missed having her in his life. He didn't care about the past. He missed the sound of her voice and the way those emerald eyes flashed at him in laughter or irritation.

It felt like he'd been around the world and back, constantly in search of something or someone and that someone was her. From the second he left her sitting by the creek behind the high school twenty-two years ago, to the instant his eyes met hers last night he was adrift. Nothing made sense in his world, nothing felt right, until now. He survived, just as she did. He went through the motions and built another life, just as she did. But he was lost without her when she was lost to him.

Chapter Three

Julia drank in Ethan as his body shook with laughter. She savored the sound of his rich, husky voice and the sound of his happy laughter filled her with joy. Her heart did its own happy conga as butterflies danced in her stomach. She loved sitting here with him, acting like they didn't have a painful past, like they had no worries in the world. She knew better.

As much as she enjoyed being near him, she had to shut this down before her heart took over. Her heart was a fool. Her brain was smarter and reminded her— friends, okay, anything else, absolutely not. She couldn't go there with him or with anyone else. Been there, done that, and almost lost everyone she cared about in the process. She gave herself a mental slap. He would be too easy to love and if she allowed it, her stupid, fragile heart would get torn into shreds in the storm that followed. Nothing good ever lasted, not for her anyway.

Lilly sat happily next to Ethan, making a hell of a mess with her breakfast. As wonderful as Ethan was with Lilly, he wasn't her father and never would be. Lilly had a father, as worthless as he was. Matt was the name of the sperm donor, not Ethan. Julia had to protect Lilly because her sweet baby was too fragile to withstand a storm. As it was, she had to figure out what to do about Matt. One man making a mess of her life was quite enough.

"Mama, more. Mama, more." Lilly held up the empty juice cup.

"Lilly, what are you supposed to say when you ask for something?"

Lilly furrowed her brow. "Um, thank-um?"

"Good try baby. Say please."

"No. No."

"Lilly, say, 'please may I have more juice?' or you won't be getting any. Do you understand?"

Julia locked eyes with Lilly across the table and a war of wills was declared. Lilly gave in first. She dropped her eyes and then the empty cup on the table. She turned and buried her head in Ethan's lap. Julia glared at a smiling Ethan and shook her head. He held his hands up in surrender, but couldn't keep the grin off his face.

"You know, Julia, I think the word 'please' is a great word to use. It's better than 'no' or 'more,' or any other word. Only big girls use the word 'please.' Do you think Lilly is a big girl or a baby?"

Before Julia could answer, Lilly's head popped up. She looked at Ethan then Julia and quickly said, "Pu-weese, Mama."

Julia stared daggers at Ethan and answered Lilly. "Okay. Good job, Lilly."

Julia flagged down a waitress and ordered a refill for Lilly. She turned back to Ethan who was coloring under Lilly's guidance.

"Tell me, Ethan, do you have children? You're pretty good with them, even for a pediatrician." Ethan's eyes clouded and a variety of emotions crossed his features before he looked away. But Julia saw the pain and was overwhelmed by guilt. After all the pain she'd already caused him, she didn't want to be the source of any more. She somehow touched on a tender topic, but after so many years there were bound to be hidden mines and grenades everywhere.

"I'm sorry, Eth, I didn't mean to pry. You're really good with her, that's all."

"It's fine. No, Alyssa and I never had children."

"Alyssa?"

"Alyssa is my ex-wife, as of a month ago. She wasn't fond of children."

"I'm sorry."

"Don't be. We married for all the wrong reasons. I wanted a family and she wanted a life of pretty dresses and parties. While we grew up in the same social circles, we were worlds apart in what we needed to be happy. Sad to say, but the wedding and the divorce were the highlights of our years together."

"God, Ethan, that sounds terrible. I am sorry. If it makes you feel any better, my story isn't much different. Matt and I were married for eight years. We've been divorced for almost two years, but we separated before Lilly was born. He was never satisfied with what we had. Actually, he was never satisfied with anything. He wanted the life you describe, the one filled with money and fancy parties. He didn't want a family or a child, and in the end, he didn't want me either."

"Sounds like he has a lot in common with my ex."

Julia shrugged. "I guess you could say that." She dropped her eyes and wrapped her arms around herself. She couldn't help but remember the mess her marriage had been and Matt's unending criticism of her. He managed to find fault with everything: how she dressed, walked, talked, wore her hair, kept the house, cooked, etc. She could do nothing right in his eyes and she took it all without complaint, trying to make him happy. Like many women, she thought if she changed, if she became what he wanted, he'd love her.

The bottom fell out when he found out she was pregnant, and all hell broke loose. On the day her divorce was final Julia made a promise to herself. No matter what, she'd never let another man make her feel so desperate to be loved, she'd lose herself in the process of making him happy.

"I'm sorry Jules. Sounds like you had a bad time of it. You know, I saw Matt with you once, at Ella's funeral. I guess that must have been around the time you were pregnant with Lilly, right?"

Julia's eyes shot up. "You were at Ella's funeral? I didn't see you."

"No, you wouldn't have. There were many people there and you were distraught. I didn't want to add to your burden. Mom told me of Ella's passing and I wanted to pay my respects. I loved her too."

Julia couldn't believe Ethan had been there. Ella had loved him like a son and she would've wanted him there. Ella died suddenly of a brain aneurysm and Julia had been out of her mind with grief. She and Matt had been arguing almost continuously at that point, and then Ella died. On top of that she started to feel sick and thought it was a virus made worse by the stress of Ella's death, not knowing she was pregnant.

"I'm glad you were there. She loved you. It was a terrible time. Her death was so unexpected. I never had a chance to tell her about Lilly. I found out I was pregnant after the funeral. I think she would have been thrilled to know she was going to be a grandma. I named Lilly after Ella. Lilly was Ella's middle name. She always said she liked the name Lilly better and one day she was going to change her name officially."

"You're right. She would've loved to meet this little angel and would've told you what a great mom you are. She would've been there for you when things fell apart with Matt. He's missing out on the best thing life's got to offer right here."

Ethan nodded at Lilly and smiled. He wiped her daughter's mouth and brushed the curls out of her eyes. Julia's heart ached. She wished she could blink and the world would be different.

Alyssa was an idiot and she bet most women in the country would agree with her.

"Thanks. Eth. You're going to be a great dad someday. Lilly doesn't share her kisses with just anyone. You have to be special for her to dole those out. I hardly get one a day."

"Well, she's sweet. She's just like her mama, all fire and attitude on the outside, marshmallow sweetness on the inside."

Julia's face burned with the compliment. It had been a long time since a man said something sweet to her. She reached for the necklace around her neck and rubbed her thumb over the heart in a tender caress.

"Well, we'd better be going. It was nice running into you today, but Lilly and I have to get back so I can drop her off at the sitter's and get ready for work."

"It was nice seeing you as well. Listen, Jules, I'd love to see you again. We have a lot to catch up on. How about we meet for dinner this week? Any day, any time is fine with me. I don't start at the hospital until next week."

Ethan wanted to see her again? She should be happy. Instead, Julia was terrified. She wasn't afraid of him, but of the feelings he awakened in her. She'd been here before with him and to a degree with Matt. Each time she was foolish enough to let someone in, she barely survived the deep wounds left behind when disaster struck. She had the scars to prove it.

Julia was still recovering from Matt's abandonment. She didn't need a psychiatrist to know her self-esteem and self-confidence took a hit. She was putting her life back together day by day, trying to find herself and she wasn't ready to put her heart or Lilly's on the line. Her first concern was to protect Lilly.

Julia was finally getting good at the single mom stuff and she couldn't be tempted to consider any other future. It had been a hard road, but she survived and embraced the fact she would be raising her daughter predominantly on her own. She and Lilly had a routine, a rhythm to their lives that couldn't be interrupted, not even for him. Their lives were busy and rich with work, friends, and new places to explore every second she was free. She couldn't rock the boat now, not when she worked so hard to find balance and peace.

"Thank you, but I don't think that's a good idea."

"Why not? It's only dinner."

"Eth, I'm not ready for this. I'm never going to be ready for this. I'm still trying to figure out my life post-divorce. You just got divorced. We have a messy past. It's not a good idea. I'm sorry."

"You know, before we were anything, we were good friends, the best of friends. I don't know about you, but I could always use a good friend. I'm not pushing for anything else. I've missed my best friend."

He wanted to be friends? After all this time and all that happened, how could he want to be friends? If she was honest with herself, she wanted this too. Next to Aimee, Ethan had been her only close friend, the only other person who knew her inside and out. But he confused her—she didn't understand his motives. Had he forgotten the way they ended?

"I'm sorry, but I have to ask. It's making me nuts. Why aren't you mad at me, at the way we ended? How could you still want to be my friend, my anything? I don't understand, Eth. You're a nice guy, but it was bad. What I did was terrible. If this is some ploy to get me in a quiet place to tell me off, let me save you the trouble. Do it now. I know I deserve it."

Julia had prepared for this moment for a long time. She wanted it to be over. She wanted him to yell and scream at her and finally put her out of her misery.

Ethan smiled and reached for her hand. She tried to pull it away, but he was stronger and held on. He caressed her palm with his thumb and said, "Easy Jules. I'm not going to hurt you. I promise. Just breathe."

She took in a big gulp of air and broke eye contact with him long enough to glance down to find Lilly engrossed in opening up all the sugar packets and pouring them into every water glass on the table.

"You know," Ethan said in a soft voice, "I've been waiting for you to ask me that question. No, this isn't a ploy to tell you off. We do have a lot to talk about. It's time we put the past to rest and move on. Two decades have passed. We both grew up. Much has happened, I…"

He released her hand and rubbed the back of his neck.

"Look, have dinner with me and we'll talk. Don't we owe each other that? Some closure after all these years?"

He was right. But there was safety here, with a whole diner of people looking on. The problem was she had difficulty saying no to Ethan when he looked at her with those soft gray eyes. She caved. "Okay, fine. Dinner. But it will have to wait till Friday."

"Okay."

"And, it'll have to be at my place because I don't leave Lilly with a sitter unless I'm working."

"Okay."

"And I'm not cooking 'cause I'll be working all day."

"I'll bring Chinese. I think I remember what you like. Anything else?"

"Yes, take that self-satisfied grin off your face. It doesn't suit you at all."

Ethan chuckled. "I'll try, but it's hard."

Julia stood, threw some bills on the table and gathered Lilly's bag.

"Come on, Lils. Say goodbye to Ethan. We have to go." Julia wiped Lilly's sugary hands with a napkin and scooped her into her arms.

"Bye, E," Lilly said, throwing Ethan air kisses with her little hand.

Ethan reached for the child and kissed the top of her head. "Bye angel. Be good for your mama today. See you soon."

All the way home, Julia floated on air while berating herself for giving in. What was the point of starting up with Ethan again? One thing would lead to another where he was concerned. She knew that with a certainty. Ella always said she never tried to keep them apart because what was the point? Whenever they were in the same room, they were drawn together like peanut butter and jelly.

Ella had been a smart woman and she tried her best to get Julia to reconsider her decision to break it off with Ethan. Although Julia never told her the real reason behind their traumatic break up, Ella was a mother and she saw the pain in Julia's eyes and the evidence of the heavy weight she carried. She lectured her for hours about secrets and how destructive they were when given power. But Julia wouldn't and couldn't listen. If only she had, things may have turned out differently.

But how was it their paths crossed again after so many years? She'd accepted the fact she'd never have Ethan in her life and built a new life without him. When that world collapsed, she convinced herself it was okay to be alone. Unlike many people in the world who never experienced true joy, she had her dose of happy and wore the evidence around her neck. The love she'd shared with Ethan was powerful. It tattooed itself on her heart and in her mind forever. She remembered every second they'd spent together and that movie reel was available for a replay at any time. That was enough for her. Few people ever experienced that type of beauty.

Julia remembered the first time she laid eyes on Ethan Sullivan. It was the first day of her sophomore year and she just celebrated her sixteenth birthday the day before. Aimee was assigned to a different section of biology and Julia sat in the back of the room nervously anticipating the start of the class. All summer she dreaded this day. The thought of having to dissect any creature was nauseating. She tried everything to get out of taking the course, but her protestations fell on deaf ears. To make things worse, all of her friends were assigned to another section. She was alone, miserable, and feeling sorry for herself as only a teenaged girl can do.

Ethan was new to the school, although everyone knew of his wealthy political family. He confidently strode into the class, scanned the room for an open seat, and locked in on her. Their eyes met and a connection was made unlike anything she'd ever experienced. He smiled at her and she melted in her chair. There wasn't any time to make introductions. The bell rang and he took a seat, right across the aisle from her. For the next hour Julia didn't hear a single word the teacher said. She'd suddenly become deaf. All she heard was the sound of her heart beating and she saw no one but him. Later, when their friendship bloomed into much more, he told her he experienced the same thing.

That day, in biology class, he passed her a note asking her out. She declined, but he was persistent, thank God. She insisted she didn't know him well enough to go out with him and he wrote, "That's easy to fix. I'm Ethan Sullivan." He spent the next forty-five minutes passing her message after message, telling her all the important things he thought she needed to know about him.

"I moved here from Chicago."

"I play football, but I'm addicted to board games. Want to play Twister with me?"

"I love pizza, but hate cherries. They're the pits."

"I don't have a favorite color, but I love the color of your eyes."

"I'm an only child and I'm used to getting what I want."

Time flew and right before the bell rang, he finally wrote, "Say yes."

By that time, she'd completely forgotten he'd asked her out and she wrote, "To what?"

"To me. Say yes to me."

She read those words over and over again, turned her head and looked right into his hopeful eyes. With a huge grin that left no doubt to what she was feeling, she whispered, "Yes."

He didn't know it, and maybe one day she'd show it to him, but she kept that piece of paper knowing, at the end of the day, she'd always say yes to Ethan Sullivan. She'd said yes then knowing she had absolutely no other choice, and she said yes today, feeling the very same way.

Chapter Four

Last night was ladies' night. As always, bonding with her girls energized and exhausted Julia and she wouldn't have it any other way. On Wednesday she texted the girls, Lexi, Christine, and Aimee, and declared an emergency ladies' night for the next evening. That was the beauty of having great girlfriends who came to your rescue at the drop of a hat. Even before Aimee moved to New Jersey three years ago, they had their ladies' night via Internet. They decompressed over wine and poured their hearts out to each other. It didn't matter if they were in the same room or even the same state. They were always there for one another.

Aimee had been in Julia's life for as long as she could remember. They first met in grade school and Julia was fascinated by Aimee's fiery red hair. In recess one day she asked Aimee if she could touch it. It was the beginning of a special friendship that spanned decades. The only thing that separated them was college, but that was physical distance. While Julia attended Holy Cross University on a full scholarship, Aimee stayed in Indiana to help her father take care of her younger sisters and her mother who had an aggressive form of multiple sclerosis.

Lexi joined ladies' night and the circle of trust a little over a year ago, bringing Christine with her. Julia was given Lexi's name from some nurses at the hospital who hired her to handle their divorce. They said she was easy to talk to, but a force to be reckoned with. This, she had in common with her brother, Adam, a well-known cardiac surgeon at Lakes Julia worked with on occasion. At first, it was all business with Lexi, but that didn't last long as the women found they had much in common.

While Christine was the same age as Aimee and

Julia, Lexi was five years younger, but she was surprisingly mature. Together the women formed a tight circle of friendship and support. There was nothing they wouldn't do for one another. They rounded each other out well, each bringing their unique life experiences and gifts to share. Julia thanked God for their friendship daily. They kept her sane and stopped her from killing Matt on a number of occasions.

Ladies' night was traditionally held once a month. However, anyone in the group could call an emergency meeting and this was a frequent occurrence. Some ladies' nights were a free-for-all with the women unloading their troubles at random. But last night was all about Julia and the men in her life. The women usually met at a nearby restaurant or bar, but this time everyone came to Julia's house because, once again, Matt decided not to show up to watch Lilly.

Lilly was too young to be disappointed by her father's absence, but Julia was beside herself. It was almost a month since Matt last saw his daughter. When he made an appearance, it would be disruptive and traumatic for Lilly. Matt was fading out of Lilly's life. Julia tried to explain to him a month away from Lilly was a year in Lilly time. Each time he stayed away for long periods, he lost any bond he built with her and had to start over again. Now when Matt reappeared into Lilly's life and tried to take her for the day, she refused to go to him. When she relented, she came back a changed little girl. Something had to be done.

It was about time Matt made a decision regarding the role he was willing to play in Lilly's life. He had to either man-up and be a real father, or get out of her life. Lexi didn't think it was going to be easy. Although she didn't specialize in custody cases, she was well versed on their legalities. She warned Julia if she went for full custody, it would be difficult, messy and costly, especially if Matt contested it.

Things could go Julia's way if she let Lexi use all the dirt she compiled on Matt. Julia, however, refused to go down that path unless she was out of options. While he wouldn't win Father-of-the-Year any time soon, he wasn't a terrible father. What Julia wanted was for Lilly to have everything she never had—a real family and father who loved her to pieces. Julia grew up craving the love and security of a family.

Then there was Ethan. Julia put the women off all week telling them she needed time to process her feelings about Ethan before talking about it. God love her, Aimee let her be, knowing when Julia was ready to talk, she would. Lexi and Christine were harder to convince. Neither knew Julia and Ethan's story, but they were smart and sensitive enough to know there *was* a story.

By the end of the night, after several bottles of wine were consumed, Lexi and Christine knew most of the story. There were some things Julia would never share with anyone other than Aimee who'd witnessed the whole sordid mess. While the other women understood her reluctance to start things back up with Ethan, they wanted her to be happy. And he was her chance at happiness. It was obvious to them she still cared a great deal for him and they told her as much. Despite her protestations and fears, they convinced her putting the past to rest would be healthy for both of them and there was no harm in having dinner with him.

Dinner with Ethan.

Crap! Where had the time gone?

Julia glanced at the kitchen clock and panicked. Ethan would arrive in thirty minutes. It was late when the girls left last night and she hadn't tidied up. She raced around the house clearing the evidence of their drinking and munching. Her house was a small multi-level structure deep in the woods. It had three small bedrooms, a bathroom, family room, and kitchen. It was easy to mess up and easy to clean. She loved her home and it showed. Every inch of it was decorated for comfort, with oversized leather furniture, colorful throw pillows, knickknacks, and photos of people and places she loved.

She and Matt lived in this house since they married. At first they were renters until shortly after Ella died. The elderly couple that owned the house said they would be happy to sell it to them when they were ready, but Matt never wanted to buy it. He complained it was old and they could do better. When Ella suddenly died, Julia was the sole beneficiary of her substantial life insurance policy. She bought the house, and with it, some security for herself and Lilly.

With Lilly's help, Julia finished the last of the dishes. She started the dishwasher and was about to sit Lilly down for her dinner when her cell rang. She grabbed it from her back pocket, glanced at the display, and sighed.

Matt. Now he calls? She wondered if he would apologize this time for missing a date with his daughter. As she wrestled Lilly into her high chair, placing her dinner in front of her, she answered.

"Hello, Matt."

"Julia, I'll be over in the morning around ten to take Lilly. Dress her up a bit. We're having a family photo taken. Nothing too crazy, please. Go for elegant and subtle. Better give me a couple of outfits in case Carla doesn't like what you've chosen."

"Hello to you too, Matt, and no, you cannot take Lilly tomorrow. You were supposed to watch her last night, remember? Anyway, we have plans tomorrow."

So much for an apology! Hearing Matt's voice

used to make Julia smile, but that was in the past. Now, she wanted to hit something every time she talked to him. It didn't help he was informing her he was taking Lilly tomorrow instead of asking if they had plans first. It also didn't help he was being a condescending ass, dictating how she should dress her child.

Julia felt her blood begin to bubble. She remembered the conversation she had with Lexi last night. She had to hold it together and not lose her mind. She had to keep communication open, be reasonable, and foster a civil relationship with Matt, etc. …whatever!

"Look, don't give me a hard time. I didn't have time for Lilly yesterday. Tomorrow is a must. Carla has the day all planned. We're going to Carla's parents' in Long Island afterward. Pack her some play clothes as well. She'll be fine. I'll bring her back around seven." After a pause, he huffed. "You said I needed to spend more time with her and now I am."

Julia turned her back to Lilly and paced the kitchen trying to control her quickly rising temper. Carla was Matt's new wife and the woman he'd been having a long-term affair with during their marriage. Her name alone made Julia see red. Carla was in her late twenties and came from a wealthy Long Island family. She was an only child and the heiress to a large fortune—she was used to having whatever she wanted. Since marrying her, Matt changed. He now lived the privileged life he always wanted and would do anything to keep his wife and her wealthy family happy.

Carla barely tolerated Lilly. She was under the impression Julia got pregnant on purpose and Lilly was Julia's way of holding on to Matt when he wanted a divorce to be with her. That was ludicrous since Julia had no idea Matt was cheating on her or he wanted a divorce. Lilly was a total surprise baby. Putting all that aside,

Carla wasn't the nurturing type. She told Julia on multiple occasions, "Children aren't my thing."

"Matt, back up a minute, would you? Yes, of course I want you to spend time with Lilly, but I need some notice and need to be consulted when you've made plans for our daughter. I don't understand the urgency."

"This is exactly why I don't come around more often. Why do you have to complicate things? Carla wants Lilly in our family photo and the photographer is free tomorrow. Have her ready, for God's sake. How hard is that?"

Julia took a deep breath and attempted a new strategy. She wanted Lilly to see her father and their plans could be changed—they were going to the Bronx Zoo. But she didn't think Lilly would do well spending the day in Long Island. Lilly hadn't seen Matt in a month so their reunion was going to be rough. Add to that wearing uncomfortable clothes, posing for cameras, and spending the day with people she didn't know, and the stress of the day would be too much for Lilly. She would most definitely have a meltdown. Matt would know this if he spent any time with her.

Julia collected herself and spoke in a low, cajoling voice.

"Okay, Matt, listen. Why don't I pick Lilly up from wherever you are when you're done with the pictures, or I could bring her to the studio and wait until you're finished? Lilly doesn't do well with strangers and she can be a handful. This way you and Carla can have your pictures and have a good day with her family."

"Julia, I'm not going to argue with you any further. Lilly is my daughter and I want her for the day. I don't have to justify my every move to you or ask your permission to spend time with her. As for her behavior, that's your fault. She's spoiled and willful, but she'll have to learn how to behave in public sooner rather than later. If you can't teach her appropriate behavior, and it appears you cannot, Carla and I have no problem doing so. Have her ready by ten sharp. Goodbye."

Julia stared at the phone. What the hell just happened? Matt was difficult, but he never acted like this before. He never went out of his way to spend time with Lilly, never demanded to see her, and never commented on her behavior. Although Julia should be happy, he wanted to spend time with his daughter, her gut told her something wasn't right.

As for Lilly's behavior, Lilly was two. Yes, she was spirited, but she wasn't spoiled. There was no way Julia was going to let him *teach* her child how to behave. She didn't like his tone or the implied threat. Julia knew all too well that kind of teaching and she'd be damned if she let him, or anyone else, lay a finger on Lilly.

The sound of the doorbell brought Julia out of her daze. Ethan had arrived and she hadn't changed out of her scrubs yet. She sighed in frustration and exhaustion. She made sure Lilly was still sitting snuggly in her chair then went to open the door for Ethan. As she walked toward the door, she ran her fingers through her hair. It was a lost cause. She was a mess. Julia took a deep breath and opened the door. Poor Ethan had no idea what he was walking into. It had been a challenging day and the phone call with Matt fried her nerves.

"Hey, Ethan. Glad you found us. Come on in."

Ethan came into the house surprising Julia with a light kiss on the cheek. His delicious scent filled her nose—cinnamon and musk.

"Hi, beautiful. Oh, oh, what's going on? What's that look on your face about?"

"Uh, nothing's going on. It's been a long day. Come on, Lilly's in the kitchen. We can eat there."

Julia turned before Ethan saw the blush that crept up her neck and face, warming her whole body. Even in her distracted state, she would've had to be blind not to notice how incredible he looked in dark jeans and a Harvard t-shirt. He was better looking than any Calvin Klein model she'd ever seen and his t-shirt was stretched to its limit, barely covering his muscular biceps and pecs. His hair was still wet from a shower and he had a sexy, mouth-watering five o'clock shadow going. The man was gorgeous and she was a hot mess. Life was so unfair.

It wasn't lost on Julia Ethan called her beautiful. The word rolled off his lips as easily as it did years ago. He needed glasses. She wasn't as thin or as toned as she used to be. Matt reminded her of that fact a million times. Her hair was a mess and needed a cut. It was a wild beast that grew thick and long. Another thing Matt hated. He said she needed to look less like Mother Earth and more like Anne Hathaway. But she was who she was.

Julia walked through the family room to the kitchen with Ethan trailing behind her carrying a couple of bags. The yummy scent of Chinese food filled the house making her mouth water and her stomach rumble. She hadn't stopped to eat all day and she was starving.

"Hi, angel baby. What are you eating?" Ethan greeted Lilly as Julia took one of the bags from him and began to empty it on the small kitchen table that served as their dining room. She glanced over her shoulder and saw Ethan doing his baby whisperer routine. Lilly was relishing in his attention and filled the room with her adorable squeals of delight. Her girl acted like all women did around Dr. Ethan Sullivan. She was drooling all over him and trying to feed him peas off her plate. One day Julia would have to get him to tell her what he whispered in Lilly's ear that gave her such joy.

"What did you do with yourself all week?" Julia

asked.

"Mainly I worked on the house and met with some contractors who will be working on the plumbing, electrical, and stonework. Although I'll be doing a lot of the work myself, I'm going to need help since I'm starting at the hospital on Monday."

"You know I think you're crazy, right? I didn't even know you liked to work with your hands. When did you learn how to do … whatever it is you have to do in that monstrosity?"

"Hey now, show some respect for my humble dwellings. You can refer to my home as the castle from now on. As for my skills for home repair and renovation, I picked it up in college and med school to make extra money. I love making old things new again, although not too new. I want the place to showcase the past in all its glory. You'll see. It's going to be fantastic."

"Okay, Tim the Tool Man, I'll try to keep an open mind. I'm starving, but I got home a little while ago. I haven't had a chance to change. Would you mind watching Lilly for a few minutes? I promise to be quick."

"I don't mind at all. Lilly and I will be fine. Dinner can wait. Go and change. Take your time. I'm in no rush."

"Okay, thanks. I'll clean her up before I go. Looks like she fed most of her dinner to her hair and ears."

"Jules, go change. I've got this. Besides, I have a surprise for my girl in this bag."

Grateful for the help, Julia escaped up the stairs to her room and shut the door. For a few minutes she stood, eyes closed, with her back against the door wondering what she was doing. She had to move. She needed to wash up, change, and get downstairs, but she wanted to hide here for a few minutes and get her racing heart under control. It was good to have Ethan in her home. She was way too vulnerable where he was concerned.

Ethan was decadent chocolate, ice cream sundaes, and fine wine rolled into one. He was something so good, but so bad. He was forbidden fruit. Julia craved him all the time and was powerless to resist him. She barely survived losing him the first time and after the last few years with Matt, Julia didn't have the strength to survive another heartache.

She studied her image in the bathroom mirror and reminded herself, for the hundredth time, tonight was about closure—not a reawakening of anything. She lectured herself on this fact all week, but that didn't stop her foolish brain from unearthing every memory she'd tried to bury. There were plenty of good memories and plenty of painful ones. The problem was her stupid brain teamed up with her heart and only wanted to dredge up the good times, disregarding the messy parts completely.

Making quick work of it, she washed up and changed into jeans and one of her favorite t-shirts, an oldie, but a goodie. It read, "I'm still mad they never actually told us how to get to Sesame Street." She brushed her hair until it fell in soft waves down her back and let it have its way and run wild and free. She told herself to behave like an adult and stop hiding in her room. Opening her bedroom door, she made her way to the stairs leading to the first floor.

Julia stopped dead.

There in the family room stood tall, muscular Ethan swaying with Lilly asleep on his chest, clutching a yellow and brown spotted giraffe around the neck. But that's not what had her frozen in her place, holding her breath, her eyes filling with tears. What mesmerized her was the sound of Ethan's husky voice singing to her baby with such tenderness her heart ached. She listened to the words and recognized Billy Joel's *Goodnight My Angel*.

It was her favorite lullaby. She played it for Lilly often. As the words washed over her, she was unable to stay upright. She sank to the top of the stairs and listened to the words he sang. She wondered what she did to ever deserve this man.

Chapter Five

Ethan finished the song and glanced up to find Julia sitting at the top of the stairs with a wistful look on her face. Her watery green eyes met his as tears slid down her cheeks. The look of longing and sadness he saw in them took his breath away. He wanted to go to his girl, gather her up in his arms, and rock her as he was doing with Lilly.

He climbed the stairs with Lilly snuggled against his heart, sat next to Julia and enfolded her in his free arm. Julia wiped her face with the back of her hand and laid her head against his shoulder. He felt like the king of the world with Julia in one arm and the world's sweetest baby in the other. That's when he decided Matt was a fool. Who could have all this and walk away from it? He would kill to have all this beauty in his life.

He kissed the top of Julia's head and gave her a gentle squeeze.

"Let's put her to bed," he whispered, nodding in Lilly's direction.

Julia stood and tried taking Lilly from him, but he shook his head and said, "Lead the way, boss. I've got her."

They passed a bathroom, the master bedroom, and then came to Lilly's room. A light pink and cream hand-painted wooden sign on the door read "Lilly's Beach Palace." The changing table, rocking chair and toy trunk were cream-colored while the carpet was a thick sandy brown. The crib was a large, solid hardwood piece of art shaped into some kind of ship with a beautifully carved footboard and headboard and high side-panels. It was pushed against a wall that was expertly painted like the ocean in soft blues and creams with gentle waves. This gave the illusion the crib-ship was floating on a calm ocean. Above the bed hung an exquisitely carved piece of driftwood—*Lilly's Ship of Dreams.*

Beach scenes covered the adjacent walls from floor to ceiling. A soft blue sky with puffy clouds covered the ceiling while seagulls flew in the distance. The room was assembled with a great deal of imagination and love. Ethan was spellbound. He'd never seen anything like this. Lilly was one lucky little girl.

He laid his precious bundle carefully in her ship and stood, watching Julia change and tuck Lilly in for the night. The entire time, Lilly never opened her eyes, but when Julia tried to take the giraffe out of her hand, Lilly held on and mumbled, "No, mine." Laughing, they hurried out of the room before they woke her up.

Ethan and Julia made their way to the kitchen in silence. While Julia warmed up their now-cold dinner, Ethan opened the bottle of wine she'd left out on the counter. She was lost in thought and he gave her space. When they were both seated with loaded plates, he broke the silence.

"Are you okay?"

"I'm fine. Sorry. It's been a long day."

"What brought on the tears?"

Julia hesitated and took a generous gulp of her wine. She looked down at her plate. "My nerves are pretty fried. Work was rough today. I lost a patient I've known for a long time."

Ethan reached for her hand and squeezed it. "I'm sorry, Julia. That's always rough. In all the years I've practiced medicine, although I've learned how to deal with death, as you have, when it happens, I still feel helpless and still grieve. Death is humbling. It reminds me despite all my knowledge and skill, I'm not God."

For a few minutes they were both silent. As he

ate, Julia pushed the food around her plate then put her fork down.

She sighed. "I'm sorry, Ethan. Maybe this wasn't such a good idea. It's been a shitty day from start to finish. I think I need to crawl into bed and forget it ever happened. If you stay much longer you're going to be an innocent by-stander to my meltdown and I'm already embarrassed."

Ethan stopped eating and studied Julia. She was as pretty as ever, but there were signs of strain around her eyes. She looked wrung out, defeated. There was more to the story than the death of a patient.

"Jules, there's nothing for you to be embarrassed about. We've been friends for decades, even if we missed a few years here and there," he said with a tender smile. "No need to hold back, go ahead and let go. I'll catch you. Why don't you tell me what's going on? Maybe I can help. I promise to only listen and not sing again since that seemed to trigger the meltdown."

She regarded him with troubled eyes for a few seconds then looked down and began shredding her napkin. "You have a beautiful voice and looked sweet with Lilly in your arms. The thing is, I had a trying day and to top it off, I got into an argument with Matt before you came. When I saw you holding Lilly and singing, it occurred to me she's never going to have what you were giving her. I never had that and I wanted it so badly for her. But, unless a miracle happens or Matt has a lobotomy, that's never going to happen for her. It's like history repeating itself and it sucks."

Julia reached for her wine glass and downed its contents then refilled her glass again and took a gulp. "Sorry, I know I'm rambling and probably not making any sense."

"No, it's okay. I'm following you. Tell me about

Matt. What kind of father is he?"

Matt sounded like an ass, but surely he loved his child.

Sighing, Julia said, "Matt never wanted children. He had a sister who had schizophrenia. She put his family through the wringer and then killed herself. Anyway, Lilly was a surprise he never wanted or accepted."

He was right. Matt was an ass. Lilly was a beautiful child. He couldn't understand how any father could resist her, but he never understood people who abandoned their children. Poor Julia carried a heavy burden. He was happy she was beginning to open up to him. The wine was probably helping loosen her inhibitions a bit and he was grateful for the help.

It was strange how one second he was comfortable with her, picking up where they left off twenty years ago, and the next second he was exploring new territory, unsure what the next step would bring. Ethan remembered feeling like this as a kid walking across a semi-frozen lake on a dare from his friends. It was March and the lake was still iced over, for the most part, but with spring around the corner it started to thaw in certain areas. He didn't know if with the next step he was going to be safe or sink. The only difference was the lake crawl was what he liked to call a *stupid human trick*—not worth the risk at all. Reconnecting with Jules, getting to know this new adult version, on the other hand, would be worth the risk … he hoped.

This Julia intrigued him. Her eyes were haunted, filled with secrets and burdens that needed to be shared. He missed his young, carefree girl who trusted him with her heart and her stories. He wanted to know what happened to her and to them all those years ago. Maybe if he said and did the right things, she would trust him once again. Some would say he was crazy. He just became a free man. Why on earth would he voluntarily walk into a storm? But this was Jules and his heart and soul recognized her and insisted he do something to keep her close and comfort her. He never understood the power she had over him and keeping her at arm's length simply wasn't an option.

"So Matt didn't want children, but she's here and she's wonderful. What kind of relationship does he have with Lilly? Does he see her regularly?"

"He sees Lilly off and on. I think she's more of an obligation to him than anything else. He's not warm or loving and she's beginning to pick up on that. I'm not sure he even knows how to love her."

"What were you arguing about before I came?"

Ethan refilled their glasses and sat back in his chair. Julia didn't have to say much, her face told most of the story. Her lips thinned and her jaw tightened. He feared she'd snap the stem of her wine glass by the fierce pressure she exerted on it.

"He hasn't seen Lilly in a month. He was supposed to watch her yesterday, but he didn't show or call. Today he remembered he had a daughter. He ordered me to have her dressed in her finest by ten tomorrow for a family picture and a day in Long Island with his in-laws."

"He's married?"

"Yup, he married as soon as our divorce was final. But that's a vodka or tequila story. Wine will do nothing to pretty up that mess," she said with a sad, self-deprecating smile. "Anyway, I tried to tell him Lilly won't to be able to handle a long day with strangers, but he wasn't having it. He told me she's spoiled and willful and he threatened to teach her some manners."

Julia stood and started straightening the kitchen while she spoke. He doubted she was even aware of what she was doing she was so agitated.

"Lilly's my child. I may not always see things clearly where she's concerned, but she's not spoiled. She's a typical two-year-old, a bit precocious, sure, but not spoiled and willful. He said it was obvious I couldn't control her and he would have to teach her how to behave. I don't know what that means, but I'm not letting him hurt her. No one will hurt either of us again."

Ethan couldn't stand to see Julia's growing distress. Her pain was palpable. He doubted she realized she referred to herself in that last sentence along with Lilly. Julia was neglected and abused as a child before Ella came into her life. She confided a bit in him when they were young, but he didn't know all the details.

He stood and walked to the sink. The water was on and she stood hugging herself, staring into space. He remembered that stance and it pained him each time she did it. He asked Ella about it years ago and she explained it was a remnant of Julia's abuse. As a young child, no one held or comforted Julia when she was in pain or afraid and thus she learned to comfort herself. Years after Ella adopted her, she continued to hold herself when she felt vulnerable. It broke Ella's heart whenever Julia escaped into the past and did this and Ethan was no better. He hated the thought of young Julia battered and terrified and he developed his own way of dealing with it. Ethan remembered how to soothe Julia. He'd done it hundreds of times and became an expert at saving her from her demons.

He turned off the water and took Julia by the shoulders turning her around. He wrapped her in his embrace and held her tightly to him. She was a tall woman, but he towered over her and she fit nicely under his chin. He stroked her golden strands and inhaled her scent. There it was, wild flowers and vanilla.

Intoxicating.

The instant Julia was in his arms, his body recognized her and knew exactly what to do to soothe its mate. Its mate? What a bewildering thought and yet it wasn't that surprising. On some level he'd known she was the one, his other half. Otherwise he wouldn't have been devastated when he lost her and he wouldn't have thought about her every day for the last twenty-two years. Simple teenaged crushes don't leave a permeant mark on the heart and soul. He wondered if she thought of him like that. There was no doubt in his mind she loved him when they were teenagers, but he wondered what she thought of him now.

"Easy, Jules. No one is going to hurt Lilly. No one is going to hurt you. You're both safe," he whispered in her ear while continuing to stroke her hair and rub her back.

After a few minutes, her body relaxed against his and he breathed easier knowing he was able to soothe her. Ethan smiled. Thank God he hadn't lost his touch.

Julia pulled away and glanced up, embarrassment evident on her face. He put a finger to her lips and shook his head.

"Nope, no apology, no embarrassment. This is me. I know you and you know me. You can trust me. It's okay. I've got you."

He walked them to the couch in the family room, noting the photos of beaches and oceans that were scattered throughout the room and the house in general. He was happy to see his girl got her wish. When they were young and silly, he would ask her, "If you could be any animal in the world, what would you be?" Her answer never changed. "A pelican, of course. I would be big and beautiful, free to soar above the oceans. I'd bask in the sun and the air and look below me at the majesty of the ocean and I'd smile every day."

"You'd smile? Pelicans don't smile."

She'd turn those big beautiful eyes on him and pierce his heart with her next words. "Oh, but you're wrong. They smile. They soar with happiness because although their lifespan is short, they're memories are shorter. They know no pain, no sorrow. They live free and die free."

Julia was obsessed with the ocean for as long as he could remember. Growing up in Indiana, she never saw the ocean except in pictures and on TV. But that didn't dull her obsession. On the contrary, she learned everything she could about oceans and seabirds, particularly pelicans. Every one of her fantasy vacations included a large body of water. He was happy she discovered so many beaches, but he wished he was there the first time she saw the ocean. They'd planned to visit the East and West Coast together when they graduated so she could see the Atlantic and the Pacific. They saved and saved for the trip, but all their plans fell apart a few weeks before graduation.

"I'm sorry, Eth. Again. I seem to be doing this a lot with you—falling apart and apologizing. I haven't been this emotional in a long time. I don't usually indulge in tears and emotional outbursts and yet I keep doing it. I blame you. I was perfectly fine without you," she said with a half-hearted laugh.

I was perfectly fine without you. Well, didn't that say it all! All Ethan's insecurities came rushing back with those few words. Why was he under the misconception she needed him now, that the past meant anything more than a teenaged crush to her? For twenty years her world went on successfully without him. She'd walked away and started a new life with another man. Yes, she married the world's biggest loser, but so hadn't he? At least she had a beautiful child to show for it. Ethan did his best to reign in his emotions and school his features. It was time for him to let her and the past go. Perhaps she was right and they would be perfectly fine without each other.

"Oh, Ethan. I didn't mean that the way it came out. I'm sorry. I meant … crap. I don't know what I meant. I'm…"

"Don't worry about it. Look, its late and I should probably be going," he said as he began to stand.

"No, Eth. Please wait. Please hear me out." Julia grabbed his hand and pulled him back beside her. "I haven't been fine without you. I want you to know. I haven't been fine. I've been far from fine."

Julia's big green eyes implored him as she continued to grip his hand with both of hers. "I've missed you. I've missed talking to you and having you in my life. I'm never this emotional and I rarely talk about anything this openly to anyone, except Aimee. It's like I've been storing it all up and all of the sudden, I'm dumping on you."

Ethan pulled his hand away and stood, needing the distance to sort through his thoughts

"Ethan, you've been back in my life for like three minutes and I'm constantly breaking down and unloading on you. I'm an adult, but with you I feel like a teenager again. I tell myself to stay strong and to get a grip. But then there you are and the words fly out of my mouth and I'm telling you things I never meant to and crying on your shoulder like I used to do. My head's spinning and to be totally honest—I'm scared. I'm a parent with responsibilities. I don't have the luxury of breaking down like this and I don't like how it feels."

She was talking, telling him all kinds of things he needed to know so he could untangle the mess she'd become, but he was stuck on, "I missed having you in my life." It was damn good to hear and damn confusing. Ethan studied Julia as she gave her impassioned speech. If she missed him so much, why the hell had she disappeared and stayed away for so long? With little effort, she could have found him. He didn't get it. He was missing something. He shook his head and sighed in frustration.

Starting up with her again was risky. She had no idea what she wanted. One minute she was hot and the next she was cold. She was scared. Scared of the past and the present. Of what exactly, he didn't know. What in the world was she hiding? Did he really want to get on this roller coaster ride again? The answer was he never got off in the first place. If he let her back in his life, he was going to do things differently. He would hold tight no matter what the past revealed or the future brought. He wasn't going to let her hide from the past or disappear out of his life again.

This wasn't going to be easy. Solving the mystery that was Julia was going to take time, patience, and skill. But as Ethan looked at her beautiful face, down her elegant neck to her hand that gripped the silver heart she wore, he knew he was up to the challenge.

He gave her a slow, genuine smile. "I've missed you too, beautiful. Every single day since the last time I saw you, I've missed you. I don't care what you dump on me. I know you're scared, terrified even, but you know damn well, I'd never do anything to hurt you. Just the opposite, actually. It's damn good to have you back in my world."

He reached down and pulled her to her feet and to him. She came willingly and he cupped the side of her face with his hand. His fingers snaked their way into her hair and his thumb caressed her soft creamy cheek and then ran across her full lower lip.

"God, you're beautiful," he whispered.

Before she had time to react, he did what he wanted to do since the second he saw her at Lexi's. He took her mouth in a soft exploring kiss that had him heating up and wanting more. When his lips touched hers, she stiffened, but as he stroked her lower lip with the tip of his tongue, she gave in, clutched at his shirt and pulled him closer. She sighed a contented sigh and sank into the kiss and into him.

He nipped her lower lip and she gasped. He took advantage and went in. She tasted so damn good. He explored every inch of her mouth and their tongues tangled in a familiar dance. There was nothing better than holding Julia in his arms and kissing her. Nothing felt so right in his life. God, he missed this. He missed her … the feel, taste, and scent of her. His Julia.

He was home.

It was she who pulled away, putting one hand on his chest, her breathing labored and her lips swollen. She looked like she'd been thoroughly kissed. She brought her fingers to her lips, closed her eyes and shook her head.

"No, no, no," she murmured.

"No?"

She stumbled back, dazed and sat as far away as she could on the couch. "Eth, no. I'm sorry. We can't do this. This wasn't supposed to happen. We can be friends, that's all. Too much has happened. We can't go back. We're different people now. It's not fair to you. I'm not good for anyone," she tripped over her words, the sentences coming fast and jumbled.

Ethan wasn't put off in the least bit because while her mouth was saying no, the rest of her body had agreed with him. She'd melted right into his arms and kissed him back. She'd held on and even pulled him closer. He didn't care what that pretty little mouth of hers was saying, they were by no means just friends. They only took a brief hiatus. It was time to rediscover and rebuild. But before they could move into the future, they had to deal with the past.

"You're right, we can't go back, but the future is wide open. Of course we've changed. Hell we've aged by two decades—just like fine wine, may I add," he said with a relaxed smile.

"This isn't funny, Ethan. There can be no future that includes anything more than friendship."

"Take it easy, Jules. Neither of us is married and there's no reason why we can't explore and see where this leads unless…"

He was an idiot. Hell, he was a damn fool. She was sweet, smart, beautiful, and single. He never considered there might be someone else. Why wouldn't she be seeing someone? The thought of someone else touching and kissing her was nauseating. He had to know.

"Are you seeing someone?" he asked, afraid of hearing her answer.

"No, there's no one else, but I can't do this again. Not with you or anyone else. I've been through too much. There's so much you don't know. I want you back in my life. I didn't lie. I did miss you, but only friendship. That's all I can offer."

Ethan took a deep breath, relieved beyond words. No other guy in the picture was a good thing because while he never thought of himself as a violent person, the image of her being with another man didn't sit well with him. "Friends is a great place to start and I'll take it, but I'm not ready to write off the future. I'm not letting you walk away from me, from us, again. I was young last time and I let go too easily. I'm not doing that again."

Julia stood and started to pace. He was pushing her, but he learned a hard lesson the last time around. He wasn't a kid anymore. He was a man ready to fight her demons and fight for both of them, even if she wouldn't or couldn't participate in the battle. He was strong enough for both of them.

"Look, tonight was supposed to be about closure, not about starting up again. I can't."

Exasperated, Ethan stood and grabbed her by the shoulders to stop her pacing. The woman was making him nuts. This had to stop.

"If tonight is about closure, then let's get that out of the way, shall we? Here is what I know. Twenty-two years ago I loved you more than life itself and I know for a fact you loved me. Then one horrific day Ella was attacked and although she survived and recovered, we never did. You pushed me out of your life from that day on. I never knew what happened. That's it, that's what I know. Now it's your turn. Let it out. Tell me what happened and have your closure."

Julia studied him, her eyes big and full of trepidation. He wanted to hold her and tell her to forget the past. While a part of him needed closure too, in some ways he didn't care about the past as long as he could have her now. But they needed to make their peace with the past before they could go on or they'd never make it. The past would always be standing in their way.

She pulled away and sat back on the couch, her arms coming around herself.

"Okay, I'm not sure where to begin."

"Before you say another word, I want you to look at me."

She raised her eyes to him. He didn't like what he saw in her eyes. The sadness and loss he could stomach, but the fear—well, that had to go.

"Before you say a word you need to know I made my peace with all of this a long time ago. It's true, I'm no longer angry, but that wasn't always the case. I was hurt, angry, confused and all kinds of things for a long time. But when you deal with death every day, you learn how precious life is and how short it is. I learned that lesson when I was an intern from a twelve-year-old boy who died in my arms from a gunshot wound. I continue to learn that lesson from my young patients who battle cancer. Jules, I let my anger go a long time ago. Now I only carry the good memories we made with me. There's nothing you can't tell me. Nothing at all."

Silence filled the room. He left her with her thoughts and went to the kitchen to retrieve their wine glasses. He made his way back to her and handed her the glass. She took it and took a sip before setting it on the coffee table.

"From the day I was born to the day Ella took me home, my life was nothing but pain and loneliness. I never felt loved or wanted even though she did her best to show me how much she loved me. Every newspaper in the country carried the story of the little girl that was found battered and half-dead that nobody wanted until a nurse took pity on her and adopted her. Did you know that? Did you know I made headlines at the age of six?"

Ethan shook his head. This wasn't a story he'd ever heard and listening to it now was tearing his heart out.

"My earliest memories are of being beaten, of being cold and hungry and terrified. I remember my mother. She was tall and thin. She had long blonde hair like mine, but it was always dirty and matted. She was always mad at me and I never knew why. I tried to be good for her, but I was never good enough. When she wasn't passed out on the couch, she was screaming at me, hurting me, or ignoring me."

She glanced toward him, but he knew she wasn't seeing him. She was far away and although he could see the pain etched all over her face and wanted to reach out and comfort her, he didn't want to break the spell.

"According to court records, my mother was a drug abuser and most likely a prostitute. My birth certificate doesn't list a father. I told you I was abused and neglected before Ella adopted me, but that wasn't the worst thing that happened to me."

Julia brought her knees up to her chest and wrapped her arms around them. "When I was six I saw my mother's boyfriend beat and kill her. When he was done, he turned his attention to me and almost beat me to death."

Ethan was stunned. God, how much pain could one person survive? Julia had survived hell and then some. He'd known she had a horrible childhood and had nightmares, but this was beyond anything he imagined. His poor girl was neglected, starved and beaten. Why would God allow something like this to happen to a child, a helpless creature? Why? For as long as he lived, he'd never understand the heavens and the decisions that came from on high. Never.

"I'm sorry, Jules. I had no idea," he said as reached for her. But her next words stopped him.

"No, wait. Just listen. Ella saved me and I owed her everything. She gave me a life I never knew existed for girls like me. She didn't just feed, clothe, and shelter me. She brought light into pitch black darkness and with it joy and laughter. She gave me love, understanding, and security. Ethan, she was all I had and she was my whole world for a long time and I was terrified if anything happened to her, I'd be alone ... again. Then my nightmare came true and my world shattered."

"I know, but—"

"No, you don't know. Let me get this out. You had everything growing up: parents who loved you and a safe and secure home, a bright future. I had Ella. You and I were as different as night and day and although you told me often enough it didn't matter, it did. When Ella was attacked, my life became an episode on *Jerry Springer* all over again. Your father was running for governor on TV and I was making the news again for something entirely different. It was too much. I had to take care of Ella. I was responsible for what happened to her and I was terrified of losing her. My world stopped and narrowed to her and me. There was no room for anyone else, not even you. I'm sorry."

Julia looked at him with sad haunted eyes that clawed at his heart. He couldn't sit back any longer, not touching her or comforting her. He reached for her hand and enveloped it in his as his thumb caressed her knuckles.

"Is that the entire story?"

She glared at him, brows raised. "Isn't that enough?"

"Yes. Of course it is."

Ethan studied Julia. She was holding something back. He didn't know how far to push, but something didn't make sense. She said she was responsible for Ella's attack. How on earth could that be? He was certain she didn't have anything to do with it. She was asleep, at home when it happened, and she was a good kid. She wasn't into drugs, didn't hang around with troubled kids. Both of them were squeaky clean, model teens. His father assured him the attack was a random act of violence. The rest of the story fit, but this part didn't make.

Yes, Ella's attack was traumatic, but he and Julia had been close as close as two people could be at their young age. Sure they had their disagreements, but she knew she could trust him. She could've turned to him and he would've moved heaven and earth to help her. Why didn't she? The way she broke things off with him, so abruptly still didn't make sense.

"Jules, I wish I'd known how you felt. I wish things had been different and I could've found a way to reach you, to help you. Why did you feel responsible for Ella's attack? You had nothing to do with that."

"I... It's complicated. Never mind. That's not important," she said and averted her eyes.

"It is important. Why did you blame yourself? It makes no sense. I know you were young and traumatized, but—"

"That doesn't matter," she said cutting him off in a tone that brooked no argument. "What I'm trying to tell you is your parents were right. Ella's attack brought home the point your parents were trying to tell us from the very beginning. We were different. We were never going to work and you deserved better. You and your family didn't need scandal and that's what I was, a hot bed of scandal."

Ethan ran his fingers through his hair and rubbed his forehead. This was an old argument, one that held no water at all and she damn well knew it.

"Julia, you knew I didn't care what my family thought. I loved you and would've done anything to help you. I guess I never convinced you of that."

"Yes, you told me over and over again. You didn't care about your family or what they thought. But I cared. I, who hardly had a family, knew the value of a family and cared for both of us. I wanted you to have the life they wanted for you. I wanted you to go to Duke like they wanted and like you wanted, not follow me to Holy Cross. In the end I had no choice anyway."

"What do you mean you had no choice? I don't get it. What am I missing?"

Her eyes met his and locked. He saw the indecision and doubt. She was trying to decide what to say, choosing her words and picking her way through the rubble of the past. In the end, she closed her eyes and shook her head. Her shoulders slumped. She was done. She was exhausted, toasted. He wasn't going to get one more word out of her.

"It doesn't matter now," she said and gave a big sigh. "It's all in the past anyway. Some things are better left there."

"I don't want any secrets left between us. Whatever it is, you can share it with me. Let me help you cast those demons out of our lives forever."

For a long time, she searched his eyes. With another heavy sigh, her big green eyes filled with sadness, she said, "No, Ethan, you've made your peace with the past and we're going to keep it that way. Now I know you're no longer angry with me, in time, I'll find peace too. Let's bury the past and never unearth it again."

Chapter Six

Saturday turned out to be a cool, rainy spring day and Lilly, who normally woke up happy, was in a cranky mood. Julia stayed up late after Ethan left, first cleaning, then talking to Aimee for hours, and finally tossing and turning for the rest of the night. She was sleep deprived and hung over and, like her daughter, was in a foul mood.

Julia dragged through her morning routine in a haze. As she fed, bathed, and dressed Lilly, the events of the night before replayed over and over again until her head ached. It was an emotional evening and although she hadn't told Ethan the entire truth, it was a relief to share some of it with him. She came close to telling him everything, but for all sorts of reasons, one of them being she was a coward, she couldn't do it. She hoped the explanation she gave him was enough. It had to be.

After convincing Ethan she was too exhausted to talk any further, he left and she opened another bottle of wine and called Aimee. Aimee was a fantastic listener. In her usual silent, yet supportive manner, she let Julia talk herself in circles until she found her way to the question she needed to ask and needed to answer. Why hadn't she told Ethan everything when she was given the chance? The truth was simple.

She was terrified.

She had every intention of telling him everything, but when the moment came, she was seized, bound and gagged by terror. What if he didn't believe her? What if he did and was furious she didn't tell him? What if this time, he was the one to walk away?

Twenty-two years ago she did what she was directed to do. She broke all ties with Ethan and kept her mouth shut. By doing so she kept herself and Ella safe from any further harm. Now their lives had collided and, like always, she would do anything to protect the people she loved. Many people, Ethan being one and Lilly being another, could still be hurt if the truth came to light. Because of that, when it came time to lift the veil and reveal the ugly truth, she couldn't do it. Right or wrong, she made the decision to hold back.

Julia settled Lilly in front of *Sesame Street* and filled the largest mug she could find with coffee that claimed to be "bold and vibrant." She sat at the kitchen table and relived the day she said goodbye to Ethan. Two days after Ella was attacked, she was released from the hospital with two broken ribs, a broken arm, and so many cuts and bruises it was impossible to catalog them all. Julia drove her home and after settling Ella in bed and giving her medication for pain, Julia penned Ethan a letter severing all ties with him.

In the letter Julia explained she wouldn't be returning to school for the last few weeks, but would finish out the year at home while taking care of Ella. She said she had plenty of time to think as she sat by Ella's hospital bed and she came to the realization his parents were right. They *were* too different and nothing could change that. She wanted to start fresh in college and he should go to Duke and do the same. As she came to the end of the letter, she sobbed and her hand shook as she wrote the final sentence, the one she knew would hurt him, the one she knew he would read over and over again and then let her go.

"I sorry, but I want my freedom. I want my wings to fly. If you love me, let me go, let me soar. Please don't hold me back, let me fly."

At first, Ethan was hard to convince, but Julia wouldn't accept his calls or his gifts and wouldn't open the door when he came by. She told Aimee the whole story one evening as she sobbed in her arms while Ella slept in a drug-induced fog. She needed to share her sorrow with someone and Aimee was the only other person on earth she trusted. She begged Aimee to help her convince Ethan they were done and he had to move on.

Aimee was hard to convince. She'd watched as Julia fell in love with Ethan and knew how much Ethan meant to her. But she relented and did her part to convince Ethan he and Julia were through. In time, Ethan stopped trying to contact Julia, until the day of their high school graduation.

Under Julia's watchful eyes and loving care, Ella healed. She was a remarkable woman who was unflappably optimistic and observant. No matter how peppy Julia acted, Ella knew there was something wrong with Julia, especially when she didn't see Ethan lurking around. For two and a half years, wherever Julia was, Ethan was sure to be. Ella loved Ethan and she was troubled when Julia and Aimee froze him out. No matter what she said or did, both girls were tight-lipped. His absence was remarkable as was the sheer misery on Julia's face. Ella couldn't comprehend what happened and no matter how often she tried to question her, Julia refused to talk about it.

After Julia's high school graduation ceremony, Ethan approached Ella and Julia asking to speak with Julia. Ella didn't wait for Julia to refuse. In a firm voice she said, "Julia, enough! I raised you better than this. You go listen to what that boy has to say and you deal with your troubles once and for all. I may be aging, but I am neither blind nor deaf. I am tired of hearing you cry every night and tired of seeing dark circles under your eyes. Child, stop running and go be the person I raised you to be. Go, do the right thing for both of you."

Turning her attention to Ethan, Ella continued. "Son, I have no idea what you did or even if you did anything to cause this, but you too must deal with this mess. I love you like you were my own and because of that, I'm interfering. This is your chance. I've bought you some time. Put an end to this nonsense and don't make me regret it."

Ethan kissed Ella's check and led Julia to the creek behind the school. They stood at the edge of the creek under a great willow tree where they often picnicked and talked for hours. Julia's heart hammered in her chest. She was panicked and terrified they would be seen together. She ached to be in his arms and hated herself for the pain she saw in his eyes, pain she'd inflicted. She refused to look at him or speak to him knowing she wasn't strong enough to do either.

She stayed silent, barely able to hold herself up as she shook with both fear and longing. When she sat on a rock but refused to meet his eyes, or answer any of his questions, and flinched when he touched her arm, he gave up. For a long time, he stayed silent, his breathing ragged, his hands ripping at his hair as he paced. Finally, he calmed and when he spoke, she could hear the defeat and utter resignation in his voice.

"I don't understand why you're doing this, ending us like this. I don't know what I did wrong and I don't believe a single word of what you wrote in that fucking letter … not a single word. I love you, Julia. I'll always love you. You'll always be a part of me." Then, he gave her the locket, turned, and walked out of her life.

Julia put her coffee mug down and reached for the locket. She opened the wings and read the inscription. It still had the same effect it had the first time she read it. Her body warmed all over and her heart soared with the knowledge at one time, someone had loved her, not because they had to, but because they chose to. Someone had loved her for who she was, the way she was. That person didn't want to change her because she wasn't good enough. To that one person, she was perfect the way she was. It was a heady feeling to be loved that way. Yes, Ella had loved her, but she was her parent, not her lover.

Julia stood and made her way to the kitchen for another mug of coffee. She shook her head and glanced at the clock on the stove. Matt would be arriving in thirty minutes. Enough of the past. She had to deal with the present. What in the world was she going to do about Matt? She had to call Lexi for some guidance.

Although it was a Saturday, Lexi would be difficult to find. The woman was always on the run. When she wasn't working, she was coordinating a charity benefit, volunteering at a shelter of some kind, or taking a class at the fitness center. Lexi was still a mystery, a contradiction, to Julia. She was young, beautiful, well spoken, and accomplished, but also the busiest, loneliest, and saddest person Julia knew. She often hid behind her attorney cloak or put on a big smile for the world to see, although her eyes told a different story.

Given Lexi's crazy lifestyle, Julia was surprised when she caught her at home.

"Hi, how are you and the world's cutest baby today?"

"Hi, Lex. We're both a bit grumpy, but fine. You?"

"I'm about the same as you guys. Just got dumped by Todd," Lexi said in a matter of fact tone.

"Oh Lexi, I'm sorry. What happened?"

"It's the usual. He wants more than I can give. Blah, blah, blah. Whatever. I don't want to talk about it. You didn't call to talk about me anyway. What's up?"

"I'm sorry, but yeah, I kind of need your advice. I

know it's a bad time and I feel bad asking, but do you have a second?"

"It's okay, tell me. Distract me from my shitty life, please."

Julia told Lexi about her conversation with Matt and her growing concern about his on again, off again relationship with his daughter as well as his latest comment about Lilly's behavior.

"Here's the thing, Jules. He hasn't hurt her or threatened to hurt her. Not really. Legally, you still don't have much to stand on, as shitty as that seems. My advice is you make it clear to him what your expectations are in the future regarding visitation and his interactions with Lilly, how you expect discipline to be handled, etc. Then stand firm. He's got to know he can't push you around and if he violates those expectations, there will be consequences."

"Okay, Lex, I'll do the best I can. I was trying to keep the peace and hoping this didn't get ugly. I want Lilly to have a good relationship with her father and I didn't want to sabotage that in any way. But he sure is making this difficult."

"Julia, you can't force him to love his child or to have a relationship with her. That's up to him. Your job is to protect your child. You've let him have all the power here and that's got to stop if you're going to protect Lilly and be her advocate. I told you to be reasonable and communicative, not let him run all over you. Come on girl, where's your backbone? If nothing else, remember I have enough dirt on this man to take him down. If you want me to. Say the word."

There was no arguing with Lexi. She was right. Julia needed to hear this and was glad she talked to Lexi. She now knew how to proceed and she felt stronger and more capable of dealing with Matt's bullshit.

As Julia hung up with Lexi, she heard the sound of a car door closing in the driveway. Spine straight and with a new sense of empowerment, she opened the door. Matt was dressed in a charcoal gray suit and tie, attempting to look elegant, but coming off as disingenuous. In her eyes, he resembled a slimy car salesman in an expensive suit. For the life of her, Julia couldn't see what she'd found so attractive in him. Thank God Lilly didn't inherit his mousy brown hair or cold blue eyes.

"Good morning Matt, please come in."

"I don't have time to come in. Carla is waiting in the car. Is she ready?" Matt said as he glanced back at the car.

As usual, Matt was in a hurry to please Carla. That was too damn bad. There was no way she was going to be rushed or rush her daughter through this reunion. She proceeded as Lexi advised and took charge. She'd been his doormat for too long and that was going to change right now. She squared her shoulders and found her voice.

"If you want to take Lilly today, you'll come inside and speak with me. We have a few things we need to talk about. This won't take long, but we will speak before you take Lilly anywhere."

Julia stood straighter and locked eyes with him. A flicker of surprise crossed his features before he folded his umbrella and walked through the door. Lilly was engrossed in *Finding Nemo* and never once looked up. Julia led him to the kitchen where she could keep an eye on Lilly. Matt passed Lilly on his way to the kitchen, but he never acknowledged her presence and in turn, his child ignored him.

"What's this about? I don't have all day," he said in a curt, cold voice that used to make her nervous and anxious to please him.

"First, keep your voice down. I don't want Lilly upset. Second, this will be the last time you pick up Lilly for anything without clearing it with me well in advance."

"This is ridiculous," Matt grumbled, crossing his arms. "I'm her—"

"Don't interrupt me, Matt. I'm well aware you're her father, although I'm not sure if you remember that fact on a regular basis. Here's the thing, if you want to be in your child's life, then you will do it consistently so she can build a relationship with you. Not this once-a-month or whenever you remember she exists business. It's too traumatic for her. If you don't want to be in her life, it's your loss. One way or another make a decision, because I'm not going to let you hurt her anymore."

"Anything else you want to lecture me on?"

His flippant manner irked Julia more than it ever had. He wasn't taking her seriously. This discussion was about their child, the most important person in her world, but not his. Lexi was on target when she said Julia had to man up and be Lilly's advocate because Matt never would. He would never be the father, the man, they both needed him to be. Lilly only had her to depend on and if she didn't get Matt's attention, Lilly would suffer.

"Yes, as a matter of fact there is, but look alive here, Matt. Perk up and listen up 'cause I'm only going to tell you this once. I do *not* believe in physical discipline. If you or your wife so much as touch our daughter in anger or in discipline, mark my words you will both live to regret it. She is not spoiled. She is two. If you feel she's too much for you to handle, then leave her to me."

Matt stood open-mouthed, glaring at Julia. She never spoke to him in that fashion and it was apparent he had no idea what to make of this new behavior. He was used to her giving in and cowering, not laying down the law and even threatening. He let his surprise show for a minute before he recovered.

"Anything else or can we go?" he said in a bored voice.

"No, that's it. Let's go see if your daughter still remembers who you are, shall we?"

Lilly was not happy to have her show interrupted. Even though Julia spent the morning telling her her daddy was coming and she was going with him for a day of fun, she was still unconvinced as Julia dressed her in her raincoat. It took some bribing and cajoling, but Lilly went with Matt. She stared forlornly at her mother as Matt strapped her in the car seat. Seeing her sad face, Julia's heart broke for her little girl. She hoped she made the right decision by letting her go with Matt for the day, not that she had much of a choice.

For the next hour and half, Julia worked off her anxiety by cleaning the entire house as she listened to the Dixie Chicks, Carrie Underwood, LeAnn Rimes, and then added a bit of Beyoncé for attitude. By the time she finished, her little house was sparkling and she felt better.

As she stepped out of the shower, she nearly jumped out of her skin when the doorbell rang. She wasn't expecting anyone and her only thought was maybe something went wrong and Matt was bringing Lilly back early. She slipped into a bathrobe and raced down the stairs, removing the clip that held her hair. Not bothering to look through the peephole, she threw open the door and came to a jolting stop. There stood Ethan with a huge smile on his face.

Dressed in another faded Harvard t-shirt and jeans, his large frame took up her entire front stoop. After all these years, he was still the most heart-stopping handsome man she'd ever known. His gray-blue eyes were filled with mischief as they devoured her from head to toe. That mixed with the wicked grin he was sporting warned the man was up to no good.

"Hi there, beautiful. Can I come in? It's kind of soggy out here."

Without a word, she stepped aside. Her cheeks turned a fiery red as she remembered what she was wearing, or more accurately, what she wasn't. She closed the door behind him and attempted to hide underneath her robe a bit more as her entire body warmed under his scrutiny.

"What are you doing here, Ethan? I wasn't expecting you."

"Well, no, you wouldn't be expecting me since I didn't tell you I was coming. If I told you, you'd be dressed and that wouldn't be any fun for me. Now would it?"

"Ethan. Honestly, I have things to do, like getting dressed for starters. I just stepped out of the shower."

"Mmh, yeah. I can see that. You look and smell delicious. Can I have a taste?" He stalked toward her slowly like a lion stalking his prey.

"Ah no, absolutely not. Stay away." She put a hand in front of her and backed away from him. He continued his pursuit, a huge grin spreading over his face.

"Oh, why not? Let me have a small, tiny taste. I promise to be quick and let you get dressed. I'll even take you out for lunch. What do you say?"

Ethan backed Julia against the wall and stood close enough she could feel his breath on her cheek. She placed her hand on his hard chest and looked up meeting his gaze as she tried to control her choppy breathing and erratic heartbeat.

"Ethan. Stop."

"Stop? Are you sure I can't convince you to change your mind? One small kiss, gorgeous, that's all."

He caressed her cheek with the back of his hand then tucked her hair behind her ear.

Julia didn't want to respond to him, but her body had other plans. It succumbed to the look, smell, and feel of him. God he smelled good. Her legs became soggy noodles, threatening to collapse. She fisted her hands in his shirt, while her nipples, the little traitors, pebbled under his gaze as everything from the waist down woke up after a long hibernation.

She dropped her eyes to his full lips and licked her lips. What was the use in arguing? She wanted this. She craved him. "Did you say lunch?"

"Mmh-hmm." He leaned into the wall and placed a hand at each side of her, essentially trapping her against his hard, muscular frame.

"Where?" she whispered in his ear, barely getting the words out as she inhaled, enjoying his mouth-watering scent. She was losing the self-control battle and she wasn't sure cared anymore. Self-control was over-rated. She was only human after all and he was… well, he was Ethan. Julia gave in. She released the death grip she had on his shirt and slid her hands up his chest and shoulders.

"Anywhere, baby. Anywhere."

"Uhm, 'kay." Her voice shook with need and her eyes hooded. She molded her body to his and was lost in an Ethan fog. It was a great place to be. The best. She wanted his lips on hers and his arms around her. For a little while, she wanted to forget all her troubles and lose herself in him. She didn't want to think about the past, present, or future. Thinking was overrated. She wanted to feel, only feel.

Ethan crushed her to him then buried his face in her hair. He licked a drop of water from her neck and kissed up her neck to the back of her ear. She hummed in delight and she shivered.

"Delicious, like I knew you'd be."

He took her lips with the hunger of a starving man and she returned his passion. She moaned in his mouth when his hand lightly grazed her breast. Julia clung to Ethan, savoring the feel of his hard chest and shoulders beneath her exploring hands and his muscular thigh pressed between hers. As their tongues dueled, she moaned again when he took her now-naked breast in his hand and kneaded it then pinched her nipple.

Julia was lost in a world of delicious sensation. She sunk her fingers in his thick hair and deepened the kiss. This time it was Ethan who moaned. He pulled away and buried his face in the side of her neck, continuing to drop kisses along her neck and jaw. As he captured her mouth in another searing kiss, she felt his hard erection press against her thigh and gasped. She sobered.

With great effort, she pulled her mouth away, gasping for air. She dropped her head against his shoulders. She knew where this was leading and she couldn't allow it, no matter how much she wanted him. She trembled all over as she tried to reign in her desire. It had been a long time since any man touched her and she needed this, needed him. In Ethan's arms she felt like a desirable and sexy woman. But good things never lasted long, not for her. Sooner or later, this too would go bad.

Julia took a deep breath and pictured diving head first into the Atlantic … in December. The time for self-indulgence was over. Gorgeous, sexy, mouth-watering Ethan had short-circuited her brain. She'd given in and allowed herself to feel and it had been sinfully good. Now it was time to get back to reality and time to re-engage her damn brain.

She reminded herself she couldn't have everything she wanted. No one could. Even if they overcame the past Ethan would wake up one day and conclude she wasn't enough for him. Then she'd be left alone to pick up the pieces of her life and her trampled heart all over again. That's what life had taught, what Matt had taught her. Men were fickle creatures that didn't stick around when they didn't get their way and not when life was too real.

Julia worked to control her emotions, but a single tear escaped and slid down her cheek.

"Hey, beautiful, what's this?" Ethan asked as he tilted her chin up and kissed her lips and cheek. "No tears now. I know I'm out of practice a bit, but I'm not that bad, am I? I'm sure with some additional practice sessions, I'll improve. You can be my tutor. What do you say?"

The hopeful, innocent look on his face had her laughing. Ethan could always make her laugh and forget her troubles.

She pushed at his chest and said, "No, I think you've been perfecting your trade over the years. You don't need any more practice. I'm the one that's out of practice. It's been a long time since anyone has been … uh. Oh, never mind. Look, this isn't a good idea. I'm sorry. We shouldn't have done that."

Julia pulled her robe closed and looked up to find him studying her with desire-filled eyes. She wasn't naïve; she knew when a man wanted her. She was surprised, however, he could still want her after so many years. She wasn't a young girl anymore and no longer had the body of a teenager. She was a forty-year-old woman who'd carried a baby and hadn't quite lost all her pregnancy weight, even after two years. Her own husband had found her lacking enough to step out and find a much younger woman to please him, and that was before she was even pregnant.

She blushed from head to toe and dropped her gaze from his, feeling exposed and inadequate.

"You promised lunch and I'm starving. I'm going to dress fast and I'll be right down. Okay?" She tried to slide past him, but she wasn't fast enough. He grabbed her hand and pulled her back into his arms. Her startled eyes met his in question.

"You do know you're a stunningly sexy woman, right?"

Julia couldn't hold his gaze and looked away. What was she supposed to say to that?

"Look at me, Jules." When she still wouldn't look at him, he tapped under her chin with his fingers. "Baby, please look at me."

Julia raised her head and met Ethan's eyes.

"I don't know what that dick of an ex-husband did or said to you to make you doubt yourself, but I can assure you of one thing. You're the most beautiful woman I've ever known. Your body is perfect and I can't keep my hands off of you. In fact, you're sexier today than you were at eighteen. You have a delicious body that one day you're going to let me fully explore and enjoy. There has never been a woman I have desired more than you. Never. Okay?"

Damn. Why did the man have to be so perceptive? How did he know what she was thinking? He wasn't lying though. She felt the evidence of his desire and saw the truth of his words in his eyes. It was good to be wanted. She nodded her head.

"I know you're scared, baby. I can feel you trembling. I swear to God I'm not going to hurt you. Try to trust me. You did once. Try and let go. I'll catch you. I promise. I'll always catch you."

"It's not that easy. I'm not sure I can. So much has happened and I'm not the same person you knew and

I have Lilly to think about too. It's too complicated."

Ethan nodded. "I get it. We've both changed and that's to be expected. You've been through a lot, but, Jules, so have I. You're not the only one who's taking a chance. The last few years have been hell for me and I don't want to revisit them any time soon. I know we still have a lot to deal with, don't think I'm fooled. But we've got time. Why don't we take it one day at a time and see where this leads to? No pressure. We were once good, no great together. Let's not try to define this, put boundaries around it, or let the past poison the future. Let's see where it leads. Okay?"

Julia sighed. Ethan was no fool. He knew she hadn't told him the full truth and he wasn't going to pressure her or rush her for more of an explanation. She was relieved. This was the Ethan from her childhood, patient and kind, but for how long? Sooner or later she was going to have to tell him everything and the truth was going to tear him up and most likely tear them apart. Could she risk her heart again knowing with almost complete certainty it would break when the truth surfaced?

She didn't have to think for long. She would always say yes to Ethan. Pure and simple, she wanted this man. She always had and she probably always would. He was it for her, her other half. She was terrified of her feelings for him. Going slow, taking it one day at a time sounded better than the alternative, life without him.

"Okay, one day at a time, but no promises."

"All right, beautiful. Have it your way. Now go dress, woman. I'm starving."

Chapter Seven

As Ethan waited for Julia to dress, he paced the length of the family room trying to control his anger at the moron Julia was once married to. He didn't need Julia to tell him all the sordid details of their marriage to know the asshole had done a number on her. Each time she spoke of him, her whole demeanor changed. She was nervous and unsure of herself. That wasn't the Julia he knew. Something changed her from the strong, confident girl she once been was, to this skittish, hesitant creature who built walls around herself and her child. Her confidence and self-worth had taken a hell of a hit.

True, she had a tough beginning, but she'd rallied. After years of Ella therapy, she learned to hold her head up high and embrace life for all its worth. She blossomed into a smart, sassy, self-assured girl who knew who she was and what she wanted from life and didn't care what anyone thought of her. She surrounded herself with a select group of people who she trusted and loved and who loved her back with the same zeal.

Beside him, only Ella and Aimee knew of her traumatic early childhood and apparently it had been a lot worse than she initially shared with him. He wondered if she was still plagued by nightmares. Once upon a time he'd been cocky thinking he knew all there was to know about Julia. Then it all fell apart and for years he questioned everything about their relationship.

Julia was a complicated woman whose past had a much bigger and deeper impact on her than his teenaged mind had understood. On top of that, she married a jerk who managed to undo some of the hard work Ella had done. So much had changed. Now she kept her head down and ploughed her way through life. Every now and then he got a sighting of the girl she once was, so all was not lost. Each time he saw Julia, he discovered something new about her and the life she was now living and he didn't like everything he uncovered. She was a complex knot he was trying to untangle and he was determined to solve the Rubik's Cube that was her life.

"Hey, stop stalling. I'm withering away here, starving to death. You ready?" Julia said as she bounded down the steps with her long blonde hair swept up in a high ponytail that swung from side to side behind her.

She wore faded jeans that fit her tall, curvy body like a glove and a God-awful lime green t-shirt that read, "I have absolutely no intention of behaving myself today!" There she was, his Julia coming out to play for the day. She was adorable. She had her own style and her own way of telling the world to go fuck itself. He couldn't stop laughing. She just made his day. He didn't know where she found that shirt, but it was the ugliest and funniest thing he ever saw.

He shook his head, grabbed her hand and pulled her in for a quick kiss.

"Come on, beautiful, let's get you fed and watered before you start misbehaving and running amuck since that appears to be your intention."

"Stop laughing. This shirt's a classic. It's both fashionable and makes a statement. In time you'll come to appreciate my fashion choices."

Chuckling, he said, "Baby, I plan to hang out a lot more with you and I very much approve of your fashion choices. I can't wait to see the whole damn wardrobe."

Ethan and Julia walked hand in hand to his truck. The sun decided to show itself, pushing the rain clouds right out of the sky. It was going to be a beautiful day after all, perfect for what he planned. Last night, on his drive home, he decided he wouldn't let Julia spend the day by herself worrying about Lilly. He knew how to get her mind off of her trouble.

"So where are you taking me in this monster?"

"It's a surprise. You have to promise me you're going to keep an open mind and try to see beyond what's directly in front of you. You'll have to use your imagination a bit."

"Huh? Oh no, no way, Eth. If your grand plan is to take me to that heap you call a home, you can turn this truck around and take me back. There is no way I'm going inside. I'm too young to die and I have responsibilities. If it collapses on top of me, who's going to take care of Lilly?"

"First, don't call my castle a heap. You haven't even seen it yet and I have a surprise for you. You'll be the first person I've shown it to. Second, if you want to eat, you'll change that attitude. Trust me, you're in for a treat."

"Fine, but I'm blaming you if anything happens to me. I'm only giving in because I'm starving and I can't make rational decisions when I'm hungry or when I'm caffeine deprived. You know that."

He reached for her hand and brought it up to his lips. "Trust me, beautiful. I promise to take good care of you." Their eyes met for a heartbeat before he turned back to the road.

Ethan couldn't wait to show Julia the glassed-in gazebo he uncovered over the last week. He started working on the property surrounding the house when the weather was good and there, in the middle of the mess that was his backyard, he discovered his very own secret garden. Actually, it was less of a garden and more of a jungle. There was so much property surrounding the farmhouse. He had no idea what he was going to do with all that land, but the possibilities seemed endless.

Over the last week he unearthed a heavy iron gate that was part of an iron and stone fencing system that surrounded the farmhouse. From what he could tell, it sectioned off a large plot of land that formed a substantial garden. No matter what he did, he couldn't seem to shove the gate open. The jungle had taken over and wouldn't release its hold on it, no matter how hard he tried. He gave up and entered the garden from inside the house through an odd-shaped door that was in the kitchen. The kitchen was massive and its ceiling slopped at one end of the room leading to an arched, heavy wooden door that was bolted and nailed shut for what seemed like centuries. It took him one full day to pry the door open and when he did, the vision that greeted him on the other side was spectacular. He couldn't wait to share it with Julia.

Ethan maneuvered his truck into the courtyard and got out to help Julia. He opened the passenger door and reached in and grabbed her by the waist, hauling her toward him. He lifted her out of the truck, sliding her down his body. He heard her quick intake of breath and felt her arms go to his shoulders and glide around his neck. He looked at her and waited, hoping she'd take the initiative and kiss him. He was certain she wanted what he wanted by the look on her face. She was aroused, but she was holding on to the illusion they wouldn't be more than friends even after that scorching kiss they shared at her house.

"Your turn, beautiful. Give it to me," he said with a slow smile.

"No."

"Okay, now I know where Lilly picked up that word. No lunch until I get what I want. Just a small peck and nothing more, I promise."

"I don't think so. You promised me lunch after

93

you invited yourself into my house and you haven't kept that promise yet. You keep adding more and more hoops to jump through. No way, Dr. Sullivan, I want lunch and I want it right now."

"Hmm, you make a good point. I did promise you lunch." He smiled but his tone became more serious as he gazed deep in her eyes. "I always keep my promises. Always. Lunch it is. Come on, wildcat. If you want to eat, I'm afraid you have no choice but to come into my humble dwelling."

Ethan drew away from her, instantly missing the warmth of her body, and pulled her behind him to the front door. He jiggled the temperamental doorknob until it disengaged and he was able to push the door open.

Julia followed him, taking it all in. All the lights were on and few blinds were wide open. There weren't many windows at the front of the house and it could be quite dark even in the light of day. The heavy stone façade made it impossible for the sun to come through, but on the positive side it also kept the house cool even on the warmest days.

The back of the house was an entirely different thing. The massive eat-in kitchen was connected to the sitting room and a dining room with an open floor plan, one room flowing right into the other. These rooms had plenty of windows and the open floor plan made the rooms appear much larger than they were.

This was his favorite part of the house. He loved the old wood-burning fireplace centered between the kitchen and sitting room. He imagined the fireplace would warm the entire place in the winter. The mantle was a mess with the stonework coming apart, but with some work it would be amazing. He glanced behind him to find Julia peering around with a look of absolute wonder on her face.

He was right, she saw it too. The potential, the possibilities of what this place could be. If he used his imagination a bit, he envisioned how the place would look furnished and fully occupied, like it was meant to be. Comfortable, over-stuffed furniture with colorful throw pillows and hand-woven Afghans filled the rooms, as a fire burned brightly in the fireplace and family pictures lined the mantle. The smell of home cooking emanated from the kitchen, while the sound of children running filled the house. Home! She saw it and she liked what she saw. Her face told it all, but he still asked. He wanted to hear the words, affirming he still could read his girl.

"Well, what do you think?"

Deep in her own thoughts, she startled.

"It's amazing, Ethan." She breathed, her voice filled with awe. "I mean, it's an absolute and utter wreck, but it's amazing. I can see what you find so appealing. It kind of draws you in, whether you want to be drawn in or not. You can't resist its charm. You can feel the history of the place and almost hear the voices of the people who used to live here. It's … enchanting. It's a home."

"I'm glad you like it. I was hoping you'd see what I see. Adam, Christine, and Lexi think I've lost my mind and perhaps I have taking on a project of this size, but I can't help myself. It's the home I've always dreamed of—well, it will be anyway. Come on. I told you I have a surprise for you and I do."

"Okay, but I hope my surprise includes food 'cause it's almost 2:30 and I could eat my arm off."

"Follow me. I shall lead you to your surprise and your sustenance."

Ethan led Julia to the door that opened to the garden. "Be careful going through. I swear the seven dwarfs must have lived here. I have to bend my body in half each time I go through."

He opened the old, wooden door and she followed him out. He heard her gasp and smiled. They stood in paradise, protected by time and space, a haven unto itself. Trees, both big and small, filled the space as well as overgrown grass and flowering bushes of all varieties. A stone water pond, much like the one at the front of the house, greeted them as they entered the garden, but this one was much larger than its counterpart. Birds flew from branch to branch and butterflies danced in the air as squirrels chased each other throughout the garden and up the trees. It was breathtaking and completely unexpected.

He waited for her brain to register everything it was seeing. She still hadn't noticed the glassed-in gazebo that stood right in the center of the garden, at a distance. It had taken him a while to figure out it was even there, hidden as it was by the overgrown grass and trees. He did his best over the last couple of days to clean a bit around it and in it. Ethan heard the exact moment she saw it.

"Oh my God, Eth. Look, look at that. It's unbelievable. Is it safe to go in?" she asked even as she started making her way to it, not waiting for him to answer.

"Yeah, it's safe. Be careful where you step. Follow the path I cut out."

Hand in hand they made their way to the gazebo. It was a bit of a hike and by the time they made it, they were both muddy and wet, but neither cared. He opened the glass door and helped her in. She gazed all around and up at the dome, glassed ceiling. It stood the test of time. Not a single pane of glass was cracked. The gazebo needed a hell of a lot of cleaning and some repair, but overall it was a treasure.

Ethan walked to the corner where he stowed a couple of blankets and a small cooler of food for them and started setting up the lunch he prepared.

"Come have a seat. Here's lunch as promised," he called to her.

Julia glanced over her shoulder and down, taking in the blanket he was sitting on and the assortment of fruit, veggies, bread, cheese, and wine he laid out.

"When did you do all of this?"

"This morning. I put everything out here, hoping it would stop raining and I could talk you into coming with me. As soon as I discovered this place, I knew I wanted to share it with you."

"You didn't know it was here when you bought the house?"

"No, I don't think anyone did. I unearthed it a few days ago."

"What a wonderful hidden treasure. I feel like Mary in *The Secret Garden.*"

"It's pretty cool and that's exactly what I thought when I found it. Come on. Eat please. I'm not much of a cook, but I'm good at throwing picnics together."

Julia sat down and smiled at him. "You did great. Thanks, Eth. You've made what I thought would be a horrible day pretty amazing."

"Then my job is done," he said with a smile and poured them each a glass of chilled wine.

"Now tell me, how did this morning go? How did Lilly do?"

"She did okay. She was pretty unhappy though. I talked with Lexi this morning and she gave me some pointers on how to deal with Matt."

"And…?"

Ethan listened as Julia told him about her conversation with Lexi, and then her conversation with Matt. He was proud of her for standing up for herself and finding her voice, and he told her so. For a while they sat in companionable silence eating and listening to the sounds of nature blooming. When they were both stuffed, Ethan cleared everything out of their way and lay down using another blanket as a pillow. He pulled her down so her head lay on his stomach and removed the tie holding her hair captive. He ran his fingers through her hair, marveling at its softness as it blanketed his stomach. They were both sated and he didn't think there was a more perfect moment.

When he thought she drifted off, she whispered his name.

"Eth?"

"Hmm?"

"Will you tell me something?"

"Sure, anything."

"Will you tell me a little bit about your life, what you've been doing the last twenty-two years? You know about mine, a bit anyway, but I feel like I've missed out on so much with you."

"Sure. What do you want to know?"

"Start at the beginning, after high school."

"I went to Duke for undergrad and then to Harvard for medical school. I met Adam at Duke and we attended Harvard together. I did my internship and residency at Mass General. Unfortunately, I married Alyssa. We lived in Boston until we divorced and then I moved here. That's the *Reader's Digest* version."

"Eth, that's your resume, not your life," she said with a giggle. "Come on, give me something."

When she started to sit, he pulled her back down so her head rested on his chest and her body was flush against his. He loved feeling her against him and he didn't want to move yet. He was in heaven.

"Okay, okay. I'll tell it all. Just don't move or I'll lose my concentration."

He felt her smile against him and he tightened his arm around her. He told her about graduating from Duke and being informed by his parents it was time to grow up and take his rightful place in the family business.

Julia stiffened at the mention of his family and he tightened his hold around her. His family had not been kind to her. They never thought she was good enough and never hid their feelings from her. While his mother took every opportunity to point out what she saw as Julia's flaws, his father ignored her presence on earth. His parents were beyond harsh to her and caused so many arguments during the time they dated, it was miraculous they stayed together at all.

Ethan loved Julia with a force that both angered and amazed his parents. The harder they tried to break the couple, the stronger Ethan and Julia's bond became. Their young love was the stuff teenaged romance novels and movies were made of. But for his parents, Ethan's fascination with Julia was the worst type of teenaged rebellion that was not to be tolerated.

"They wanted me to settle down with a girl of their choosing, the daughter of one of Dad's business associates. When I refused to meet her or any other girl and insisted on continuing my education at Harvard, they cut me off. Plain and simple, it was their way or the highway."

"I'm sorry, Ethan. That must have been very hard on you." Julia said in a quiet, solemn voice and he gave her a reassuring squeeze.

"It was and it wasn't. I knew a showdown was coming sooner or later. I never thought they would go that far. They left me no choice. That day I packed up everything I owned, called Adam, and started driving across the country to Maine. I stayed with Adam's family and tried to figure out the rest of my life. His parents were more supportive of me than my parents ever were."

"They sound like great people."

"They were terrific, warm, generous, and loving people—nothing like my folks. They were both killed two years ago in a small plane crash. It was a real tragedy."

After a minute of silence, Ethan continued. He had little in his bank account and although he had a partial scholarship to Harvard, there was no way he would be able to pay all of his expenses. If it wasn't for Adam's family, he didn't know what would've happened to him. Adam's father, a Harvard alum, made some calls and within a few days, Ethan's partial scholarship turned into a full ride.

Ethan recalled how he stayed estranged from his parents until a few years ago when his father had a stroke and asked to see him. Slowly but surely, they mended fences and it was through them he met Alyssa. At first Alyssa was a nice distraction and nothing more. But before he knew it, one thing led to another and he was proposing to her and then marrying her. It was the single biggest mistake of his life.

"I was lonely and plain sick of being by myself. I missed you terribly even after so many years had passed and I needed to move on and share my life with someone. I wanted to start a family. I couldn't have you so I threw myself into the relationship and fell in love with the dream of love and a family more than the actual woman. Do you understand?" he asked squeezing her against him and kissing the top of her head.

Ethan needed Julia to understand he'd chosen to move on only because he had no other choice. Although she'd moved on as well and built a life without him, he never wanted her to doubt he hadn't thought about her every day, loved her every day, even when he was in the arms of another.

"I get it, Ethan. I'm sorry. You don't owe me an explanation. I never wanted you to be unhappy. I never expected you to give me a second thought after the way we broke up. I wish things had been different. You deserved to be happy. I'm sorry, I ..." Julia pulled away from him and sat up and he followed.

"Hey, I'm not telling you this because I want you to feel guilty and apologize. We already visited that part of our history last night. I only wanted you to understand I didn't let go easily either. You wore my heart around your neck every day and I had a part of you with me, inside me, always. That's all. Okay?"

Her big green eyes met his and he saw the impact his words had on her. There it was, she finally got it. She finally understood he never let her go. Ethan took a deep breath and positioned his back against the gazebo wall. He pulled her into his arms and between his legs so her back rested against his chest.

"Want to hear the rest? It's not fairytale material, more like what nightmares are made of," he asked as he entwined their fingers.

She nodded her head and settled back against him with a sigh. "If you want to tell me, I want to hear."

He hated reliving the past and the next part was a doozy. He hadn't talked about this to anyone other than Lexi and Adam and although it was in the past, he still had a visceral reaction every time he remembered how he was manipulated. But if he wanted Julia to trust him and open up to him, then he had to set the example. She needed to understand she wasn't the only one shit happened to.

"No, it's okay. I want you to know."

"Even though I hated all the society bullshit, I wanted Alyssa to be happy. I really tried. I went to the parties that were important to her and entertained all her friends at our ridiculous house she decorated like a museum instead of a home. It worked. While she was having the time of her life, I was miserable, but she didn't care. When I reached my limit and couldn't continue with the charade, our lives became a series of arguments that never seemed to end."

Julia squeezed his hand in hers. "I'm sorry, Ethan. That sounds painful and the arguments remarkably familiar."

"Yeah, we have a lot in common, but at least you have Lilly. I wasn't so lucky. Alyssa knew I wanted children. We discussed it before we married and she said she wanted them too. Because we were both older, we agreed to try for a child right away. After a year of trying without success, I suggested we see a fertility specialist. She flat-out refused to go and told me she was certain she'd conceive soon."

Julia turned in his arms and placed her palm against his cheek. "And did she, Ethan? Did she become pregnant?" Julia asked in a soft voice.

"That's the thing … I have no idea. A month later, she showed me a positive pregnancy test and we celebrated. I was overjoyed and wanted to go with her to her doctor appointments, but she told me I was suffocating her. So, I gave her space. But when she was seven weeks pregnant, I came home one night to find her crying. She said she miscarried." Ethan shook his head and ran his fingers through his hair.

"I was beside myself and wanted to take her to the hospital, but she told me she'd already seen her doctor and there was nothing to be done. Over the next two years this pattern repeated itself three more times."

Julia turned completely around and straddled him. Surprised, he wrapped his arms around her loving the feel of her body against him and the familiar and easy manner she adopted with him. This was the first move she made on her own to come closer to him and he was delighted. "God, how sad. I'm so sorry, Ethan. But I don't understand what you meant when you said you have no idea?"

"Yeah—it's a bit of a sordid story. You sure you want to hear more of this mess? I'm supposed to be taking your mind of your troubles, not giving you more to worry over."

Julia met his eyes and touched her lips to his. "Tell me."

That's all she said and he saw the sincerity in her eyes. His little warrior was ready to carry his troubles along with hers and she wasn't going to take no for an answer. Sighing, he kissed her and told her the rest of the story.

Ethan considered himself a smart man and something wasn't right. While he was beside himself after each miscarriage, Alyssa bounced back fast and never seemed concerned or upset. One evening after she went out with her girlfriends, he was looking for something. He didn't remember what now. He pulled out the drawer of her nightstand too roughly and it fell to the floor scattering all its contents. When he bent to clean the mess, he discovered birth control pills. As far as he knew she'd never been prescribed birth control pills. Things unraveled after that. When he confronted her, she informed him she never had any intention of having a baby and was going through the motions for him, just to keep him happy. She told him she disliked children and would never ruin her body by carrying a child, not for him or anyone else.

"That was the last straw. I left her that night and started divorce proceedings the day after. I knew my marriage was over. I could never trust her again. I don't know if she was ever actually pregnant and aborted our child, children, or whether she somehow faked the pregnancy tests. In the end, it didn't really matter. Whatever she did, it was done and there was no going back. She'd lied to me over and over again and had gone to such lengths … it was done."

"I don't know what to say. I'm so sorry. What kind of relationship do you have with her now?"

Ethan gave a harsh laugh. "I wouldn't call what we have now any type of relationship. She killed any hope of that. It took two years and a hell of a lot of time, energy, and money to be rid of her. She tried every trick in the book to keep me tied to her, but in the end, she failed. And that's the highlight of my life for the last two decades. Not a pretty story, is it?" Ethan said in a weary voice.

Julia touched her forehead to his. "I'm sorry you had to go through that. I'm sorry I made you talk about it when all you probably want to do is forget it. But, Ethan, she's a fool. Alyssa is a fool." Placing a tender kiss to his lips, she whispered against his lips, "She has no idea what she lost."

"Thanks, baby. It's done and I'm glad you know. I told you my ex and yours have a lot in common."

"Yeah, I guess they do. I knew Matt didn't want kids and honestly, I was okay with it. I wasn't sure if I could really be a good mother anyway. Lilly was a total surprise."

"You're a fantastic mom. That kid loves you to death and you're great with her. Why did you think you wouldn't be a good mom?"

Before she could answer, Julia's cell rang. She pulled away and stood pulling the cell out of her pocket and glancing at the display.

"Sorry, Eth, it's Matt. This can't be good."

Ethan studied her as she spoke with Matt and saw the worry cloud her features. He heard Lilly screaming her head off through the phone. He stood and grabbed Julia's hand. Without a word he headed for the door. The one-sided conversation he heard was enough to make his blood boil. That son of a bitch was letting his daughter cry her heart out as he screamed obscenities at Julia.

It was time he met Matt and showed him Julia was no longer on her own and no longer his to do with as he liked. That nonsense was going to stop.

Chapter Eight

Julia and Ethan made it to her house in record time—way before Julia expected Matt and Lilly to arrive. Matt called from the car and said he was on I-80, about thirty minutes away. All Julia heard was her baby sobbing in the background, asking for her mama over and over again while Matt screamed at her to stop crying. Julia had no idea what happened to bring on Lilly's complete meltdown, but as she heard her child weep, she began to lose her mind and a hot, blinding rage built.

Matt used a hands-free telephone system in the car. Therefore, Julia knew Lilly could hear her voice throughout the car as she spoke with Matt. Julia tried to interrupt Matt so she could talk to Lilly and calm her down, but he ignored her and his shouting escalated. He was livid and said Lilly had been intolerable—out of control all day.

He told Julia it was evident she was incapable of parenting a child and called Lilly a little brat. He spewed something about Lilly biting him, vomiting on everything, holding her breath until she almost passed out, and crying most of day. The more he talked, the angrier he became until Julia worried for Lilly's safety. She interrupted his rant in a firm tone and told him she would meet him at the house where they would talk more. She told Lilly she'd see her soon and everything would be all right. Then, she hung up feeling helpless.

Ethan listened to every word as he shepherded Julia out of the gazebo, into his car and started driving her home. She glanced at him as she spoke to Matt and she saw his jaw harden as he gripped the steering wheel, his knuckles turning white. She felt the waves of anger coming off him and filling the car. Although Julia understood his anger was not directed at her, she worried how he would channel it. She couldn't handle another man losing it at this moment.

Once they arrived at the house, Julia thought Ethan would drop her off and go, but he followed her in. When she suggested he leave, she could handle things from here, he glared at her, with thunderous gray eyes, and said in a tight voice, "There is no way in hell I'm leaving you to handle that son of a bitch alone. Got it?"

She took in his unwavering stare and the hard set of his jaw and realized there was no use in arguing with him. She may not have seen him for a couple of decades, but she remembered that stubborn look. She paced around the house, looking out the window every time she thought she heard a car. Finally, Ethan stood from the couch, walked over to her, and hauled her into his strong arms.

"I know you're sick with worry, but it's going to be all right. She's going to be fine. Please, baby, take a deep breath and try to calm down."

"I can't calm down. She was sobbing, calling for me, and I couldn't help her. She needed me and I couldn't get to her. I shouldn't have sent her today. I didn't listen to my gut. I'm her mother and I failed to protect her. I promised her the day she was born I would never let anyone hurt her. I failed her."

Ethan grasped her shoulders and held her away from him. "Jules, listen to me. She's going to be all right. It sounds like she had a tough day with her father, but most likely she'll be fine. You didn't fail her, he did. You'll take care of her and comfort her. She'll be fine and we'll both deal with him. You're not alone anymore. Do you understand?"

"Ethan, this isn't your … wait, that's them."

Julia rushed out of his arms, across the room and

flung the front door open. She heard Lilly's sobs and her heart sped up as she ran to the car. Before Matt had a chance to get to Lilly, she opened the back passenger door and reached for her child.

Lilly was halfway strapped into her car seat and she was sobbing her little heart out. Julia noted her child had been in a car for God knows how long without being properly strapped in and the pressure in her skull ballooned until she was certain her head would explode. Then she studied Lilly's face and she gained a new understanding for the words justifiable homicide.

Lilly's cheeks were tear-streaked and the right side of her face was reddened with a distinct handprint. Her child had been slapped! Julia closed her eyes and breathed in deep, trying to control the trembling that took over her body fueled by the all-consuming white-hot rage that flowed through her veins like lava.

She examined Lilly again and saw the child's eyes were red and puffy and her nose was runny. She was still in the formal dress she put her in that morning, although it was an absolute mess. The two-hundred-dollar white taffeta dress had ruffled sleeves and red dots, a collared neckline with three little red buttons that flowed down the center of the bodice and large fabric rosettes around the bottom of the skirt. Where this morning she looked adorable, now she looked like a sad, disheveled and distraught little girl.

Julia worked to free Lilly from the few straps that held her in her seat as Lilly reached out to mother, her sobs escalating. Finally free, Lilly wrapped her arms around her mother's neck and her legs around her waist, molding her tiny body to Julia's like a baby koala bear. She buried her face in Julia's neck and continued to sob. Her little body trembled against Julia's and all Julia could do was hold her as she tried to control her own trembling limbs.

"It's okay, Lilly. Shh, shh, Mama's here."

She repeated this mantra in the most soothing voice she could muster as she rubbed circles against Lilly's back. Before he could get one word out, Julia pushed past Matt and walked up the concrete stairs and into the house, leaving him to get Lilly's belongings. She didn't trust herself to speak. She had to calm Lilly down first and get her out of earshot before she dealt with Matt. And she was sure as hell going to deal with Matt.

She entered the house and saw Ethan standing with Lilly's stuffed giraffe in his hands.

"How's our girl doing?" he asked as he walked toward them.

"She's okay, aren't you, baby? You're fine now you're home."

Although Lilly's crying had eased some, she kept her head buried in her mother's chest. Looking at Julia, Ethan raised an eyebrow and nodded at the open door in question.

"He's bringing her stuff in."

Ethan took over rubbing Lilly's back. Lilly stopped crying and was hiccupping and sniffling as she tried to catch her breath.

"Hey, angel face. What's this all about? Why all the tears, sweetness? Look what I have for you. George the giraffe missed you."

Lilly raised her head and looked at Ethan. Then she threw herself out of her mother's arms and into his as Matt came through the front door.

"E!" she wailed as she reached for him and her giraffe at the same time.

Lilly buried her tear-streaked face in his neck and fisted his shirt. Julia saw the instant Ethan noticed the redness on Lilly's cheek because his jaw tightened even more.

"Hey, angel. Come on baby, you're breaking my heart," he cooed as he continued to rub her back. "No more tears or you're going to make George and me cry with you and that would be a real mess."

"Who the hell are you? Get your hands off my daughter this instant." Matt's voice roared through the room and Lilly began sobbing again as she held onto Ethan with all her might, trying to crawl into him. Julia didn't know what to do as she looked between Matt who began stalking toward Ethan and Ethan who looked like he would crush Matt with one arm as he cradled her daughter with the other. She didn't have to do or say anything. Ethan raised his head and said one word aimed at Matt.

"Stop."

It sounded more like a growl and there was no doubt at his meaning. He gave Matt the most formidable glare she'd ever seen. His eyes were glacial and, although he never stopped rubbing Lilly's back, his whole demeanor changed and a tick was now visible in his jaw. In all the years she'd known Ethan, she'd never seen him look this angry or this deadly, and in all the years she'd known Matt, she'd never seen him take an order from anyone. Matt froze in his tracks openmouthed and stared at the giant of a man in front of him.

Julia intervened before the men went at it and further upset Lilly.

"Matt, this is Ethan Sullivan. Ethan is a good friend of mine."

A few seconds ticked by with the men sizing each other up until Matt looked away. Muttering he'd talk to her about this after he emptied and cleaned the car, Matt walked out of the house. Lilly settled again, her body going limp against Ethan. She closed her eyes and fell into a fitful, exhausted slumber.

Matt returned with the rest of Lilly's belongings from the car and dropped them inside the front door. In a much more subdued, but no less nasty tone, he commanded, "Julia, we need to talk. Now. Outside."

"That's fine, Matt. Outside is a good idea. Ethan, are you okay with Lilly or do you need me to take her?"

"Lilly and I are fine, but let me put her down and we can all talk."

"This doesn't concern you in any way. I will talk to my wife alone and without your interference."

Lilly whimpered in Ethan's arms again.

"Shh, I've got you angel. You're safe," Ethan whispered to the child in his arms, then glared back at Matt, pinning him with a hard stare.

Keeping his voice low and controlled, Ethan said, "Here's how this is going to work, Walker. You go ahead and talk to Julia, but let's be clear about a few things. First, she's no longer your wife; you lost the privilege of calling her that a while back, so check yourself. Second, the only thing saving you from me right now is the child I have in my arms. So be careful what you say and how you say it. I can be a protective son of a bitch with what's mine. Are we clear?"

Matt gave Ethan a hard, assessing look, and then turned to Julia. "Yours? Fine with me. You can keep Julia. I don't give a damn. You're right. She's no longer my problem. But that's my daughter you're holding. So don't threaten me, you prick. I'll say and do what I like."

"Matt, don't…" Julia started.

Ethan walked to Julia and put an arm around her and squeezed her shoulder. Never taking his eyes off Matt, he spoke in a low, even tone.

"It's okay, baby. Looks like Matt and I need to get to know each other a little better. Why don't you take

Lilly and put her to bed while we get acquainted?"

"I don't think that's a good idea, Ethan. I need to handle this on my own."

Julia's voice was filled with apprehension and her eyes darted between them. Matt was being an asshole and Ethan had gone all possessive caveman on her. Matt had no idea who he was messing with. Ethan was twice his size and, if her memory served her, when his voice dropped and his eyes narrowed, it meant he was barely keeping his temper in check. God help the idiot who got in his way. While Matt deserved anything Ethan dished out, she didn't want a brawl in her home.

She could give in and let Ethan take care of the situation for her. She didn't doubt he could convince Matt to leave, but she knew Matt. He may give in and go this time, but he would be back and he would make her life, and possibly Lilly's, miserable. He was accustomed to bullying her and putting her on the defensive. It was time she stood up for herself and her child. Enough was enough.

"Beautiful," Ethan said. "Look at me. You really want to do this?"

"Yes. I can handle this just fine," she said in a stronger, more convincing voice as she met his eyes.

"Okay. But, there's no need to take this show on the road. Why don't you stay here? I'll take Lilly, clean her up, and put her down."

"You sure?"

"Oh, for God's sake. Are we going to do this all night?" Matt bit out. "I don't have time for this nonsense. Are you going to hide behind your boyfriend or are we going to discuss the disappointment that is our daughter?"

Julia put a hand on Ethan's chest to stop him from taking the bait. She turned and walked toward Matt.

"Oh, we are most definitely talking and we're

doing it now."

She glanced over her shoulder at a very pissed-off Ethan. "Eth, it's okay. I've got this. Please take care of Lilly. She's had enough drama for the day. As soon as I'm done with Matt, I'll be up. It shouldn't take too long."

Ethan nodded and gave Matt another hard stare that delivered a message of warning so clear it needed no translation.

Julia gave her full attention to Matt and decided right then and there it was time to do what she was put on this earth to do—protect her child and introduce Matt to the definition of *enough*. She'd been patient and put up with his array of shit for way too long. Enough was enough. Matt crossed the line when he rained pain down on her child. For her, it was the point of no return and in that minute, all the rage that had built over decades made its way to the surface and exploded.

Before he could get out a single word, she spoke in a tone she knew he never heard coming from her before. She barely recognized her own voice. She opened her mouth and fought for the little girl who was abused, neglected, and left in the hands of a monster who almost killed her. She fought for her child who wanted so much to be loved by her father, a man who barely tolerated her and thought of her as a problem, an obligation, and finally a disappointment.

"I don't know what happened today and I don't care. I'm going to be as clear and as succinct as possible so you fully understand the message I want to relay to you."

"No, I think it's time you listened to me, Julia. I've had about—"

"Enough! I am through, so very through listening to you. I am through putting up with your bullying and your insults and cowering in the corner, all because I wanted our daughter to have a healthy relationship with her father. Well, now I'm done. We're done!"

She walked closer to Matt so they stood eye to eye. Matt was speechless. His eyes were wide and his mouth hung open.

"We've been over this before, but I am going to review this with you one last time. I am well aware you never wanted children, but Lilly is here to stay. She was a surprise for me too, but I, unlike you, do not see her as a nuisance or a disappointment. She is a blessing, a joy, and the most important person in my life."

"She is out of control and you have no idea how to raise her. You don't discipline her whatsoever. You're raising her to be as wild and unrefined as you are. That is evident in the way you dress her to the way you let her do and say whatever she wants. You think any form of discipline is abuse because someone took a firm hand to you. It's obvious by her behavior today she needs a much firmer hand."

Julia froze. Matt knew her story well enough to know she survived much more than a "firm hand." He never liked her talking about her past and thus he only knew the basics. He was smart enough to understand the difference between discipline and abuse; at least she thought he was.

"I can't believe you said that, but I'm glad you did so I know what you believe is appropriate discipline. Thanks for making this even easier for me, for giving me the ammunition I need."

"Look, Julia, I didn't mean that. I know you were abused, but Lilly was impossible today, right from the beginning. She was into everything, refused to sit still, mind her manners and was as demanding as hell. When Carla tried to change her, she started screaming for you and then held her breath. Carla had no choice but to slap her."

"No choice? Have you lost your mind? You let that woman touch our child in anger. You stood by and let someone hurt our baby and you condone this behavior?"

"Julia, you're blowing this out of proportion. It was a light slap to the cheek and it worked. She took a big breath in, but then started screaming her lungs out again. She was in such a state. She even bit me when I tried to buckle her into her car seat."

"So you decided it was safe to leave her unsecured in the car? Are you insane? Not only did you allow her to be slapped while you stood by and did nothing, then you threw her in the car without care for her safety all because she was crying. Why, why would you leave her unharnessed? She could have been injured or even killed."

"Stop it, Julia! She's fine. You're making a big deal out of nothing. A light slap on the cheek did not mortally injure her. Hell, she deserved a lot more than that. I've had enough of her antics. I won't put up with this type of behavior, even if you will. It's simply not acceptable."

She couldn't believe what she was hearing. It was no big deal? Was Lilly's safety so irrelevant to him he put her at risk? Did he believe slapping a two-year-old child was an acceptable way of discipline? She studied him and saw a stranger, an unfeeling, self-absorbed stranger. She questioned her own sanity for ever loving him and marrying him.

"Matt, you're not listening to me. When I said we're done, I meant just that. It's over. Since you never wanted Lilly and since you only see her as an obligation, consider yourself off the hook. You'll never have to deal with her behavior and her antics, as you put it, because you'll never be given the chance again to touch my child, hurt my child, or discipline my child. Never."

"Lilly is my child as well and I will see her where and when I want to. Furthermore, I will discipline her how I see fit. You cannot keep me away from her and if you try, you'll regret it. Unlike you, my resources are vast. Don't force my hand, Julia. You don't want to go there."

As Julia was about to answer him, she heard footsteps and turned to see Ethan coming down the stairs. His eyes met hers and it was evident he'd heard their conversation. His eyes were on fire. The house was small and they hadn't been keeping their voices low. Julia sighed and wrapped her arms around herself. Her shoulders slumped in exhaustion as adrenaline filtered out of her body. She didn't have the energy to run interference between the two men *and* tend to her daughter.

Ethan must have read and interpreted her body language. He ignored Matt, took sure, steady strides to her and pulled her in his arms, taking her by surprise. She stiffened, unused to being in another man's arms in front of Matt, but then thought the better of it and relaxed against Ethan, letting the warmth of his body seep into hers and the strength of his arms hold her up. She breathed in his familiar scent, closed her eyes and let his words soothe her.

"It's okay, beautiful. She's okay and sleeping soundly. You're okay too. Remember what I said. You're not alone," Ethan whispered in her ear so only she could hear.

She sagged, nodded and looked up to meet his eyes. In his eyes she found tenderness and determination.

"Julia!"

Julia jumped as Matt's voice thundered throughout the room. Ethan steadied her as she turned in his arms. For a minute she'd forgotten Matt was in the room. When she tried to pull away from Ethan, he wouldn't let her, and held her tighter, her back to his front.

"Matt, keep your voice down. Lilly is asleep and I'd like to keep her that way," she said.

"Should we finish our discussion about our daughter or do you feel it's more important to make out with your boyfriend in my presence?"

"That's uncalled for. Grow up, Matt. As for our discussion, I think we're done. You can threaten me all you want, but after today, if you ever want to see Lilly again, you can do it in my presence or not at all. It's your choice. I won't risk her safety or her emotional health again. I'm giving you an out and I suggest you take it."

"If you insist on this nonsense, you'll be hearing from my attorney. I don't think the courts will choose to leave a child with an emotionally scarred woman with limited financial means who is inappropriately consorting with a man, while that child could be with her father who can provide her with a stable family and financial security. When your background is revealed to the courts, no judge in his right mind will give you custody."

Julia pulled away from Ethan's embrace. Had Matt just threatened to take her to court and take her child from her? Why would he do that? He didn't want Lilly. She was certain of that. Would he take Lilly away from her mother out of spite? To what end? Julia's breath caught and her heart slammed against her ribcage like a trapped bird fighting to break free.

"Let's think this through, shall we? You never had a father and you're mother was a drug-abusing whore. Even the woman who raised you had a colorful past. Hell, the only reason she got custody of you was nobody wanted you in the first place. You're nothing more than damaged goods—emotionally unstable, held captive by your past and incapable of raising or disciplining a child. I tried to mitigate some of that damage when we were married, but I failed and frankly you're no longer my problem."

Damaged goods. Emotionally unstable?

Is that what he thought of her? Is that why he left her? Each word out of Matt's mouth was like a slap to the face. Hearing the man she once loved and trusted be so cruel was devastating. She wanted to shatter, to fall to the floor in pieces and give in to grief. She couldn't. Not now. That's what Matt expected and what he wanted. She wouldn't give him the luxury. Julia had no idea why Matt was hell bent on hurting, not destroying her, but she wouldn't give him the satisfaction.

Man-up. She remembered Lexi's words. What the hell was wrong with her? When did she become so weak? She finished her self-directed pep-talk and pushed her sorrow and pain aside. She would examine her feelings later and if she needed a good cry, she'd allow herself that extravagance later, in private where no one would judge her emotionally unstable.

Now, however, was the time to push up her sleeves and fight for her child. No one but Ella ever fought for her, but she knew what she had to do and how to do it. She'd fight and she'd fight dirty. If Matt planned to devastate her life by take her child away, he had no idea what he unleashed. Let him think she was damaged goods and emotionally unstable. Perfect. He was a damned fool. She may be a lot of things, but first and foremost she was a mother. She would go to any lengths to protect her child. He left her no choice. She would destroy him.

Chapter Nine

"That's enough! Not another fucking word out of you, Walker," Ethan said through gritted teeth.

For a few seconds Ethan's vision went red as he fought to control the blinding rage that consumed him. If he hadn't seen Julia's whole body tremble, he would have been on top of the asshole giving him the beating of his life. Although Julia hated violence of any kind, even she could see this guy was asking for it. He laid a hand on her shoulder for a second before facing off with Matt. He stood as close to her as possible and reached for her hand, squeezing it.

"Earlier I warned you to check yourself and I see you didn't take me seriously. I don't have a child in my arms anymore and if you think for one second I'm going to let you speak to Julia like that, you're sadly mistaken. She's no longer on her own, no longer your punching bag. This conversation is over. Get out and if you don't, I'll be happy to help you."

"Are you going to hide behind your boyfriend from now on Julia? Is that how I can expect all our conversations to go?"

Julia straightened her spine and squared her shoulders.

"There won't be any more conversations and I doubt there'll be any lawyers. I've never asked you for much, just that you be a decent human being and father, but since that's not possible, you've left me no choice. Have your lawyer call me. Better yet, have him call Lexi, because this is the last time I'll speak to you without my attorney present. You should know I am a mother who is willing to do anything to protect her child," Julia said in an eerily calm and cold voice, one Ethan never heard before.

"First your boyfriend threatens me and now you. Really, Julia, you've reached a record low. We'll see what the courts think about the use of threats and violence as a way to problem solve."

"Oh, I'm not threatening you. I'm simply reminding you that you, more than most people, have a few skeletons in your closet you may not want your new wife and her wealthy, upstanding family to know. I too have resources. I hoped I'd never have to play dirty, for Lilly's sake, but I will."

"I have nothing to hide, and do not bring Carla or her family into this. They're not your concern," Matt said in a much less cocky voice. He ran a hand through his hair and a nervous tick started in his right eye-lid.

Well, that was interesting. Matt was actually nervous. He was hiding something. Whatever Julia had on him, it had to be good.

"If you have nothing to hide then Carla must already know she wasn't the first or only woman you cheated on me with. She was the wealthiest and the best pick of the bunch, I suppose, but certainly not the only. Don't look so shocked. I know all about the other women you had on the side over the years. But you know what they say, once a cheater, always a cheater. Lexi can provide Carla with some pictures of today's flavor of the month. Now, how do you think Carla's parents will feel about the way your treating their little heiress? Hmm? But hey, let's not get hung up on those tawdry details."

Matt's face turned a volcanic red and he visibly trembled. His fists clenched at his sides. He was about to erupt.

Ethan took a protective stance next to Julia, positioning his body slightly in front of hers.

"Wait," Julia said, "I'm not through. We're

getting to the most important part. Before you decide to take me to court, save yourself some time and money and inform your lawyer you never wanted your daughter. You even threatened to leave me, via email of all things, unless I aborted her. Yes, I kept that little love note, for an occasion like this. I hoped I'd never have to use it. I foolishly thought…" Julia's voice hitched and she looked away. Then she took a breath and with a slight tremble to her voice said, "I thought over time you'd fall in love with your child … as I did."

For a few seconds, not a sound could be heard in the room. Ethan caressed Julia's hand with his thumb. Her hand was cold and trembled in his. She was putting on a strong front, a fantastic illusion of strength and will while she battled her own nerves beneath the surface. By facing off against Matt, she was reliving and admitting some ugly truths about her marriage and the father of her child. It had to be painful and yet, she appeared composed and confident, except for the slight tremble he heard in her voice and felt in her hand.

"Matt, for all our sakes please think things through a bit more before you drag us both through what is sure to be a lengthy and long court battle. No, don't say anything more," Julia interrupted Matt before he could go on the attack.

"I'm sorry it had to come to this. But if you're honest with yourself, you'll admit you want Lilly now, I'm sorry to say, for all the wrong reasons. You weren't there for her birth or when she had pneumonia and was hospitalized a month later. You weren't there for so many difficult times and you missed out on even more wonderful times. You didn't see her first smile, hear her first word, or hold her hand as she took her first step. You missed it all. You could have seen your child as often as you wanted, but your visits were infrequent, obligatory, and brief at best."

Julia released Ethan's hand and took a few steps toward Matt. "Matt, you've never been there for Lilly emotionally or even financially. Since the day she was born, you haven't spent a single penny to support her, not when we were married and not after we were divorced, even though the court mandated you to do so. There's nothing left to say and nothing left to do except for you to go now. This is done. We're done. Do what you have to do, but remember an innocent's life is at stake."

Matt studied Julia for almost a minute, their eyes never leaving each other. A variety of emotions crossed his features. His jaw was set in stone and his hands were still fisted by his sides. Eventually, without a single word more, he broke eye contact and shook his head. Then he turned, stalked to the door, and slammed out of the house.

Julia stood as still as a statue, staring at the door. Ethan didn't know what to do first, kiss her or strangle her. He was proud of her. She found her voice and stood up for herself and for Lilly. But he couldn't believe she let Matt get away with so much for so long. No wonder the guy thought he could do and say anything.

When she began to tremble and her arms went around herself, he went to her side before she collapsed. He reached her just as her knees gave away. Without a word, he gathered her up and carried her to the couch, cradling her in his lap. She'd been strong, did what she had to do, and said what she had to say. Now her body and mind were shutting down as she became aware of the enormity of what just occurred. Most likely, it was the first time she stood up to Matt. As he suspected all along, his Jules, the one who had a voice and a strong one at that, had been lost. She just made her debut to Matt and shocked the hell out of him. In Ethan's estimation, it was about damn time.

Now, it was time to deal with the fallout of emotional overload. At first she didn't cry, but shook violently, to the point her teeth shattered. He reached for the afghan that covered the back of the couch and wrapped her in it as he held her body closer to him and whispered words of encouragement. She'd been by herself for so long and he wanted her to know she wasn't by herself anymore. He was by her side in battle and would stay there if she let him. But if she didn't want that, he'd be happy waiting at home to clean and dress her wounds and hold her until the pain and terror past, just as he was doing now.

Ethan watched her react to Matt's digs about her childhood. She stood strong, absorbing each blow, and never showing the impact those words were having on her heart. She shoved each painful word to a corner to deal with later because at the time she needed to unleash her anger and pick up her weapons and fight. Now that the battle was won and she lay down her weapons, he was certain she was revisiting each scene and replaying the conversation. This time the pain was rolling through her and over her.

"Jules, baby, it's over now. You did good. It's over and I'm so proud of you."

She didn't say a word. She held tight to his shirt and silently wept. He tightened his arms around her and rocked her. She didn't need him to say anything or to try to dissect what occurred. There would be plenty of time for that later. No, the best thing he could offer her was the strength of his embrace and his understanding and support. They stayed like this with her soft cries the only sound in the house until she, like her daughter, fell into an exhausted sleep.

The sun went down and the room darkened. Ethan looked down at the face of the strongest, bravest woman he knew … his Jules. She was a survivor; there was no doubt about that. He brushed the hair away from her face and wiped the wetness off her cheeks. Shit, she was still crying, even in her sleep. He bent and brushed a light kiss to each of her eyelids and her lips. He told Matt she was his, and he meant it. Julia was his and he loved her.

Ethan loved Julia.

Why was that thought so surprising? He had always loved her. He never stopped, not when she'd ripped his heart out and rejected him and not when she left. It took them twenty-two years to find each other again and just a few days for them to pick up almost where they left off. Yes, they were all grown-up, adults with complicated lives and complex problems. But they gravitated to each other like they always had and they always would. They belonged to each other. Ethan was convinced of that. Now he had to convince Julia of the same.

Ethan scanned the small room with its cozy, if worn, furniture. This house held everything that was dear to him, everything he loved—the beautiful, strong, yet fragile woman in his arms and the little spitfire she created slumbering upstairs. Both were precious to him and he'd work hard to make sure they both knew they could trust him and they were loved. He would make damn sure neither were hurt again by Matt or anyone else.

Julia still cared for him. There was no doubt in his mind. But she could be stubborn and she was going to be wary after this mess to give all of herself and her baby to him or anyone else. He couldn't blame her. He would bide his time and earn their trust and love. He was up for a good run if at the finish line he could have Julia and Lilly.

He stood with Julia in his arms and debated

whether to tuck her in her bed or lay her on the couch. He wasn't leaving her tonight, no matter what she said. She would have nightmares and he wanted to be there when they came. They always came after a traumatic event. Once she battled through one nightmare and woke up, she'd stay up for the rest of the night so she wouldn't have to experience more. When they were younger, after a bad night she would have dark circles under her eyes and her vibrant green eyes would be dull and haunted. He was powerless to do anything about the nightmares then, but that wasn't the case now.

Ethan lay Julia on the couch and checked on Lilly. Lilly was waking up as he entered her room. He was glad he was there when she awoke because he didn't want her to cry out and wake her mama. She smiled sleepily the second she saw him and reached out to him to.

"Hello, angel baby. All better now after your nap?"

He picked her up and held her to him as she wrapped her arms around him and settled against his chest. The poor kid was still wiped out.

"Mama?"

"No worries, angel. Your mama is downstairs taking a nap. How about we go make something to eat? You want to help me cook?"

"Okay, E," she sighed.

He carried her down the steps and to the kitchen pointing to a still-sleeping Julia so Lilly saw her mother was nearby. Lilly looked at her mother and lay back against his chest, sticking her thumb in her mouth. He rubbed her back and whispered to her while he opened cans of soup and took out the bread, butter, tomato and cheese he needed to make grilled cheese and tomato sandwiches.

He wasn't much of a cook, but soup and

sandwiches he could handle. He had to do everything one-armed because Lilly refused to be put down, even when he tried to bribe her with a cookie. He gave up and went about preparing the simple meal as he whispered to Lilly.

"Angel, do you know I love you more than there are stars in the sky?"

"No."

"Angel baby, do you know I love you more than a world of hugs?"

"No."

"Do you know I love you more than there are fish in the sea?"

"No."

"Angel eyes, do you know I love you more than there are angels in heaven?"

With a big sigh, she lifted her head off his shoulders and studied him with her big, green Julia-eyes. She smiled a sad, wistful smile and said, "Okay, E."

His heart broke a little more. He brought his face to hers and gave her butterfly kisses until she giggled her happy baby girl giggles. He heard movement and looked up to see Julia watching them, her eyes filling with tears again. Ethan walked to Julia and brought her into their embrace.

"Oh no you don't. No more tears. Angel, want to help me give your mama some butterfly kisses too so she doesn't cry?"

"Yesh," Lilly said with such enthusiasm it had him grinning.

"Okay sweetness. I'll get this side, you do the other."

He brought his face close to Julia's cheek and fluttered his eyelashes so they stroked her cheeks while Lilly attempted the same on the other side.

"Butterfly kisses for you, beautiful," he whispered in Julia's ear and then brushed her lips with his.

She smiled at him. "So that's what you've been doing when you whisper to Lilly. Sweet, yet sneaky."

Julia took Lilly from him and gave her a kiss and hug. "Hi, baby girl. How're you doing? Did you have a good nap?"

Lilly was happier now and allowed Julia to put her in her high chair without a fuss. Julia stood next to Ethan as the soup warmed and he made sandwiches in a practiced manner.

"I'm sorry about all the drama, Eth. I'm sure this wasn't how you planned to spend your weekend. I'm sorry about, well … everything."

Ethan turned off the stove and took her in his arms. He searched her eyes, not knowing where to begin. There was so much to say.

"First, there's nothing to apologize for. Not a darn thing. We have a lot to talk about, but what we all need now is food. Then, once everyone is fed, if you're still up to it, we can chat. If not, there is always tomorrow or the next day or the next. Okay?"

Imitating Lilly, she smiled and said, "Okay, E."

They ate in comfortable silence, each lost in their own thoughts with Lilly's babbling filling the silence. As he did the dishes, Julia took Lilly up for a long bath. He heard her reading Lilly a story. It wouldn't be long before Lilly would fall asleep and Julia would come down. He busied himself opening a bottle of wine and searching for wine glasses.

Julia joined him on the couch after she changed into yoga pants and a long-sleeved t-shirt. She'd washed her face and pulled her hair back with a clip. Her eyes looked bigger than ever. She was exhausted. She tried to put distance between them by sitting at the far end of the couch, but he wasn't having any of that. He reached for her and hauled her into his arms, forcing her to look at him.

"No, Jules, no way."

"No what?"

"No distance, no walls, no excuses, and no apologies. Just you and me and just now, not the past rearing its ugly head. Do you understand? I know we have a lot to talk about and a lot to deal with, but we'll do it together."

"It's my past and my mess. I appreciate you being here and wanting to take care of Lilly and me, but this is my life, not yours. You just ended a messy painful relationship and you don't need another."

Julia tried to pull away from him, but he tightened his hold.

"I appreciate you trying to protect me, but I know my needs the best. What I need and want are you and Lilly. I'm not walking away. I know you're scared, but baby, try to have a tiny bit of faith in me. Remember, we agreed—day by day."

She shook her head and pulled away. This time he let her.

"I told you. I'm not ready for this and I'm not sure I ever will be. I'm not good with relationships of any kind. They don't seem to work for me, not in the long run, anyway. Matt wasn't entirely wrong. I am a bit of a scarred mess."

"That idiot wasn't right about a single thing." Ethan didn't like how this conversation was starting.

"Look, it's time you knew the full story. He was right about my birth mother and my father and even Ella and her past. My parents never wanted me. No one wanted me but Ella. I thank God for her, but Matt's right. Ella's husband was incarcerated. He was on death row for murder the last time I heard. Although she was never involved in his mess, she would've never been able to adopt me if anyone, including the state, had any idea what to do with the damaged little girl I was. He was also right about having children. I agreed never to have children when we got married. Look what I came from. I didn't want to pass that on to my children. So he wasn't entirely wrong, not about the past anyway."

"Jules, you're a wonderful mother. You had a terrible start in life, but that has nothing to do with the kind of person or mother you are. Don't let his bullshit become your reality. You're better than that."

"No, I know I'm not like my parents. I know I'm a good parent. I know I'm not damaged or emotionally unstable. That was devastating to hear coming from his lips, but I don't buy into that nonsense. I do know though, I'm not great with relationships. After I left Indiana and started undergrad, I didn't date for years. In fact, Matt was the only man I ever agreed to go out with since you. I fell for him and wanted a family so badly, I didn't see what others did. Ella and Aimee saw how he always criticized me, how he wanted to change everything about me. I wanted to please him. I tried to be what he wanted, but I was never enough. At first our marriage was good, I thought, but he always wanted what others had and what he didn't. Nothing was enough."

Julia stood and started to pace.

"I knew something wasn't right between us for years, but I ignored everything. I overlooked all the signs of his cheating. He stopped coming home, lied about his whereabouts and became defensive if I asked where he was. So I stopped asking because I was terrified of losing him. Shortly after Ella died, I found out I was pregnant. Aimee had just moved here and was staying with us for a few weeks. She convinced me everything was going to be okay and to just tell him. To say he was furious is putting it mildly. He left that night, telling me to get rid of it."

Ethan could tell Julia was lost to the past. She stopped pacing and stood in front of the bay window that faced the forest. He sat motionless wanting to go to her, but not wanting to break the spell. He needed to hear the whole ugly story to know what he was dealing with. The more she talked the more the pieces fell in place, explaining so much of her past and present behavior. His heart ached for her.

"Aimee found me that night half out of my mind. I think I would have lost it completely if it wasn't for her. I woke up to an email from Matt telling me to get rid of it or our marriage was over. He was my only family, the only person I had in the whole world other than Aimee I could depend on. So, although I didn't want to and knew it was the wrong choice for me because I'd already fallen in love with my baby the second I knew she existed, I agreed to have an abortion. Can you believe I was that needy, that stupid, that damaged?"

Not waiting for his answer, she continued talking.

It pained Ethan to know he hadn't been there to help her and protect her when she needed him the most. It was illogical to feel this way since she was the one that left him and married another man, but he couldn't help feeling like he let her down.

"I couldn't do it. I stopped right before the procedure began. I started crying and couldn't stop. I begged them not to take my baby. I wanted her. I loved her already and I will never forgive myself for almost letting her go."

Ethan had enough. He stood and walked to her. He slid his hands around her waist and fit her back to his front. He held her tightly against him, kissing the top of her head, saying nothing. He walked them slowly backwards, sat on a big leather rocking recliner, and pulled her to his lap. Julia came willingly and nestled in with her head against his chest. He smiled because he didn't think she even knew what she was doing. Her head and her heart were at war. Her brain worked overtime to find all the reasons why she couldn't be with him. Her heart took the lead, knowing it was safe.

"He called that night to see if I had the procedure and when I said no ... we ended. He moved out the next day. When I had Lilly, I was by myself except for Aimee. If it wasn't for Aimee, I don't know what I would've done."

"I'm sorry, baby. I wish I had been there. I wish you hadn't been alone and feeling desperate." Ethan had to say the words. It was how he felt. When you loved someone, logic didn't have a role. When you loved someone, even if they hurt you, you didn't want them to ever feel pain.

Julia straightened in his lap and laid her palm on his cheek. "Ethan, how can you even say that? This was all my doing and Matt's doing. This life, this mess, I created is mine to own and mine to fix. You are a good man. You always have been, but this isn't yours. Do you understand?"

He understood more than she realized. She was punishing herself for her past mistakes, even some that weren't hers to own. She didn't believe she deserved his help or his love. She didn't trust herself where relationships were concerned and she sure as hell didn't trust others. This wasn't the time to convince her otherwise. He needed the whole story so he could plan.

"We'll talk about us later. For now, help me understand why you never confronted him about his affairs?"

Julia sighed. "I found out he'd been having an

affair with Carla for at least the last year of our marriage a few weeks after he left me. I was hurt and angry. I did confront him about her, but it was a wasted effort. At first he denied it, but then he was matter of fact about it. We were done and he didn't feel he needed to answer to me for anything. It was Lexi who found out all about the rest. I refused to use any of the information she compiled on him in court and I never discussed it openly with him. By that time, he started to show some interest in Lilly and I didn't want to antagonize him. I wanted him to develop a relationship with his daughter so she would at least have a father. Is that so wrong?"

Ethan wanted to say yes, it was wrong. She allowed Matt to mistreat her during their marriage and by not holding him accountable she'd given him license to continue doing so for years after. But Ethan wasn't her. He hadn't survived what she had. He hadn't been abused and neglected. He hadn't lived with insecurity and doubt. He didn't have the right to judge her.

He also wasn't a parent. But he could understand her need to give her child a chance to have two loving parents. It would do no good to share his thoughts with her. The important thing now was she found her voice.

"No, I get it. But why didn't you at least ask him to pay child support? It's the least he could have done for his child."

Julia shook her head. "He said it was my choice to have Lilly, not his. He threw that in my face on a regular basis and when the topic came up and I challenged him, he punished Lilly by not seeing her for weeks afterward. In time, I stopped bringing it up all together. Lexi was angry when she found out he wasn't making the payments. She has a growing file of all his exploits and has been waiting for the day to make him pay."

"And are you ready for that?"

Julia looked away from him for a few seconds contemplating his weighty question. Then she turned her head and met his eyes and the fire he saw in them gave him hope.

"You know, I never intended to do anything with all that information. I didn't want that legacy for Lilly. But I'd rather her grow up safe, happy and healthy without a dad, than anywhere near Matt. If the day comes when she uncovers all of this, she'll know I went all out to protect her. She'll know someone loved her enough to jump in front of a moving bus just to make sure her life was never touched by ugly."

Chapter Ten

Julia woke up Sunday morning nestled in her bed and in Ethan's warm embrace. For a few seconds her heart picked up speed and she panicked. She couldn't recall why she and Ethan were in her bed—together—or what they had done all night. Her eyes flew open and just as she was about to jump out of bed and out of her skin, it all came rushing back. She took a deep breath and settled her racing heart.

She and Ethan stayed up for a long time talking and eventually she fell asleep right there on his lap. She woke up as he laid her in her bed. She was beyond exhausted and didn't have the strength to argue with him when he told her he would be spending the night on the couch downstairs in case she or Lilly needed him. She sleepily pointed out the linen closet where he could find a pillow and sheets and fell into a deep sleep.

Her dreams were filled with images of a child being beaten and crying out for help. The little blonde girl was tiny as she huddled in the corner, in a ball, her arms wrapped around herself, on the floor of a cold and dirty room. Normally, the child in her dreams was herself, but last night, it was Lilly's face she saw. Julia must have cried out in her sleep because the next thing she knew she was being cradled in a warm, strong embrace until she fell asleep again. The dream repeated over and over again with Lilly crying out for help and Julia unable to reach her. Each time she awoke, Ethan reassured her she and Lilly were safe.

Now in the bright morning sun, she was mortified. She hadn't had this bad of a night in a long time and Ethan was there to see it all. Not only did he have to deal with Matt and all that drama, she too had fallen apart. For a person who hated crying, she did an awful lot of it lately and all of it in his presence. She'd kept her emotions bottled up, but in his presence she let go—too damn much. And he was always there to catch her.

Ethan took it all in stride. God, he was such a good man. The best man she knew. He took care of her and he took care of Lilly like she was his. The boy she loved so long ago had grown up to be a wonderful man any woman with half a brain would love. She wasn't an exception.

She sighed. She was falling hard and fast for him all over again. He was impossible to resist.

She remembered how he called her his in that caveman, protective way that sent tingles throughout her body. He didn't hide the fact he found her attractive and he wanted more. God, she wanted to give him more, so much more. But, she didn't know if she could. What if she gave it to him and she ended up hurt again? This time, Lilly was falling in love too and if he left them, the storm wouldn't just wreck her, it would touch her precious baby too. He asked her to trust him and if there was one person left in the world she knew she could trust, it was him. She needed to let go, a tiny bit, and trust he would continue to catch her as he said he would.

Julia snuggled deeper into Ethan's hard, warm chest and felt his arms tighten around her. She didn't think he was awake yet and she didn't want to wake him. The poor guy had barely gotten any sleep last night and it was still very early. She loved lying close to him, listening to his heartbeat and feeling the rise and fall of his chest and his warm breath on her hair. Their legs were tangled and although he had a muscular leg thrown over hers that was getting pretty heavy, there was no other place she wanted to be. It felt incredible to wake up with a man's strong arms around her again. What made this perfect was those arms belonged to Ethan. Her Ethan. She'd always think of him that way and no matter what happened. He was hers.

One of Julia's arms was thrown over Ethan's flat, hard abdomen and the other was trapped between them. They were still dressed in yesterday's clothes, although he'd taken off their shoes and socks. Slowly, so as not to wake him, Julia explored the man she last touched this intimately when she was barely eighteen. He was her first and her best. She only had two lovers in her life, Matt and Ethan. Matt was a selfish lover and he could get rough, especially if he was drinking. She shivered as she remembered the harsh way Matt had taken her at times. Why hadn't she stopped him? Why hadn't she protested?

The answer was simple. She wanted to please him. She wanted to be loved. Thank God that part of her life was over. She was better, stronger. She would never allow herself to be treated like that again. Ethan would never touch her in anger or disgust. She wasn't insignificant, damaged, and imperfect in his eyes or in his arms. This she knew to be true and real.

Julia buried her face in Ethan's chest, inhaling his musky scent. She couldn't resist running her fingers through his thick unruly hair. It was divine. Her fingers glided over his cheeks and jaw, his morning stubble scratching her palm and fingers. She traced his soft, full lips with her thumb, licking her lips at the same time. She studied him, but he continued to sleep peacefully.

Julia slid her hand tentatively under Ethan's shirt and then stopped moving. She listened for any change in his breathing, warning her he was awake. When he continued his deep even breathing, she closed her eyes and let her hands explore. Everywhere she touched, she felt firm well-defined muscles and smooth, warm skin. The light scattering of hair tickled her hand as she glided it across his chest and pecs. Lord, he felt good. Her body agreed and responded to the feel of him.

Ethan introduced her to lovemaking when they were seventeen. He was young and inexperienced, but even then he was a generous lover. That first time, her young body responded to him with a hunger that surprised them both. Even though he was her first and she was scared, she wanted him badly and trusted him. As soon as he kissed her and touched her, she gave herself to him. He was a tender, thoughtful lover.

Julia felt a little guilty taking advantage of Ethan while he slept, but she couldn't help herself. He felt and smelled too good to resist. She pushed his shirt up and turned her head into him. She kissed him right over his heart. Unable to resist, she kissed him again, this time her tongue darted out to taste him. She heard his quick, deep inhalation and knew she was caught. Julia tried to pull away, her face flaming, but he rolled and his heavy body settled even more on top of her, trapping her between the bed and him.

"Morning, beautiful. Don't stop. I was enjoying myself," he said in a gravelly morning voice as he shifted completely on top of her.

"Morning. Sorry, but you're kind of hard to resist." She hid her face in his chest, unable to look at him. Her face was on fire.

"Hey, I'm not complaining. Come on Jules, show me those emeralds."

Pulling up her big girl panties, she met his gaze.

"There she is. Hi, baby. Did you enjoy your exploration this morning?"

"Oh God, you were awake? The whole time?" Mortified, she pressed her face in the side of his neck, hiding once again. Bravery was overrated. This was embarrassing.

Ethan chuckled, enjoying her discomfort. He rolled them so she was lying on top of him and she gasped at the unexpected move. Wide-eyed, she looked at him as he held her to him, her hair falling all around them. He ran his fingers through it, pushing it off her face and behind her ears and she melted more into him, letting her whole body relax against his, luxuriating in the feel of his body beneath her.

"You have the softest hair I have ever felt. It's like silk and it smells so good, like wildflowers and vanilla," he said as he buried his face in her hair and took a deep breath. "I love your hair, don't ever cut it."

"Really?"

"Yeah, really. It's gorgeous."

"He hated it," she said without thinking. "He said I should cut it because it didn't have style and I didn't look sophisticated enough with it."

"He's an ass, baby. It's perfect. It's you."

Ethan captured her mouth in a kiss that started out soft and exploring, but turned hot and demanding. Julia liquefied on top of him and raked her hand through his hair, loving the feel of it between her fingers. Her nipples pebbled as they rubbed against his chest and wetness flooded between her legs. She wanted him and from the erection poking her in the belly, he was just as aroused.

Julia made an instant decision. She wasn't going to overthink this. She wanted him and he wanted her. There were both unattached and despite all her fears about relationships, the past and starting with him all over again, she was going to reach, for once in her life for something she wanted without worrying over every detail about the future. She was going to be reckless … for just this once.

Julia pushed at Ethan's t-shirt and he stopped kissing her long enough to pull it off and throw it on the floor. She straddled him, her eyes taking in every inch of him. He was magnificent. He folded his arms behind his head and smiled sensuously at her. He was sexy as sin with his morning stubble and his sleep-tousled hair. There wasn't an ounce of fat anywhere on him and his muscular chest had a delicious smattering of dark hair. She ran her fingers over his cheeks and travelled over his shoulders, biceps and chest, learning him once again. But when she reached his abdomen she looked up, seeking permission. He stayed still, giving her time to explore, and when she looked at his face, she found a naughty smile on his lips.

"Having fun? Is it my turn yet?"

Julia saw the desire in his hooded eyes and felt his growing erection jump and jab her. She couldn't wait for him to touch her. She was wet just exploring him. She smiled and nodded. She took off her shirt, never taking her eyes off him. Ethan's smile grew into a full grin. He ran a finger over the upper edge of her cream lacey bra and rubbed his thumbs over each hardened nipple. She couldn't hold back the small moan his touch elicited. Hearing it, he reached for her and kissed her slowly and sensually.

Within seconds he had her bra off and he rolled them again so she was underneath him. He continued his lazy exploration of her mouth, tasting every inch of it. His hands cupped her breasts. He kneaded them and pinched her nipples between his thumb and index finger. She arched her back and whimpered into his mouth wanting more. She clutched him to her, one hand fisting his hair, the other digging into his shoulder.

She was sure he could feel how wet she was through her thin yoga pants, but she didn't care. She wanted him to know she wanted him. It had been so long since any man had touched her this way. She was hungry, no, starved for him. When he kissed his way down her neck and then took one nipple into his mouth while his hand continued to caress the other, she saw stars. Lord, the man had a gifted tongue. Julia tugged at his hair and whimpered. She needed more and she needed it now.

"Eth, please. I need…"

"Shh, baby. I know."

He took her mouth again as his hand found its way into her yoga pants and past her thin thongs. The second he touched her, she arched into his hand and moaned. She was going to lose her mind. She wanted him deep inside her, but this was the next best thing. He'd learned a few things in twenty-two years and as he ran his fingers through her folds and then lightly brushed her clit, she couldn't hold still. He was teasing her and she wasn't sure she could take it. She writhed underneath him, trying to get closer, trying to get his hands where she needed them.

"Eth… I… Please," she begged shamelessly.

With one hand at her hip he stilled her movements. He held her firmly in place while he plunged two fingers into her wet heat as his thumb pressed over her clit. That was it, she saw heaven! Julia cried out her release as he took her mouth with his and swallowed down her cries. Her body trembled as she clamped down on his fingers. She clung to him, holding him to her as she came and came and then came down slowly. She opened her eyes and looked at him with a dazed expression. He held her eyes as he removed his fingers from her and put them into his mouth, licking them clean. It was the most erotic thing she'd ever experienced.

"Delicious!"

Julia dropped her face into the side of his neck. Holy shit. Did he just do that? Did she just do that? She hadn't let herself go like this with anyone for a long time.

When she and Matt first got together, their lovemaking was good, but never as good or as satisfying as it had been with Ethan. She held back with Matt, especially at the end when his lovemaking was perfunctory. Part of herself she kept untouched by anyone but Ethan, only for Ethan, always for Ethan. Matt never knew about Ethan, but he wasn't a stupid man. The more she held back, the more frustrated he got by her lack of response. Eventually, he stopped caring about pleasing her and focused only on his needs.

"Hey, beautiful, look at me."

She lifted her head and their eyes met.

"That was the hottest thing I've ever seen. I love watching you come apart in my hands. You're beautiful, baby, and there is nothing for you to be embarrassed about. Okay?"

She reached for him and kissed him, her tongue exploring his lips and every inch of his mouth.

He broke the kiss and framed her face between his hands.

"Please tell me you're on the Pill," he begged in a husky voice.

She nodded. They should have had this talk before they were this far, but here they were and they had to act like grown-ups.

"Yes and it's okay, I'm clean. I haven't been with anyone since Matt left two years ago. But…?"

"I'm clean too, sweetheart. I swear. I swear you're safe with me. In every way possible."

Without hesitation she nodded. "I trust you, Eth. I've missed you so damn much. I'm not going to lie. I'm scared to death because if this doesn't work out between us, it won't be only me who gets hurt, it'll also be Lilly."

He tightened his arms around her and kissed her eyes, nose, and finally her mouth.

"I can't read into the future, but what I can promise you is I will do everything in my power not to screw this up for all of us. But you have to work with me. I know you're scared, but I've got you and I've got Lilly."

Julia studied Ethan's eyes and the promise she saw burning there left her no doubt Ethan was all in and would do everything in his power to hold them together. Could this really be happening? After all these years, did they really have a future together as a family. The thought excited and terrified her.

The past.

No. No. She couldn't, no wouldn't spoil this moment. The one she waited a lifetime for. Ethan had come back to her. This wasn't a dream. Her Ethan had come back to her and wanted to try at a future together. Her dreams had come true and she was going to reach for happy, even if she didn't deserve it.

"Okay, sweetheart," she whispered.

Ethan stilled at her words and stared at her in surprise.

"Eth, sweetheart? What's wrong?"

She wasn't sure what she said or did to cause him to go so utterly still.

She brushed his cheek with her fingers. "What is it? What did I say?"

He cleared his throat and said, "You said 'sweetheart'. No one has ever called me anything other than my name. It took me by surprise and I—"

"Ethan, if you don't like it, I won't, I'm sorry. I didn't even think; it just came out."

"No, no, I love it. Don't stop." He crushed her to him, and then pulled away so he could kiss every inch of her face. He took her mouth in a scorching kiss that would have led to other things if it weren't for Lilly's voice coming over the baby monitor.

"Mama, Mama! Up."

Ethan and Julia pulled apart and he smiled at her. He shook his head and chuckled. "Sounds like our girl is up. She's got interesting timing. I'm going to have to have a talk with my little angel."

"God, I'm sorry, Eth. If I don't get her, she's going to scream the place down. She wakes up raring to go and with a hell of a lot of energy."

He kissed her soundly on the lips, rolled off her and reached for his shirt.

"Baby, there is no need to apologize. Don't worry. I don't give up easy. Lilly is going to keep me on my toes. We'll have our time and when we do I don't want us to be rushed or distracted. Why don't you girls get ready for the day while I go home and shower?"

At the mention of him leaving, her face fell.

"Hey, beautiful. I need a shower and clean clothes, but I'm coming back to my girls after and we can spend the day together. Okay?"

Julia felt foolish. She was acting like a lovesick horny teenager. "It's okay, really. You probably have a million things to do before you start work tomorrow. We'll be fine. I've got to go grocery shopping anyway."

"Perfect. Why don't we meet at the diner for breakfast and then we can go shopping? I need groceries as well. You ladies can explain to me how to get the damn cart free from the chains holding it hostage. I tried to go shopping at the monster-mart last week, but I gave up when I couldn't even get a cart." He grinned.

"Monster-mart?"

"The grocery store on 202. It's a massive, intimidating monster."

She smiled at him and shook her head. She wondered how a grown man, a physician of all things, could be intimidated by a simple grocery store.

"Are you sure you want to shop with Lilly and me? She loves the grocery store. It's more fun than any playground I can take her to."

"Yeah, I'm sure. I hate grocery stores; maybe she can teach me a thing or two."

An hour later, Lilly and Julia met Ethan in front of Frank's ready to start the day. Despite all that had happened the night before, both of them had recovered and she looked forward to spending the day with Ethan. Waking up in Ethan's arms erased much of the ugliness of previous night. They still had a lot to deal with and a lot to talk about, but for once, she was optimistic about the future.

As Julia and Lilly waited for Ethan to park the monstrosity he drove, Julia couldn't help but think of his parents. If their relationship progressed, Ethan would have tell his parents about her and that thought made her physically ill. She avoided all conversations having to do with his parents. But she couldn't do that for long and she didn't want to. She wanted to feel brave enough to tell him everything so they could go into the future with nothing between. She wasn't there yet. Sooner or later it would come to a head, though, and there would be no delaying the inevitable. For now, she wanted to enjoy one day, just one day together without drama.

Ethan got out of his truck and came toward her Honda CR-V. He strode toward her looking all kinds of sexy. The man made an art out of wearing jeans and t-shirts. He opened her door, pulled her out, and gave her a deep, passionate kiss that left her wet, breathless and clinging to him in the middle of the road. Her hormones spiked and if they weren't in the middle of the street and didn't have Lilly, she would have held him hostage as her love slave in bed. When she opened her eyes, he was grinning. The rat knew exactly what he was doing.

She shook her head and leaned against her car catching her breath as Ethan tackled the web of harnesses holding Lilly secure in her car seat.

"How the hell did you get her into this medieval torture device?"

"Torture device? It's just a few buckles and straps." Julia laughed. "I'm sure you can figure it out."

Julia stood back and watched him flounder. It was entertaining watching him pull at the harnesses and get absolutely nowhere. Meanwhile, Lilly looked like she was about to hit him over the head with her giraffe. After a few minutes, Julia took pity on him.

"Push the big red button, Eth. She'll do the rest. If you can't get her out, how on earth are you going to get her in? That takes real skill."

Muttering under his breath—that Lilly was more secure in the seat than a racecar driver—he followed Julia's directions and depressed the red button. In an instant, Lilly pushed the straps aside over her shoulders and reached for him.

"Out, pu-weese."

Ethan shook his head and lifted Lilly and George into his arms and out of the SUV.

Julia enjoyed dressing her daughter up. She didn't spend anything on herself, but Lilly always got the best and looked like a little doll everywhere they went. Today the child was dressed in a sporty pink and white striped rugby Ralph Lauren dress with a Peter Pan collar and matching bloomers with white ruffles. She had a sparkly pink and silver hairband holding back her curls and equally sparkly sunglasses perched on her little nose. She was edible.

Lilly made a complete recovery overnight and was happily into everything possible at breakfast. Ethan used his charm on the same waitress that served them the last time they ate at Frank's. He secured Lilly a coloring book and crayons. More importantly, their meals came out in record time. As they chatted and ate, Lilly decided to test her boundaries. Halfway through breakfast, after she'd been told by Julia several times she couldn't play with the glasses of water on the table, she reached across the table for Ethan's. Quickly, he pulled it out of her hands before it could spill.

"Lilly!" Julia admonished her, but Ethan shook his head. Julia let him take over, interested to see how he would handle the situation.

"Lilly, the water on the table is for drinking and not for playing with. Your mama told you no earlier. The answer is still no."

Lilly gave him her best innocent, big-eyed, pouty-lipped look and said, "Pu-weese, E."

"No angel. These are not toys. You can color instead."

"No."

"Okay. No it is, but if you want to go shopping with us and not home, you will listen. Got it?"

After a second of looking between Ethan and Julia, Lilly smiled an angelic little smile and said, "Kay." Then she went back to coloring like nothing happened.

"Okay, baby whisperer, that was impressive. Where did you learn that trick?"

"*Super Nanny* of course. It's where I get all my good material."

Chapter Eleven

An hour later Julia and Ethan arrived at Food-Feast in separate cars so they could each go home afterward, unload their groceries, and prepare for the week. Unlike Ethan, Lilly knew how to free shopping carts from the chains. The ransom was a mere quarter pushed into a slot on the cart's handle and bingo, the chains dropped. Ethan had lived in two other states and travelled to many more and yet he never saw anything like it. He had no idea what the purpose was because when shoppers were done utilizing the cart, they got their quarter back when the chain was placed back into the slot on the cart. It was a mystery to him why the market tortured its patrons in this manner.

At Frank's, Julia asked him what he needed from the store. He stared blankly at her and mumbled, "Ah, everything."

"What do you mean everything?"

"I mean I have coffee and beer at the house and, of course, running water. That's it."

"Ethan, you've been at that house for at least two weeks and you only have coffee and beer? What have you been eating?"

"I go out to eat or grab food and bring it home. I hate shopping and frankly grocery stores of this magnitude freak me out."

"Sweetheart, what do you mean they freak you out?" she asked, trying not to laugh, but failing.

He didn't care. She called him sweetheart again, the word flowing effortlessly off her lips. He smiled at the sound of her happy laughter; that too was music to his ears.

"Baby, it's not nice to laugh at someone with my

type of disability. We can't all be perfect like you."

"Okay, tell me about this disability you have and I'll see what I can do to help you."

"It's simple. I get lost and confused in stores that big. I'm used to shopping at small neighborhood grocery stores, not stores the size of an entire mall. Who needs so many choices?"

After she listened to him complain while barely keeping a straight face, she promised to help him if he kept track of Lilly who loved to shop and refused to sit in the cart. That was easy. Ethan picked Lilly up and placed her on his shoulders. He and Lilly followed Julia around and placed whatever they liked in the cart, half of which Julia took out when she thought he wasn't looking. He told her to put whatever she thought he needed in the cart because he needed everything. Other than some sports drinks and coffee, Ethan let her choose everything because frankly he didn't care what they bought. He was in it for the pure joy of being with them, not the food.

After a while, when it was obvious by Julia's harried expression and her clipped answers he and Lilly were getting on her last nerve, Ethan took Lilly to explore the store. Every few minutes they returned with a new, very cool item and begged Julia to buy it.

Guava juice.

Ugly fruit.

Canned sardines. Lilly thought the can was pretty and shiny.

Julia considered each item, frowned, rolled her eyes and firmly shook her head refusing to buy it. When they both begged, "Pu-weese," in unison, she relented and scowled at Ethan. Each time, she told Lilly Ethan was misbehaving and he wouldn't be allowed to come shopping with them again. All in all, it was a fun outing for everyone.

It wasn't until they were at the checkout counter their sunny day turned stormy. Ethan was helping Julia place all of their groceries on the belt, when they Lilly screamed.

"Mama, Mama. No."

Ethan turned and saw Lilly on the floor behind them, scooting away from a well-dressed, blonde woman who was attempting to grab her arm. He dropped the item in his hand and went to Lilly. He scooped her up before the woman had a chance to touch her. Ethan had no idea who she was or what she intended to do with Lilly, but he wasn't about to let her get away so she could terrorize another child. He held Lilly to him with one arm and grabbed the woman's arm with his other hand.

"Get your hands off me. I wasn't going to hurt Lilly. I was trying to help her up off the floor."

Before he could say anything or process the woman called Lilly by her name, he felt Julia next to him.

"It's okay, Eth. Let her go. This is Carla, Matt's wife."

Ethan released Carla and tried to comfort Lilly who held on to him like her life depended on it. She trembled in his arms. In his mind there was only one reason a child reacted this way to an adult she knew and the thought of it sickened and enraged him.

"It's okay, Lilly. Shh, Angel. I'm here. Your mama's here and everything is going to be okay. You're safe." Ethan whispered to Lilly as he stared daggers at Carla who rubbed her arm and looked at him in bewilderment. She was a petite woman in her twenties who looked remarkably like Julia. Matt certainly had a type.

"Who on Earth are you? How dare you lay a hand on me."

"Calm down, Carla. This is Ethan, my…"

Ethan heard the hesitation in Julia's voice as she searched for the right word to describe their relationship.

"I'm her boyfriend," he said for her, "and I wouldn't have had to touch you if you weren't terrorizing Lilly. Do you want to explain why a child who knows you so well is scared of you? She is trembling in my arms."

"Ahh, so you're the infamous Ethan my husband told me about. Well that explains everything. I have nothing to say to either of you. As for the little brat in your arms, I have no idea why she behaves the way she does except to say she runs wild and is completely undisciplined. I was trying to help her up. My mistake. Next time, I'll let her roll all over the dirty floor. She's no longer my problem anyway."

"Carla, she was never your problem and never will be. We're done here," Julia said.

Julia turned away from Carla and looked at Ethan. "Can we finish checking out, please? It's almost time for Lilly's nap."

Ignoring Carla altogether, Ethan gathered Julia in his arms and kissed the top of her head, knowing Carla was watching them.

"Sure, beautiful. Let's get home and put our girl down."

Ethan followed Julia home although she insisted he didn't need to. By the time they got to the house, Lilly was asleep. As Julia put her down for a nap, he brought in Julia's groceries. He heard Julia coming down the steps and went to her. Ethan hated to leave, but she was right, he had much to do before tomorrow. It was going to be a busy week learning the hospital and getting to know his new colleagues on staff. But before he left, he wanted to make sure his girls were okay.

"How's our girl?"

Ethan noticed Julia's soft smile every time he referred to Lilly as theirs. Every time he held her, played with her, or kissed her, Julia's face softened and that smile melted his heart. He wanted Julia to know how much he wished Lilly were theirs, but it wasn't the right time. Anyway, it didn't matter Matt was her biological father. If Ethan had his say and things went as well as he hoped they would, one day he would make Lilly legally his.

"She's fine. Asleep. You know that woman must have done something to her for Lilly to behave that way. I feel terrible she was so scared. I wish she could talk to me and tell me what happened."

Ethan reached for Julia. He brought her to him and held her close, breathing her in and rubbing her back.

"I know, Jules. I wish she could tell us what happened too. We'll have to watch her for any usual behavior. It's probably just the trauma of yesterday. It's still fresh, but in time she'll forget it."

"I hope you're right." She hugged him and laid her head on his chest. "You've got to go and empty all those groceries before something goes bad."

"Yeah, baby. I guess I do and I have to get ready for the week. Will you two be okay tonight?"

"Sure, we'll be fine. We're used to being on our own. Having you here is an added bonus and a blessing."

Ethan looked into Julia's eyes. He saw sadness creeping back in. He didn't want to leave her. Spending time with her and Lilly came naturally. They were the family he wanted and Julia was the woman who roamed his dreams and held his heart. It was amazing how attached he was to them in such a short period of time. At times it felt like he and Julia had never been apart. Talking to her and being with her was easy and so, so good.

"Jules, you're not alone, not anymore. I'm a phone call away and I'll call you before I go to bed tonight. Okay?"

"Okay, Eth."

"How about we do lunch tomorrow?"

Julia stiffened in his arms. Surprised, he looked down at her, raising an eyebrow.

"No lunch?"

"Ah, no. Lakes is like any other hospital. It's a gossip mill and I don't want to be the new topic of the day. Can we keep our personal life at home, until we know for sure where we're headed? Please?"

He gazed into her troubled eyes and understood what she was asking. She wanted to be viewed as a professional, not another hospital affair to be gossiped about. He was okay with that, but he wasn't okay with her not sure where they were going. He had to give her time, to have patience.

"Okay, Jules. No new hospital romance for the gossipmongers. We'll keep it all business at work, but not because I don't know where this is going. I do and so do you. Now, I've got to go. Bye, baby."

Before she could say anything he kissed her hard, wet, and long so she wouldn't forget him or the way he felt about her anytime soon. He drove home knowing he had plenty to do to get ready for the next day, but unhappy to be leaving Julia with time to think and time to doubt. Before he left he suggested Julia call Lexi and tell her what happened with Matt and Carla. It was time to get some expert advice. Lexi had plenty of colleagues who specialized in custody cases. Julia told him that's what she intended on doing as soon as she put away the groceries.

Ethan kept busy all afternoon, first putting away the groceries, then doing laundry at the local Laundromat since he hadn't figured out where or how he could hook up a washer and dryer in his mansion. After the laundry was done, he made his way back home and folded it, utilizing the laundry basket as a dresser. He had no real furniture and it was becoming a problem he would have to rectify soon. Finally, he started sorting the moving boxes until he found what he needed to take to his new office tomorrow. He loaded those into his truck and then called it a day.

It was almost 8:30 p.m. by the time he showered and changed for the night. He got himself a beer and although he had every intention of cooking, he settled for a sandwich instead. He checked his phone throughout the day and he hadn't received any phone calls or texts from Julia. He itched to call her, just to hear her voice, but now he was worried about calling and waking up Lilly. He sent her a text, asking her to call when she was free. A minute later she texted back saying she'd call him as soon as she got off the phone with Aimee.

Ethan knew what that meant. If Julia was chatting with Aimee, it was going to be a while. He used the time to call and check on his parents. His father was already asleep and he spoke to his mother. He was tempted to tell her about Julia, but it didn't seem like the right time and he thought he should talk to Julia before they advertised their relationship to the world.

Ethan sensed Julia still had some unresolved feelings where his parents were concerned. He couldn't blame her. His parents were a handful back then, especially his father. When he was a kid he had no idea how to handle them. He ran interference between Julia and them on a regular basis, but it was never enough. He was caught in the middle never satisfying them or Julia. But that was in the past. He learned to handle them a while back and they now had a healthy respect for one another. He wanted them all to work out any old feelings that still lingered and put the past to rest once and for all.

Ethan didn't like the world his parents lived in, where everything revolved around money and social standing. He tried to live in that world with Alyssa and that experiment was a colossal failure. Now he accepted their world was all they knew and all they wanted. They did their best, which often fell short, to accept his "lifestyle," as they called it. That was their way and while he didn't like it, he accepted it. He knew his parents loved him and wanted him to be happy and he hoped they would understand Julia made him happy. He wasn't naïve enough to think they'd all fall in love, but he'd be happy if they came to a place of mutual respect and understanding.

Ethan was in bed wide-awake waiting for Julia to call, when she put him out of his misery an hour later.

"Hey, beautiful. How was the rest of your day?"

"Hi. I'm sorry I lost track of time talking with Aimee. Is it too late? Are you in bed?"

Julia sounded anxious. He wondered what that was about.

"Jules, it's fine. It's not late and I am just lying around. Is everything okay?"

She sighed. "Yes, everything's okay. I was worried you'd be angry because I didn't call you back right away."

"Baby, I'm not angry at all. Why would I be? I'm glad you have Aimee and the rest of your girls to talk to. Now tell me, what did Lexi say? Did you get to speak to her?"

"Lexi is going to give my information and my entire file, including all the dirt she has on Matt, to an attorney that deals in child custody matters tomorrow. She was glad I came to my senses, as she puts it. She said not to speak to Matt's attorney myself if he calls, but to give him her number."

"Okay, that's good. So how is Lilly?"

"She was a bit clingy, but otherwise fine. She went down right before you texted. Did you get everything done that you needed to?"

"Yup, all ready for tomorrow. Are you ready for bed?"

"I'm in bed, but, as usual, I have too much on my mind to sleep."

"Want me to tell you a story like I used to when you couldn't sleep?"

"I can't believe you remember that."

He hadn't forgotten a single detail of their time together, but he didn't tell her that. When they were young, he called every night and he could tell by the tone of her voice if she needed soothing. Sometimes his made up stories were short, other times they were long and lasted deep into the night. He would weave stories for her until her breathing evened and he was certain she drifted off, or on rare occasion, until Ella picked up the phone and told him to hang up.

"Yeah, I remember. Shut the lights, lie back, and I'll tell you a special story, one I've been waiting to tell you for many years. This one I didn't have to make up, though."

He waited until he was certain she was lying still under the covers and then told her a story his Grandma Mildred told him the day she turned 71 and he was the only one of her family to turn up to celebrate with her. Not even her daughter, his mother, bothered to come and wish her only living parent a happy birthday. It was ten days after Ella's attack and as was his usual habit on Saturday morning, Ethan dressed and went to have breakfast with his grandmother. He was her only grandchild and they formed a special bond from the second he was born.

Grandma Mildred was a warm, loving person, unlike the child she gave birth to, and he knew that day was going to be tough for her. It was the first birthday she'd be celebrating without his Grandpa Frank. Grandpa Frank died a year prior and Ethan's mother stopped speaking to Grandma Mildred a short time after. That day, Ethan bought his grandma a small coconut cake, her favorite, and red and white mums. He went to celebrate her birthday with her, though he was heartbroken Julia wouldn't see him.

The second she saw him, his grandmother knew something was wrong. He'd introduced Julia to her a few months after they started dating. He and Julia visited her together on a number of occasions. The women liked each other from the start and in many ways, Julia was the granddaughter his grandmother never had. When he told his grandmother what happened to Ella and then of Julia's refusal to see him, she held him in her arms as he cried like a child. She listened, saying little. Then she dried his tears and told him she had something for him—the angel-winged, heart-shaped locket with the inscription embedded in its center. She told him she was certain if he gave it to his sweetheart, she would always remember him, know he loved her and one day, she would make her way back into his life. Grandma Mildred explained how the locket came to be hers.

In the winter of 1941, when Mildred was nineteen, she was in love with a young man named Charles Laraby. She'd been seeing him for a year behind her parents' back and they planned one day to be married. When the United States entered World War II, he was drafted and she was beside herself. They, like many, decided to elope and when he returned from the war, they would tell her parents.

Mildred and Charles spent one night together as man and wife; that was all they had. As a wedding present he gave her the locket with his picture inside it. He told her she was his angel and no matter what happened he would always be with her. Charles's final words to Mildred were, "Remember you are the love of my life and I'll love you forever."

A month after Charles went to war, Mildred found out she was pregnant. She was ecstatic and terrified. Mildred shared the news with Frank, Charles's best friend who had a heart defect and could not join the war effort. Before leaving for war, Charles made Frank swear he would take care of Mildred. Frank and Mildred had grown close over the last month and were good friends.

Frank and Mildred each sent Charles a letter telling him of her pregnancy, hoping one of the letters would reach him. They never received a response. She was nearing her second trimester and was about to tell her parents about the pregnancy and her marriage to Charles, when she received word Charles was killed in the line of duty.

Mildred was devastated and fell in a deep depression. Only the thought of Charles's baby growing inside her kept her from taking her own life. Still, she had no idea how to tell her family and she knew she couldn't take care of the baby by herself. Her options were limited and she was running out of time. Frank was with her every step of the way, sharing in her grief and offering warm, strong arms to comfort her.

A few weeks after they received notice of Charles's death, Frank sat her down and told her he wanted to marry her and give her and Charles's child a home and a future not marred by scandal. At first, she refused. She told him she didn't love him and he deserved better. Eventually he convinced her although he wasn't her first choice, he still cared for her and marrying her would not be a burden, but a joy.

By that time Mildred's parents suspected their daughter was in trouble. When Frank asked them for her hand in marriage, they agreed to a small quick wedding. When Ethan's mother was born a little earlier than expected, everyone turned a blind eye.

Mildred and Frank built a wonderful life together and had three other children of their own. Over time they grew to love one another with a ferocity and a passion few ever experienced. Frank had given Mildred and her child a home and a great deal of love. In return, she loved him back for the extraordinary person he was. Frank and Mildred were married for fifty years and for all those years, she wore the locket Charles had given her. It became a symbol of true love for both of them.

Frank developed an aggressive form of lung cancer and although he fought it with all his might, he knew he was losing the battle and would soon be leaving his Mildred. Before he went, he wanted to do something special for her, something that would mark the incredible life they had together. Thus, for their fiftieth anniversary, he took the locket that meant so much to both of them and had it inscribed with the words, "RILY, forever" and he placed his picture alongside Charles in the center of the heart. He gave it to Mildred and told her he wanted her to know she'd given him the best life a man could ever dream of and like Charles, he loved her forever and beyond.

This, Ethan explained, was the locket his grandmother gave him to give to Julia on a cool May day when he sat at her kitchen table and wept for the girl he loved, but who wouldn't have anything to do with him. His grandmother kept the pictures of Charles and Frank, and gave him the locket assuring him Julia would indeed use those wings to fly back to him one day.

She hadn't been wrong.

Chapter Twelve

By the time Ethan finished telling his story, Julia was weeping. It was a beautiful story. She couldn't believe he gave her Grandma Mildred's locket. Julia treasured the locket because Ethan loved her enough to give it to her even when she was at her worst. To her it symbolized the story of their love, but she never dreamed it held the story and secrets of other grand loves, too.

She told Ethan how touched she was by the story and asked him if the locket should be returned to his mother. Although she couldn't stomach the idea of being without her locket, she had to ask. It was the right thing to do, even if that woman had been such a misery to her. Ethan explained his mother knew nothing about the locket. The day his grandmother gave it to him, she was adamant Julia have the locket and his mother never know of its existence. Thus, it was in the hands of its rightful owner and that's where it should stay until Julia handed it down to Lilly.

Ethan's mother didn't know Frank wasn't her birth father until after his death. She was helping his grandmother go through some of Frank's personal papers when she came across the letter he'd written to Charles before her birth. It had been returned to the sender and Frank had held on to it. Grandma Mildred did her best to explain to her daughter all that happened so long ago and why she and Frank never told her about Charles, but his mother couldn't or wouldn't understand and her relationship with her mother was deeply affected for good.

It was well after midnight when Ethan and Julia agreed it was time to hang up and attempt to get some sleep. Julia assured Ethan he gave her a sweet story to dream about and she was sure she could drift off. She lied. She stayed up the rest of the night thinking of Mildred, Charles, and Frank, and her own growing feelings for Ethan. She knew without a shadow of a doubt she loved Ethan. What she didn't know was what was holding her back from saying the words.

At first she was unsure of his feelings toward her, but now there was no doubt in her mind. He adored Lilly and Lilly adored him. He knew all about Matt and their crazy relationship and instead of running, he was ready to do battle on her behalf. He was every woman's dream—smart, successful, sweet, and sexy. What the hell was wrong with her? He was the love of her life and she should be jumping for joy he was back in her life and wanted her and all the baggage she came with. And for the most part she was. Still she kept experiencing fleeting moments of dread. It was her own fault. Guilt crept in on a regular basis, filling up all the open spaces and crevices of her mind. She didn't tell him everything about the past and even a lie of omission was a lie. Relationships built on lies were doomed to fail.

Monday morning came too fast and Julia was sleep deprived. She went through the day feeling groggy, irritable, and unsettled. In the short time Ethan was back in her life, she became accustomed to hearing his voice and seeing him, neither of which happened until late Monday evening and then their contact was brief. Ethan hit the ground running at the hospital and he didn't make it home until well past 10 p.m. By the time he was able to call Julia, she was half asleep.

The next four days weren't much better. She was busy at work and poor Ethan seemed to be running from dawn till well past dusk. Although they exchanged texts and brief phone calls, by Thursday the weekend they shared seemed like a lovely dream. She almost wondered if it actually happened. Julia's body remembered just fine. Every time she recalled how he touched and kissed her, her entire body warmed all over again and she ached for his touch.

On her lunch break Thursday, Julia returned a call from Leslie Donaldson, an attorney specializing in child custody Lexi recommended. They spoke briefly and made plans to meet the following week for an official intake. Talking about fighting for custody made Julia anxious and she lost her appetite. She was tempted to call Ethan to see how his day was going and to tell him about her conversation with Ms. Donaldson, but after staring at her cell for ten minutes, she decided it could wait until the evening. Although she and Ethan hadn't made any specific plans, she thought she would see him that night for a quick dinner. She was wrong.

Right before she picked up Lilly from the sitter, she received a text from Ethan saying he was invited to dinner with the Chief of Staff and had no choice but to go. He asked how she and Lilly were doing. Feeling anything but cheerful, she forced herself to sound peppy and sent a text back saying all was well, not to worry about them and to have a good dinner. Then she told herself to get a grip. They were both busy people, this was to be expected. Unfortunately, the lecture she gave herself wasn't convincing because her mood plunged even lower.

It was late by the time Julia got Lilly fed, bathed, dressed and in bed. After cleaning up the kitchen and family room a bit, she gave into her bad mood and total body and mind exhaustion. Settling for a glass of wine and a handful of peanuts, Julia lay in bed with the TV on. She vacillated in and out of sleep when she her cell vibrate. She grabbed it sleepily. It was Ethan.

"Hi," she mumbled as she glanced at the bedside

clock and saw it was 11 p.m.

"Hey, I'm sorry I woke you. I wanted to see how my girls are doing."

His girls … she loved it when he called them that. The implication of ownership and belongingness warmed her each time he said it. She tried to de-fuzz her brain enough to have a real conversation with him, but she was exhausted and had downed a large glass of wine on an empty stomach.

"We're okay. Lilly is asleep and I'm almost there. How was your day?"

"My day was fine. Long, but that's to be expected. Are you all right? You sound funny."

"I'm fine. I've had a long day too. I'm wiped."

"Okay. I'll let you go back to sleep then and we can chat tomorrow. Sweet dreams. Give angel a kiss for me in the morning."

"I will. Goodnight."

Julia hung up feeling remarkably lonely. The house was silent and felt empty. She grabbed the pillow Ethan had slept on and brought it to her nose. She smelled traces of his cologne and the scent soothed her. She hugged the pillow and fell into a fitful sleep.

Friday morning Julia woke up to the sound of heavy rain pounding the roof. Mother Nature was making a show of force: thunder, lightning, hail, and wind. You name it, it was happening. Lord she hated rain! She considered calling in sick, but thought better of it and dragged herself out of bed. By the time she got out of the shower, she missed a call from Ethan. Although she called him back after she dressed and was attempting to feed a cranky Lilly, she never got a hold of him.

The day went to hell from there. Traffic was a nightmare and she was late dropping Lilly off, late to work, late for a meeting, and then to make things fun, a patient threw up on her. By lunch, she wasn't fit to be around humans. Noticing it had finally stopped raining, she sat outside on one of the picnic tables behind the hospital and deep-breathed until she felt more settled.

Unfortunately, peace wasn't in the cards for her. She was forced to listen to a bunch of staff from the pediatric wing discussing a hot new pediatrician who had a sexy smile and smoldering gray-blue eyes, but no wedding band. They discussed Ethan's many assets openly admiring every inch of his body and she wanted to get up and scream at them, "Hands off and eyes off. He's mine!" Then she realized she was behaving like a teenage girl, mentally slapped herself, and went back to work.

At 4 p.m. as Julia got in her car, she received a text from Ethan saying he had a late consult and didn't know what time he'd be done. She rested her head against the steering wheel and sighed in frustration as tears filled her eyes. She was being ridiculous. The man was a physician, what did she expect? His hours were going to be shit for a while. He had to re-establish himself in a new city. It wasn't his fault.

The more she thought about it, the more frustrated she became with herself. She didn't want to want or need someone like this again. Becoming dependent on someone for her happiness couldn't be healthy. Her foul mood wasn't due to a bad day, or even missing Ethan, but of being scared of her growing feelings for Ethan. The problem was her heart knew what it wanted and as usual it acted alone, not consulting with anyone before it gave itself away. She loved Ethan and when she wasn't with him, she felt like she was stumbling through the day like a blind person.

As if reading her mother's mood, Lilly adopted the same outlook on life and was irritable and difficult to deal with from the second Julia picked her up. She refused to sit in her car seat and no amount of reasoning or bribing seemed to work. Finally, Julia wrestled her into it and listened to her scream all the way home. At home, Lilly picked at her food, barely eating any of her dinner. Looking at her daughter, Julia knew she would have a devil of a time getting Lilly down for the night unless she was able to change both of their moods.

Julia started a bubble bath for Lilly and then hopped in with her. That did the trick, at least part way. They played in the bath with the variety of toys Lilly amassed until the water cooled. Then Julia dragged them both out, wrapping a now-crying Lilly in a fluffy towel and slipping on her bathrobe. She sighed, then put Lilly's PJs on and broke a cardinal rule and let the child sleep in bed with her.

As she got them situated under the covers with Lilly holding tightly to George, Julia's cell rang. The second Julia saw Ethan's picture flash on the screen, she felt the weight of the world shift off her shoulders. All it took was a second, however, before nimble little fingers snatched the phone out of her hands and began tapping on the screen while happily crying out, "E! E!"

Julia wrestled the cell out of Lilly's hands as she answered the call and turned on the speakerphone.

"E!"

"Hi, Angel, how did you hijack your mama's phone?" Ethan's laughing voice came over the phone.

"E! Come!" Lilly ordered as she continued to wrestle Julia for the phone.

"Hi, Eth. I'm here. I'm having some issues with little miss demanding today." Julia's voice was weary as she tried to be heard over Lilly's continuous yelling for Ethan and the phone.

"Angel, you're wearing Mama out. Be a good girl and settle down so I can talk to her and then I'll talk to you. Okay?"

"Okay," Lilly said and immediately settled back on the pillows, stuck her thumb in her mouth, and cuddled with George.

"You have to tell me how you get her to do that. She and I are in my bed because she has worn me down. This is the first time all night where she is actually looking angelic. This baby whisperer thing you've got going should be bottled and sold somehow."

Ethan chuckled and said, "Hi, beautiful. You sound tired. What's going on with you girls?"

Julia took the phone off speaker and Lilly lost it and let out an ear-piercing, "Nooo, Mama. My E. Nooo." Then she burst into tears.

Seeing Lilly unraveling, Julia quickly put the phone back on speaker. "Ethan, for God's sake man, say something. Have pity on me and talk. I made the mistake of taking you off speaker and she's become unglued. I don't get it."

"Angel baby, what's this all about?" Ethan's low soothing voice came over the cell.

"E, mine," Lilly sobbed.

For a few seconds both Ethan and Julia were silent, stunned at what Lilly said. But Ethan recovered.

"Lilly? Angel mine? Stop crying. I'm here sweetness. How about I tell you a story?"

Lilly stopped crying and with little sniffles and a sad little voice said, "Okay, E."

Lilly settled back against the pillows with her thumb back in her mouth and George clutched tightly to her. Julia lay next to Lilly and gathered her in her arms, waiting for Ethan to begin his story. As Ethan told Lilly the story of the *Three Little Bears*, Ethan-style, Julia watched her daughter's eyelids become heavier and heavier and then close.

Lilly said everything Julia wanted to say with that one word, *mine*. Lilly staked her claim on Ethan, just as he, seconds later, claimed her as his, *angel mine*. Julia's heart ached for her child who never cried like this for her own father, but knew where she could find love and without hesitation reached out and grabbed it. She wished she were as brave as her girl. Her day had been shit because she started it without him and she felt his absence deep all day. Now, like her child, she was soothed by the sound of his voice.

"Jules," Ethan's soft whisper broke into her thoughts.

Julia glanced at Lilly. She was deep in slumber. Julia took Ethan off speaker. "Hey, Ethan. Thanks. She's asleep. You're off speaker now."

"Glad she's down. Now what's going on with you two? What happened today?"

Julia hesitated. She didn't want to sound needy, but the truth was she needed Ethan. He knew her too well and would know if she lied. It was now or never. She took a deep breath.

"Jules? Come on baby. Just tell me."

"I'm well, that is … I think Lilly and I missed you," she said, trying to get the words out as fast as she could before she chickened out.

When he didn't say anything and there were a few seconds of total silence, Julia panicked. Had she misread him, misunderstood him somehow?

"Ethan, I'm sor—"

"Julia, don't finish that sentence. Come downstairs and open your front door. I'm here."

"What? You're here?"

"I was driving home from dinner when I called you. Will you come downstairs and let me in before your neighbors call the police, please?" he said, a grin evident in his voice.

Julia jumped out of bed, tucking Lilly in the center of the bed and placing pillows all around her so she wouldn't fall out. A grin spread across her face so wide she was sure she looked like a lunatic. She was thrilled Ethan came to her and she wasn't going to hide it.

"I'm on my way down," she whispered. "Hold on."

She glanced down at the pink tank top and boy-shorts she wore; not very glamorous, that's for sure. Her hair was a mess. She was a mess, but she didn't have time to change. She flew down the steps and scanned the family room and kitchen. It looked like a toy store threw up all over the house, but there was no time to rectify that either. Ethan would have to accept her as is. This is what single working moms and their homes looked like.

Her heart did acrobatics in her chest. She stood in front of the closed door feeling a little like a wobbly bowl of Jell-O. She tried to will her body to open the damn door. So she'd admitted she missed him, what was the big deal? Taking a deep breath, she opened the door and was swept up into strong arms that held her so tight she could barely breathe.

Ethan kicked the front door shut as Julia wrapped her arms around him. She stood on tiptoes, buried her face in the side of his neck and breathed him in. Every single damn thing that had gone wrong all week slipped away. She was in Ethan's arms and all was good again. The elephant that had made himself comfortable on her chest all week stood, stretched, and sauntered off. She was as light as a butterfly floating in the summer breeze and it felt great.

She rained kisses up the side of his neck and under his ear and whispered, "You're here. You came. I missed you, sweetheart. We missed you."

"My girls needed me and I needed them. And Julia?" He pulled her gently from him and raised her chin with his fingers, forcing her to look him in the eye. "I missed you too. I missed both of my girls. It's been a shit week without you guys."

Ethan brought his mouth down on hers in a hard claiming kiss that seemed to last an eternity and took stole her breath. His lips devoured hers and his tongue dueled it out with hers, rediscovering and reclaiming every inch of her mouth. By the time he finished kissing her, her legs were Silly Putty and she clung to him for support. Sometime during the kiss, he walked them over to the couch and pulled her down on his lap. As he held her in his lap, she burrowed into him and rested her head on his chest, trying to catch her breath and slow her galloping heart. She wrapped her arms around him and squeezed. Looking up at him, she studied every inch of his face and slid her fingers in his thick, wavy hair.

Smiling, she said, "Hi."

"Hi, beautiful. Better now?" He brushed the hair away from her face and attempted to gather it into his hand.

Julia noticed every time they were intimate like this, he played with her hair and would try to gather it in one hand. He was like her personal human hairclip. She loved the way he touched her with such passion and how he never hid his desire for her. When he wanted her, his eyes would change to an intense dark gray and his voice would go all husky. He always put his feelings out there, never hiding any of it from her. He made her feel sexy, beautiful, and wanted.

"Now, tell me what happened this week and don't leave anything out."

Julia recounted the week's events, including her conversation with Ms. Donaldson and her appointment with her the following week. When she was through, she admitted with the exception of the conversation with the attorney, the last few days were not that awful. Without him, though, every minor hiccup seemed so much bigger than it actually was.

"I'm sorry, Eth. I haven't been myself for the last few days. Lilly picked up on it and had a meltdown. We're not usually this needy. I'm fine now. Tell me about your week."

He tugged at the ponytail he formed in his hand until she looked up and their eyes connected. In his eyes she saw the truth of the words he said next and was assured of his sincerity.

"First, there's nothing for you to apologize for. From now on I don't want you holding back anything. I want to know it all: good, bad, everything. You're not being needy and even if you were, I love hearing my girls missed me as much as I missed them. Jules, I know you're scared and I know it was hard for you to tell me you missed me, but you're not the only one who has needs in this relationship. It's *good* to be needed and wanted. Thank you for giving me that."

Julia laid her palm against his face, leaned in, and gave him a long, slow kiss. What did she do to deserve this incredible man? He gave himself completely to her. He trusted her with his heart just as she trusted him with hers and Lilly's. She wasn't in this alone. She could do this. She looked into his eyes and gave him what he'd been waiting for, what he needed to hear and she needed to say.

"I love you, Ethan. I love you, as does Lilly."

Without even a second of hesitation, Ethan smiled and said, "I love you too, baby, both of you. I've loved you for as long as I can remember. I've never stopped. You've always had me. Do you know that? You've always had me."

Grasping the locket in her hand, she brought it up so he could see it. "Yes, I know. I've worn the evidence of your love around my neck for twenty-two years and I have loved you in return. I've never, not for an instant, stopped loving you. I never believed I'd have you again. I convinced myself that this is all I would ever, could ever have of you. Now"—she looked back into his eyes— "now I know better."

"Thank God for Grandma Mildred. I'm glad she gave me that locket to give to you. I can't tell you how happy I was when I saw you still wore it."

"I never took it off, not even when I was with Matt, I couldn't. I knew it was wrong, but you're the only man who's ever loved me just the way I was. I couldn't have you away from me. I needed you close and it was all I had of you."

"I can't believe Matt never questioned it."

"He never knew about you. He thought Ella gave the necklace to me. He never opened it; never saw the inscription. I tried to take it off and put it away when we first got married. Aimee and Ella told me I should, but I think I lasted about a month. One day I opened my jewelry box and there it was. I couldn't help myself. I put it on and the relief I felt was so immense, I never took it off again."

"I'm here now and I'm not going anywhere. We somehow found each other again. This is a gift we've been given, this second chance. Let's put the past behind us, all of it. I meant every word in that locket and nothing has changed except I love you even more, if that's possible."

Chapter Thirteen

By the tender look on Ethan's face, Julia was sure she made the right decision. She was glad she told him she loved him. He said he loved her and Lilly and she believed him. She hadn't thought about how he felt and what his needs were. She was selfishly thinking only about herself and Lilly while this man, the man she loved, needed her and Lilly to love him and need him. Well, that wasn't a hardship. They could give him that. He was easy to love. He wasn't going to let her and Lilly down, but she also vowed she'd be there for him and not let him down, either.

"Eth, I know you've had a long day, but will you stay? I mean, I … I want you to … uhm…"

Julia's cheeks warmed and she dropped her eyes. She felt ridiculous. She was a grown woman, not a skittish virgin and yet she was blushing. Asking a man to spend the night and make love to her shouldn't be this hard, should it?

"Jules, there's nowhere else I'd rather be. I want you too baby and I'm not going anywhere. Come on, let's go put Lilly in her own bed. I want to love my woman in a comfortable bed where I can take my time and not on this couch."

With that, he took her mouth in a deep devouring kiss that had her melting into him as her body caught on fire. That was all it took. She wanted him badly and she could feel by his growing erection, he wanted her no less. He ended the kiss and stood leading her up the stairs and shutting the lights as they went up.

In her bedroom he made his way to the side of the bed where Lilly lay in deep slumber sucking her thumb and holding George close. Ethan scooped her in his arms.

Lilly stirred and drowsily opened her eyes, looked at Ethan, smiled a sweet smile, and nestled into him.

"E," Lilly mumbled and smiled as her eyes closed again.

"Shh, angel mine. I'm here. It's okay now, sleep baby," Ethan cooed as he rocked her and walked to her room.

Julia made sure the baby monitor was on as Ethan returned and shut the door behind him then began undressing. She'd been too distracted before to notice, but the man looked sinfully delicious in a black tailored suit, white dress shirt, and gray silk tie. The suit fit his muscular body perfectly and he looked professional, powerful, and unbelievably sexy. No wonder every female in the hospital drooled over him.

Julia sat on the edge of the bed and watched Dr. Sexy remove his jacket, tie, shoes, and socks. He looked up and smiled when he saw she was perched at the end of the bed watching his every move. He didn't seem to mind and continued the show for her by unbuttoning his shirt and then taking it and his white undershirt off. Next he undid his belt and pants, letting them fall to the floor, leaving him only in snug-fitting boxer briefs. The evidence of his desire filled his boxers and bulged impressively.

He prowled toward her and gave her a slow sexy smile filled with promise of what was to come. When he made his way to where she sat on her high four-poster bed, he ran his hands up her bare thighs applying slight pressure until she opened and he could stand between her legs. His hands wandered up to the edge of the snug boy-shorts she wore and his thumbs began a slow caress of her inner thighs.

Julia was lost to the delicious ripples of pure lust that ran through her as his thumbs continued their slow exploration, getting closer and closer to her center. The feeling of his naked, muscular thighs rubbing against hers was exquisite and she couldn't stop herself from running her hands over his chest, feeling his muscles ripple underneath her palms. She heard his swift intake of breath as her fingers rubbed over his nipples until they hardened. Lost in the wonder that was him, she reached up and pulled him to her. He didn't resist.

He kissed her and it was deep and wet as she raked her fingers through his thick hair. His hands traveled under her tank top and he broke their kiss to remove it. With his eyes blazing, he took in every inch of her.

"You're beautiful," he said in a husky whisper.

Without warning he bent down and captured one of her nipples in his mouth and sucked hard as his hand captured her other breast and kneaded it. Her nipples instantly hardened and she arched her back as she held him to her. She felt her panties getting soaked and knew he would see and feel evidence of her overwhelming desire for him. She was lost to the delicious sensations he was evoking in her.

When one of his hands made their way under her boy-shorts and his thumb lightly ran over her wet panties, applying slight pressure right over her clit, she started to tremble and used all of her will to hold back her quickly approaching orgasm. She arched into him and moaned in his mouth. His thumb continued its exploration and caress as his other hand ran up her side and over her breast lightly caressing the already-hardened nipple over and over again. She saw stars. It wouldn't take much more to push her over into complete bliss. She was putty in his hands and she clung to him, whimpering his name.

He kissed her again, a long, demanding, hot kiss that had her wild with need. Suddenly, they went at each other, starved and needy. They took turns touching, kissing, sucking and tasting every inch of each other. She took what she wanted, needed, and what she'd been waiting so long for. She took everything he gave and she gave him everything he demanded and everything he needed. Mouths locked, tongues danced and tangled, and before she even knew what had happened, they were both naked, limbs tangled in the middle of the bed.

She arched into his mouth as he kissed and licked down her stomach and then parted her legs. Before she had time to protest or feel embarrassed, he licked her folds and plunged his tongue deep inside her. Her eyes rolled to the back of her head in sheer ecstasy and she was mindless with need. Her body trembled uncontrollably as she fisted his hair in her hands and moaned his name over and over again.

"Oh God, Ethan!"

"Shh, baby. It's okay, I got you, but you have to let go of my hair or I'm going to be bald by the time we're done." He looked up at her and chuckled.

She tried to loosen her grasp as she involuntarily arched into his talented mouth that licked and sucked every inch of her except the place she really wanted him to. When she whimpered his name again and applied pressure to the back of his head, he got the message and took her clit in his mouth, sucking at it while he plunged two fingers in her. That was it. She screamed his name and shuddered, her body clamping down and holding his fingers deep inside her.

Before she fully came down, he was on her. He covered her with his large powerful body and took her mouth in a long, passionate kiss. She opened her legs even wider for him as she held on to him and dug her fingernails into his back. She felt his long, thick, rigid erection at her center, but as he slowly began to enter, her eyes widened and her breath caught. He was so big and she hadn't done this in a long time. What if she wasn't good enough? What if she couldn't give him what he needed? She stiffened and clamped down so he was forced to stop.

"Jules, look at me. Give me your eyes," he said, his voice tight, giving away just how much control he was using. "Baby, please, let go. Just give me your eyes. You're beautiful, perfect and I love you. I've got you. Let go and I'll catch you."

Looking up at him, she saw the tenderness and love he felt for her reflected in his eyes and on his face. She touched his face and kissed him. "I love you, Ethan."

"I love you too, so damn much."

Her eyes locked with his and she could do nothing but trust him and let go. The second she did, he plunged all the way in until he was planted deep inside of her. They both moaned. It felt so good, so deep, but she wanted more. She wrapped her legs around him and threw her arms around his back, effectively cocooning him in her embrace. She squeezed him using every muscle she could and he plunged even deeper, harder in her.

"God, you feel so good," she said in a husky voice as she dug her fingernails in his back and her heels in his buttocks.

"More?" he asked as he trembled underneath her hands.

He was holding back, trying to be gentle for her, but she wanted all of him. "Eth, more, yes. Give me all of you. Don't hold back. I need you, all of you."

He went wild. Within seconds he turned her on her belly and pulled her up on all fours as he plunged again and again into her until a fine sheen of sweat covered both their bodies.

"Come on baby, just let go. Come for me, Jules."

Ethan reached down and around, using his thumb, he rubbed her clit in a circular motion with just the right amount of pressure. That drove her over the edge. Her arms collapsed and she screamed out her release into the pillow. He thrust deeply a few more times and then with one hard, deep thrust he let go and buried his head into her hair as he groaned out his release, his body trembled and spasmed and she could feel the warmth of his release inside her.

He kissed the side of her neck right up to her ear and said, "Remember I love you forever."

They stayed that way, him buried deep inside her and his body covering hers for a long time as they both caught their breath and came down to Earth. Finally, he pulled out and rolled to his back, turning her and gathering her close to him. Her muscles were nonexistent and her bones had liquefied. She felt like a boneless puppet as he positioned her to lie on his chest and held her to him. He brushed her hair off the flushed face and kissed the top of her head.

"You okay, beautiful?"

"Mmh."

"Does that mean yes or no?"

"Mmh."

"Okay, I need a little more. Think you can say a few more syllables?"

"Yes … no."

She forced the words out of her hazy brain. She was sated and only wanted to cuddle next to his warm body and sleep. She hadn't felt this good, this satisfied, and this, well, *loved* in so long. Why did the man want to talk?

"Jules, did I hurt you? I'm sorry if I was too rough. It's been a long time for me too."

Julia heard the uncertainty in his voice and roused herself. She squeezed him and kissed his chest. "No, sweetheart. You didn't hurt me, far from it. I was with you all the way. I haven't felt this good or come that hard ever. I'm Jell-O, chocolate mousse, crème caramel. Choose your dessert. Can't move, talk, and won't be able to walk for a week. You've learned a few things since we did this last time."

Ethan hugged her to him, stroked her back, and chuckled. "Okay, you had me concerned with your ... mmhs. You're amazing. Do you know that? I don't think I'm going to be able to get enough of you or that sexy body of yours."

She didn't know what to say. He was being sweet. Self-conscious all of the sudden, she reached for the sheet to cover herself. She knew it was stupid to feel shy after what they just shared, but she couldn't help it. The euphoria was fading and she remembered the last time Matt saw her naked.

She was pregnant and didn't even know it yet. Her body had begun to change, her breasts a little bigger and her tummy a tiny bit rounder. He walked into the bathroom as she was getting out of the shower. He stopped and stared at her with visible disgust.

"You need to take better care of yourself. You've let yourself go, like all women do once they're married. Really, Julia. I expected better of you. You need to watch your diet and exercise more or you're going to go from curvy to fat fast." He shook his head and walked out as she collapsed onto the edge of the tub and cried, humiliated beyond belief.

"Jules?" Ethan interrupted her thoughts. "What's going on in that head of yours? Why are you trying to hide from me?"

She shook her head and started to sit up, dragging

the sheet with her. Giving him her back, she tried to steady her voice. Why do memories of her nightmare with Matt come at the most inopportune times? Damn it, even though he wasn't there, Matt was ruining this beautiful night for her.

"Nothing, Ethan. I'm going to clean up and get a t-shirt. I'll be right back."

Ethan wrapped a muscular arm around her waist and dragged her back toward him, positioning her underneath him, effectively trapping her. Putting two fingers under her chin he forced her to look up at him.

"No hiding, Jules. Not now, not ever. Let's promise we'll always be honest with one another. That way we'll learn from our past mistakes and not make the same ones going forward. We're starting fresh here, baby. We've got to stay honest. It's the only way we'll make it."

He was right. If they were going to do this and make it work, they had to be honest. But she carried a lot of garbage in her head from her childhood and her marriage and there was a lot she still hadn't told him about their past. She was afraid what he would do when she did. She couldn't think about that now.

"Okay, Ethan, I'll try. Be patient with me. Some things aren't that easy to share. They're embarrassing and painful."

"I've got all the time in the world. Now, what's with the hiding?"

She couldn't hold his gaze and focused on the hollow of his throat. She told him about Matt and the bathroom incident as she struggled not to die of humiliation. He was silent as she talked and even after she finished. After a couple of minutes, he rolled off of her, stood, and scooped her out of the bed. She gasped in surprise and grabbed onto his shoulders.

"Ethan, what are you doing?"

"I'm going to show you how I see you," he said in a firm voice as he strode to the bathroom with her in his arms.

In front of the full-length mirror, he put her down in front of him so she was facing the mirror. She felt vulnerable and exposed and tried to turn away.

"Uh-uh. No, don't turn away. Look. This is how I see you. Stay with me."

He gathered her hair in his hands and ran his fingers through it. He pulled it to her back, as their gazes locked in the mirror. "I love the feel of this gorgeous hair in my hands and caressing my body."

He ran the back of his hands down her breasts and cupped each one, playing with her nipples. "Your breast are perfect, soft mounds that fit my hands just right, like they were created for me."

He ran his hands lightly down her sides and then across her flat abdomen stopping right above her mound. "Your skin is so incredibly soft and I love the way it flushes with desire. You have curves in all the right places, a sexy body with a delicious belly button. And here"—he cupped her mound—"is where I'd like to stay all day if I could."

It took a while, but she saw the honest desire and appreciation he had for her in his eyes. Seeing that gave her the confidence to stand tall, confident and beautiful in her sensuality. She turned in his embrace and met his eyes.

"Thank you," she whispered.

"For what, beautiful?"

"For giving me back … me."

Chapter Fourteen

The six weeks that followed were the happiest Ethan could remember in his life. He, Julia, and Lilly fell into a routine of domestic bliss. They worked, they played, and he and Julia made love every second they could to make up for all the years they missed. Most nights Ethan ate dinner at Julia's and slept at her place so Lilly's routine was not disturbed and because his place wasn't quite ready for a curious toddler. Lilly thrived under his attention and always squealed in delight when her E came into view. Each day Ethan fell deeper and deeper in love with his girls and started thinking of forever.

Julia met with the custody attorney several times and although she was prepared to move for sole custody, she elected to wait Matt out. Matt had been surprisingly quiet, too quiet in Ethan's opinion. Since the day Matt stormed out of the house after bringing Lilly home, he hadn't contacted Julia and hadn't tried to see his daughter. Although Ms. Donaldson thought they should act first and put him on the defensive, she acquiesced to Julia's insistence they take a sit-and-wait approach. Over the last six weeks, Julia's temper cooled and although she still wouldn't let Matt take Lilly out of her sight again, she hoped they could come to some sort of understanding and avoid a nasty court battle.

Ethan wasn't sure he agreed with Julia. Ultimately, this was her decision and he tried to be supportive. He loved Lilly and thought of her as his already. He wanted children and she filled a hole in his heart. Ethan was determined no one, not even her bastard of a father, would ever hurt her again. Lilly captured his heart and even Julia thought it was amusing how her precocious child had charmed and conquered Ethan so quickly.

To say Ethan spoiled Lilly was an understatement. Evidence of this could be found any time they were together, but especially at the Sullivan Castle where they spent much of their free time. While Adam and Ethan spent hours demolishing, repairing or remodeling walls, floors, and ceilings, Aimee, Lexi, Christine, and Julia worked on furnishing and decorating every room that was completed.

Then there was the garden. Julia claimed it as her domain. Over the weeks, and with the help of a few gardeners, the wild jungle garden was transformed into paradise complete with a baby play space containing a swing set, sandbox, and baby pool for Lilly's enjoyment. Ethan took over outfitting Lilly's playground with every imaginable toy a child could want, including an outdoor dollhouse. No matter how much Julia complained he was spoiling Lilly, Ethan told her nothing was too much for his angel.

Only two things marred their perfect existence. The first was easier to deal with than the second. Around the first week of June, Alyssa contacted Ethan. At first he avoided her calls and let the calls go to voicemail. He deleted her texts unanswered. Finally, he decided to put an end to the constant calls and messages by answering the phone. He prepared himself for her usual tirade filled with accusations and ugly comments, but what he got perplexed him. Alyssa apparently just figured out he no longer lived in Boston and, for some odd reason, felt the need to call him and try to reconnect.

She was civil and asked about his new life in Jersey and his new job. She even went as far as to apologize for her outrageous behavior over the last few years. Ethan wasn't fooled. He gave her the briefest of information, accepted her apology, just to put an end to the bizarre conversation, and wished her well. He thought that was the end of it until she called again a week later.

This time Alyssa asked if she could come to Jersey to see him or if they could meet up somewhere in Boston. When he said he didn't think it was a good idea to meet and he saw no reason to do so, she became more demanding. He didn't know what her game was, but there was no way in hell he was letting her back into his life. He told her, in no uncertain terms, they were over legally and otherwise and he had no interest in rehashing the past or having her in his life. When she ignored what he said and continued to insist they meet, he snapped.

"Alyssa, listen carefully because this is the absolute last time I will speak to you. I've moved on and so should you. You destroyed any hope of us being friends or anything else by your destructive behavior. While I once wanted you in my life, that has changed. We are completely and utterly done. Stay out of my life and I'll do the same for you. Do not contact me again." With that, he hung up. She hadn't called or texted since.

Julia listened to him speaking with Alyssa and said nothing. She fixed him a drink, gave it to him, and walked out of the room. Later that night in bed, he brought up the subject.

"We don't have to talk about this. Really, Ethan, I'm fine. I'm just tired," she said and turned on to her side, giving him her back.

She wasn't fine. He wrapped his arm around her and dragged her stiff body against his. Inhaling her sweet scent, he kissed her hair and neck.

"Baby, I want you to listen to me. I'm not Matt and I never will be. Alyssa and I are over. We have been for a long time and nothing will ever change that. What it comes down to is this. Do you trust me? 'Cause if you don't something or someone will come between us. You have to talk to me. Tell me what you're thinking and feeling and give me a chance to chase away your demons."

A few minutes of silence went by and then her body melted against him. She turned in his arms and burrowed her face in his neck as her arm snaked around his waist and around his back. She fisted at his t-shirt in her hand and held him close.

"I'm sorry, Eth," she said and kissed his neck. "Of course I trust you. I know you're not Matt. I love you, sweetheart. Please don't give up on me, on us."

He gathered her hair in his hand and pulled on it until she lifted her face to him, but she kept her gaze on his chest. He touched his lips to her forehead and said, "Eyes, beautiful. Let me see those beautiful emeralds." When she lifted her gaze to him, he saw the uncertainty and fear. He took her mouth in a deep scorching kiss that had her moaning in his mouth and arching her body into his.

"I love you, Jules and I'm never going to give up on you. Never!"

The second thing that shook Ethan was harder to put his hands around and continued to trouble him. One night, as he lay holding Julia in the dark after a long, satisfying session of lovemaking, he casually mentioned he needed to call his parents in the morning to check on his father. The last few times he talked to him, he sounded more tired than usual. The second the words left his lips he felt Julia stiffen in his arms. In the darkness of the room he couldn't see her face to read what was going through her head, but her body language gave him concern.

His parents had given Julia a hard time when they dated in high school, but that was a long time ago when they were just kids. Both his parents had been unwavering in their disapproval of their relationship. As hard as they tried to convince Ethan to break up with Julia, he wasn't remotely convinced. He told them they didn't know her well enough to disapprove of her and their differences in social status and back accounts had no bearing on their relationship.

During the time they were together, Ethan brought Julia to dinner a number of times hoping if his parents got to know her, they would see how wonderful she was and change their minds. He couldn't have been more wrong. Each time his parents met Julia, their meeting ended in disaster. Julia always left feeling humiliated. He'd apologized for his parents' behavior and spent hours talking to Julia, repairing the damage they did to her self-esteem. Then he'd come home and spend even more time arguing with his parents, mainly his mother, about their unfair treatment of Julia. Still he was hopeful they would accept her in time, if not love her as he did.

Six months before his high school graduation, all hell broke loose. One evening, after they finished dinner and were waiting for dessert to be served, he reached for Julia's hand and told his parents he had an announcement. He finally decided which university he was going to attend in the fall. He would not be attending Duke, as his father and grandfather had done. Instead he would attend Holy Cross University with Julia.

To say his father was livid was an understatement. Mayor Sullivan had ignored Julia's presence in his son's life other than to tell him not to get her pregnant. But, that night he made it clear he would not entertain the idea of his son not following in his footsteps like they planned for the last four years. From that moment on, war was declared and Julia was no longer welcome to dinner or any other event his parents were in attendance. They'd reached their limit and refused to continue pretending Julia would ever be an acceptable choice for their son. Life became a living hell for him at home.

In the end, Julia broke up with him and he gave in to his parents' wishes and attended Duke. The Sullivan's never once discussed Julia's sudden disappearance from his life, his depression, or the reversal of his decision to attend Duke. It was like she never existed. They threw him a massive graduation party attended by all their friends and toasted his fine accomplishments and his future at Duke. As a graduation present they packed him off to Europe for two months and before he knew it, he started his studies at Duke.

Twenty-two years passed since all that drama took place. Julia might still have some painful memories, but they were adults now and his parents lived hundreds of miles away and had no influence on him whatsoever. His parents had aged and softened quite a bit over the past two decades. Although he hadn't told them Julia was back in his life, he was fairly certain they would be happy to see him happy again since, Alyssa, their choice for him, had made his life a living hell.

As Ethan lay in the dark next to Julia that night, he tried to talk to her about his parents. They seemed to do all their serious talking at the end of the day in bed these days. But she made light of the issue. She gave him a peck on the lips and said, "I don't want to revisit the past when the present is so much better."

Ethan wasn't fooled. He knew she didn't sleep that night or the night after. Out of the blue, her nightmares returned. After that, he decided not to bring the topic up again and give Julia time and love. He hoped in time she'd open up to him on her own.

Weeks later he sat at the kitchen table talking to his mother on the phone and watching Julia prepare the potato salad they were taking to Lexi's for the July 4th cookout. Although she lost her smile the second the conversation began, she seemed to be okay. When he started talking about his father and his mother's growing concern about his health, however, Julia froze in her place, staring out the kitchen window with her arms wrapped around herself.

That was it. They couldn't put this conversation off any longer. It was obvious Julia was never going to open the subject herself. It was the final stumbling block between them and he was going to have to storm the castle and bring Julia out of the past and fully into the future.

He ended the call with his mother, promising her he would call back in the evening to check on his father who at that moment was preparing to take part in a July 4th parade and then give a speech. He made his way to where Julia stood, wrapped his arms around her and pulled her into him. Her slender frame trembled against him.

"Julia, what is it? Please, tell me what's wrong. I can see something's eating at you, something to do with my parents. I can't help you if you won't tell me what's got you so upset."

Julia shook her head and said nothing.

"Jules, please. Whatever it is, you can trust me. Don't you know that by now? I'd never let anything happen to you. I can't stand to see you so upset. I want you to be happy and healthy and whatever you're holding in is standing in the way of you reaching both those things completely."

When he got no response, he turned her around in his arms so he could see her eyes and what he saw in them made him flinch. His girl's eyes were big and absolutely terrified. What the hell? He cocooned her in his arms and rubbed her back until she stopped quivering.

"Ready to talk?" he whispered in her ear.

She pulled away and the resignation he saw on her pale face was both a blessing and curse. She was giving in, but it looked like she was also giving up.

"It's a long story, Ethan, and not a pretty one. We have to be at Lexi's in an hour. I promise to tell you everything, but let's enjoy the day and then we'll talk tonight after Lilly is down. Okay?"

"We don't have to go, we could call Lexi and give our apologies. She'll understand. We could spend the day quietly together and work through this," he offered, wanting to get it over with.

She shook her head. "No, I want to go. I need to go. Please I promise we'll talk as soon as Lilly is down."

"Okay, Jules. Whatever you need. Just remember I love you when you are talking with your girls today. I understand you need them. I get it. But remember there's nothing you can't tell me and we can't share. Okay?"

"Okay, Ethan. I'm sorry," she said in a small, resigned voice.

"Nothing for you to be sorry about. I'm not upset you need your girls. Now come on, let's get the day started. I'll go see if Angel is ready to get up from her nap and you get the food packed."

Ethan gave Julia a soft kiss and caressed her check with his thumb. "It's going to be okay, baby. Whatever it is, we'll work through it together."

By the time Ethan and Julia arrived at Lexi's, the celebration was in full swing. Everyone was dressed in casual summer clothes and looked relaxed and happy. Music played in the background as people lounged around talking, munching on chips, and drinking beer. Lexi immediately took the salad from Julia, handed them both beers, and directed them to the deck.

As they walked to the deck, Julia tried coaxing Lilly out of Ethan's arms, but she refused to budge. Lilly was uncharacteristically cranky and clingy since she got up from her nap. She didn't look like she felt well and pulled on her right ear. Ethan worried she may have the beginnings of an ear infection. She wasn't running a temperature, but her nose was runny and she refused to eat anything.

"Angel mine, want to get down and see what the other kids are doing? Looks like they're having fun."

"No." Lilly said and laid her head on his shoulders.

"Lils, come to Mama for a while," Julia tried as they made it to the deck.

"No, mine. My E," Lilly insisted as she wrapped her small arms around Ethan's neck, holding him tight. Although Ethan hated Lilly wasn't feeling well, he loved it when she called him hers and he couldn't help the easy, self-satisfied grin that spread over his face.

"It's okay, Jules. I've got her. Angel mine, I'm yours, always baby. But, could you ease up on trying to choke me?" he said, chuckling as he tried to loosen the stranglehold Lilly had on him.

Smiling, Julia shrugged her shoulders at their friends gathered around them on the deck and said, "She gets him more than I do."

Julia strolled to Aimee's side and whispered in her ear. She was doing her damnedest to put on a happy face and overall she was doing a good job, but Ethan could tell she was troubled and so could Aimee who immediately turned and walked inside, hauling Julia behind her and disappearing in the house. Julia needed Aimee and would feel better after speaking with her. Ethan was happy Julia had that kind of support, but he couldn't help feel a little bit jealous. He wished Julia felt comfortable enough and trusted him enough to talk to him about this and everything else. Logically, he knew he couldn't take Aimee's place in Julia's life, just as Aimee couldn't take his.

Whatever Aimee and Julia talked about seemed to brighten Julia's mood and for that Ethan was grateful to Aimee. Forty-five minutes after she walked off with Aimee, Julia returned to his side with a genuine smile on her face and the anxiety gone from her eyes. The short emerald-green sundress she put on this morning molded to her slim figure from her breasts to her tiny waist and then flared in a full skirt that ended right above her knees. The color matched her eyes and every time she moved its lightweight material made it shimmer and ripple around her. He couldn't keep his eyes or his hands off of her.

"Hi," she greeted him, standing on her toes and placing a kiss on his lips.

"Hi yourself. Have I told you how beautiful you look in that dress?"

"Not in words. But your eyes have relayed the message ever since I put it on and showed it to you. In your eyes, I always feel beautiful. Thank you, sweetheart."

He pulled her close and gave her a deep sensual kiss that was only interrupted when a few people jokingly yelled at them to get a room. Julia hid her face in his chest and blushed, but didn't pull away. He loved she wasn't ashamed of their relationship and didn't care who was around. Unlike Alyssa who despised any public displays of affection, even holding hands, Julia gravitated toward him in any room they were in and reached for his hand and for his mouth whenever she could. It was a heady feeling to be loved openly.

By 8:30 the barbequing was done, as was the feeding frenzy that followed. Everyone enjoyed a glass of wine on the deck as they waited for the fireworks to begin. Lilly ate little, but eventually released her death grip on Ethan and went to play with the other kids. Julia sat next to Ethan on the outdoor loveseat, cuddled in his embrace, watching Lilly play on the grass. Everyone's belly was full and they were almost lulled into a food and wine coma, when Lilly's scream jolted them to their senses.

Julia and Ethan separated and stood so quickly it was almost comical. As they both rushed in unison to the stairs leading to the garden, they froze as they heard Lilly cry out, "Mama! Daddy! E!"

Julia stood at the edge of the deck, rooted in her spot. Ethan, not missing a step, continued down the steps to Lilly's side. When he saw his little drama queen had tripped and had a tiny scratch on her knee, but was carrying on like she was bleeding from a major artery, he breathed out in relief. His baby girl wanted her daddy.

Daddy. Lilly fell and wanted him. In her eyes, he was her daddy. His heart filled and overflowed with love for the beautiful child with blonde ringlets and big green eyes that captured his heart the first time she smiled mischievously at him. Mini-Julia had him wrapped around her little finger. Now he knew what that phrase actually meant, because he had to admit if his angel asked for the moon, he'd do everything in his power to get it for her.

He didn't know what Julia thought of the whole thing, but by the way she stood staring at them from the deck, he thought she was in shock. He never heard Lilly say the word "daddy" before, but he wasn't upset or even shocked. He was delighted. Lilly hadn't seen her father in a month and half and Ethan formed a tight bond with the child over the last few weeks. For a child her age, it was inevitable she referred to the man who took care of her daily as her daddy, especially when her real father was missing from her life.

Seeing him standing above her, Lilly raised her tear-streaked face to him and held up her arms.

"Daddy, up, up." She sobbed.

Ethan scooped Lilly up in his arms and cuddled her close. He climbed back up to the deck where there was more light and he could assess her injury better. She clung to him, crying dramatically.

"Angel, you're okay now. I've got you. It's just a little scratch. I promise to kiss it and make it all better. Stop crying, baby. You're fine."

Back on the deck, he noticed everyone was watching them as Julia made her way over to them and started fussing over Lilly.

"Hey, Lils, what happened?"

Enjoying the attention, Lilly hiccupped and said, "Mama, I fall. See?" She pointed to her knee.

"Yeah, baby, I see. You have to be more careful. Remember I made you from—"

"Scatch," Lilly answered in a serious tone.

"That's right, Lils, Mama made you from scratch. Now come to me and I'll get you taken care of."

"No, Mama, my daddy," Lilly said as she shied away from her mother's outstretched arms and clung to Ethan.

"Lilly, Ethan's not…"

Ethan laid a hand on Julia's shoulder before she could complete her sentence. He squeezed it and shook his head. "It's okay. It's good."

"My daddy, my daddy!" Lilly repeated, staring her mother down.

Ethan shifted Lilly in his arms and threw one arm around Julia's shoulder drawing her close to him. He gave her a soft kiss on her temple and then whispered in her ear. "If it's okay with you, it's more than okay with me. I can't tell you how much I love hearing her call me daddy. I'll guard her heart as if it was my own. I swear, Julia."

He gazed into Julia's tear-filled eyes. He hoped those tears were the happy variety and was relieved when she gave him a watery smile and nodded. He wished they weren't in public right now so they could talk more about this and all it implied, but they'd have to do that later. He hugged her close and gave her another quick kiss. "Thank you, beautiful."

Then he turned to the bundle of curiosity in his other arm that watched them closely. "Okay, angel. I'm yours, but be sweet to your mama or you're going to make this daddy sad. Got it?"

Looking up at Ethan, Lilly smiled. "Yesh. Saw-ee, Mama."

Ethan kissed Lilly's head. "Well done, Lilly. Let's get that booboo cleaned and bandaged before the fireworks begin."

Chapter Fifteen

By the time Ethan and Julia left Lexi's it was late. It had been a lovely evening with great food and friends, even with Lilly's drama. They drove back home in companionable silence while Lilly dozed in her car seat and Julia stared out the window recalling her conversation with Aimee. When they got home and put Lilly to bed, they'd finally have the conversation she'd been putting off since the moment Ethan came back in her life. If she didn't face the past and tell Ethan everything, the past would come between them, like an unwelcome visitor at the most inopportune time, and tear them apart.

After her long chat with Aimee, she felt much better. Aimee had lived it all with Julia. Although she understood the root of Julia's fear, she was adamant it was time for Julia to share the past with Ethan since it involved him as much as it did her. Aimee was certain after he got over his initial shock, Ethan would be glad Julia shared the past with him so they could overcome it together.

Then they would be able to build a life together without secrets blocking their way. Julia couldn't avoid Ethan's parents forever—they were a part of his life and he would tell them, sooner or later, that she was in his life again. They were all adults now and his parents didn't have power over them as they did when they were teenagers.

The problem was Ethan's father may be older, but he was still powerful. Twenty-two years ago he was powerful enough to shatter her world to get his way. Things hadn't changed much except now she had Lilly to worry about and to protect. She survived Mr. Sullivan's destructive reach into her life the first time, but if anything happened to Lilly because of her relationship with Ethan, she wouldn't survive it. Aimee assured her Ethan would never let anything happen to them. Once he knew the truth of what happened to her and to Ella, he'd protect her and Lilly from everything and everyone, including his father.

Julia was so lost in her thoughts she didn't realize they arrived home until Ethan opened her door and guided her out of the car. Startled, she let him pull her into his arms.

"You okay?" he asked as he kissed her forehead.

"I'm fine. Just thinking."

"You know nothing you tell me is going to change the way I feel about you."

The night was dark, but the full moon and bright stars gave her enough light to see the sincerity and love in his gray-blue eyes. "Yes, sweetheart. I know. It's time we talked."

He touched his lips to hers then laid his forehead against hers. "I'm glad to hear that. Why don't I put Lilly down while you shower and change? We can relax and chat after I've done the same."

"Sounds good."

Julia took a long, relaxing shower. It had been a hot, sticky day and it was good to clean up and cool off under the gentle spray of the cool water. She finished and liberally applied the wildflowers and vanilla lotion Ethan loved. Finally, she brushed her teeth and dressed in a rose-colored tank top and shorts. Not finding Ethan in the bedroom as she expected him to be, she searched Lilly's room. Lilly slept peacefully, but Ethan was nowhere in sight.

As she made her way down the stairs, she heard Ethan's voice coming from the back deck. Puzzled at who he could be talking to so late, she walked toward the deck, opened the door, and stepped outside. Ethan turned around and by the strained look on his face, she knew something was wrong. She had no idea who he was talking to, but there was a lot of medical jargon being thrown around and she thought perhaps he was talking to a patient's family or to the hospital.

He ended the call telling the caller he would leave tonight and be there as soon as he could and to call him if there were any updates.

Julia went to him and placed her palm against his chest. "What is it, Eth? What happened?"

He gazed at her with troubled eyes. "It's Dad. It sounds like he's had a massive heart attack. I've got to go home right away. He's in critical condition and mom is overwhelmed."

Julia did her best to control her reaction. She hugged him to her. "I'm sorry, Ethan. Of course you have to go. How can I help? Want me to pack for you while you shower and make travel plans?"

He studied her face and then hugged her back. He sighed and ran his hand through his hair. "That would be great. I don't know how long I'll be gone. I'll call Lakes in the morning. Will you and Lilly be all right?"

"Please don't worry about us. We'll be fine. Go be with your family."

Julia saw Ethan was struggling, torn between her and his parents. She touched his face and kissed his lips. "Ethan, sweetheart, I promise Lilly and I will be fine. We'll talk when you get back. This can wait. Go be with your parents. We'll still be here, where you left us, safe and sound when you return. Until then, we can FaceTime every day. Okay?"

That seemed to do it. He gave her a small smile and touched his lips to hers. "Okay, FaceTiming it is. I want to talk to Lilly every day so she doesn't get confused when she wakes up and finds me gone."

God, how she loved this man. Even in times of crisis, he thought of her and Lilly first. "Yeah, sweetheart. That would be good. She'll like that. You know possessive she is about her daddy."

The next hour passed in a blur as Ethan booked a red-eye to Indiana, showered, and dressed while Julia packed for him. He left with a quick hug and a kiss and drove himself to the airport saying he would park the car in long-term parking and deal with it later.

After he left, Julia was wide-awake. She stalked around the house straightening up here and there and when there was nothing left to do, she went to her bedroom. Ethan wouldn't land in Indiana until the crack of dawn and then he planned to rent a car and drive straight to the hospital to check on his father. He promised to call her as soon as he landed, but that wouldn't be for hours.

She lay in bed remembering the last time she saw Ethan's father. She was young then, barely eighteen, and Mr. Sullivan was the mayor of their city, although he was well on his way to being governor. When Mayor Sullivan entered the ice-cream parlor where she worked late one night, she was surprised and a bit fearful. She didn't think he knew where she worked, but that had been a stupid thought. Mayor Sullivan knew everyone who lived in his city and everything that happened in it.

Julia hadn't seen Mr. and Mrs. Sullivan in weeks, not since Ethan made his grand announcement about Duke. While she could say with all honesty she disliked Ethan's mother, she never knew what to make of his father. Mayor Sullivan was a formidable figure that focused all his attention on his dinner and his newspaper whenever she was in his presence. He was a man of few words, but when he spoke, he expected to be heard and obeyed. He was never warm toward her, but he wasn't hostile like his wife. Mayor Sullivan barely acknowledged her presence one way or another, not until the day his son crossed him. Then, he turned his scowl on her and his laser-like stare penetrated her and almost liquefied her in her seat.

The night he visited Julia at work the mayor didn't waste any time getting down to business. He waited until she served the last customer and locked up for the night. Then he offered to fund all of Julia's education and pay for all her expenses for the next four years if she broke up with Ethan and never contacted him again. Julia knew the Sullivan's didn't like her, but she was shocked at the lengths they'd go to cut her out of Ethan's life. Although he intimidated the hell out of her, Julia refused him without a second's delay.

"I know you think I'm trash and honestly, I don't care anymore. I love your son and that's the only reason I've put up with so much from you and Mrs. Sullivan. I'd do anything for him. He's everything to me and I'll never leave him. If he wants to break up with me, he's going to have to tell me himself. I'm not interested in your money, not now, not ever."

The mayor, nonplussed, gave her a hard look and in a smooth, menacing voice said, "Young lady, you're making a grave mistake. I dislike being crossed. You've caused my family a great deal of turmoil and I've been a patient man. But I think this teenaged crush you and my son share has gone far enough. Now I'm a reasonable man," he continued with a cold smile that didn't reach his eyes. "I'm going to allow you a week to think about my rather generous offer. Remember your choices have consequences."

Julia was petrified. Did the mayor just bribe her

and then threaten her? She didn't have time to analyze their conversation. With her spine straight and her legs shaking, she walked to the door, unlocked it, and opened it. Then in the strongest voice she could muster said, "Please leave sir. I think we're done here." When he left, she locked the door and collapsed on to the nearest chair trembling all over.

True to his word, he came back a week later. This time their conversation was much briefer.

"Have you made your decision?"

"Sir, the answer is still no and will always be no. Please leave me alone. Don't do this. Don't break your son's heart."

Mayor Sullivan studied her for a full minute. Then with a resigned sigh, his lips thinned and he said. "You've made a bad choice for both you and your mother." Without another word, he turned and walked out leaving a stunned, scared and confused Julia behind.

That evening, Ella never made it home from the hospital. At 1 a.m. Julia woke up to the sound of the doorbell and a persistent knocking on the front door. Two police officers informed her Ella was attacked in the hospital parking lot and offered to give her a ride to the hospital. They waited as Julia, with shaking hands and a racing heart, changed and got into the back of the cruiser. In front of the ER, one of the officers came around to let her out of the car. In a low, cold voice meant to intimidate, he told her he had a message from a friend.

"The mayor is deeply concerned about your future and some of the poor decisions you've been making. He expects from now on, you will make better decisions and do what he asked you to do. He wants you to understand your actions and the choices you make have consequences. Do you understand?"

Julia was bewildered. When the burly officer

repeated his question as he squeezed her upper arm painfully, her eyes filled with tears and she nodded and whispered, "Yes. Yes, I understand. Tell him I understand, please," as the tears streamed down her face.

Now, as she lay in bed with only the sound of the ceiling fan whirring overhead, she felt tears slide down her face once more. This time she wasn't afraid when she recalled those memories. She was hopeful. God help her, but she hoped he died. If these thoughts made her a monster, so be it. The man almost destroyed her life and she'd lived in fear for twenty-two years. Although she never saw or heard from him or his goons again, he effectively delivered his message in a way that impacted her life for decades.

Undoubtedly, Mayor Sullivan knew all about her past—those records were easy to retrieve. He played on her fears and won. After the childhood she endured, she hated violence of any kind and wouldn't even watch violent movies or TV shows. By hurting Ella and taking Ethan out of her life, his actions had triple the effect he probably intended or maybe he was smart enough to know the damage he'd do and didn't give a damn.

As Ethan raced across the country, probably praying for his father's life, she lay in bed and prayed for the opposite and she wasn't the least bit sorry. She was, however, completely unsure of what to do and what to say to Ethan. She couldn't tell him what his father had done, not now anyway. If his father died, there would be no reason to tell him anything. The person who'd separated them would be dead and there would be nothing to gain from hurting Ethan with the past. Even if he lived, she wasn't sure she could tell Ethan after all.

Julia felt Ethan's loss profoundly. She rolled onto her side and grabbed his pillow, burying her nose in it. It was all Ethan. She cuddled it close and closed her eyes, willing her brain to shut down so she could get some sleep before Lilly woke up. Although Julia had taken the next two days off to spend them relaxing with Ethan, Lilly didn't understand the term vacation and relaxation. She would be up at her usual, ridiculously early time, and Julia would walk around like a zombie all day if she didn't sleep.

Morning came too quickly and after a night spent tossing and turning, Julia woke at 6 a.m. to the buzzing of her cell. She grabbed it and answered knowing it had to be Ethan.

"Hi, Eth."

"Hi. I'm sorry I woke you up. I wanted to let you know I arrived and am on my way to the hospital. You okay?"

"I'm fine. Lilly's still asleep. I'm glad you called. How was the flight? Did you get any sleep?"

"The flight was fine, but no, I couldn't sleep. You?"

"Not really. Any news from the hospital?"

"I just got off the phone with Mom. Nothing new. The hospital is about thirty minutes from the airport. I should be there soon."

"Okay, sweetheart. Drive safely and let me know if anything changes. I love you."

"Love you too, Jules. Give Lilly a hug and kiss from me. I'll try to call later and chat with her."

"Okay, bye."

Julia hung up and heard Lilly call for her. She dragged her body out of bed to get her daughter and start the day. Julia and Lilly spent the day lazing around the house because Lilly was running a temperature and was fussy. She gave her a dose of baby Tylenol and encouraged her to drink juice. Julia hoped this was nothing more than a summer cold. As an infant, Lilly had ear infection after ear infection, but she hadn't had one in a long time.

At 7 p.m., Ethan called sounding exhausted and stressed. He said his father was in much worse shape than he thought and the next forty-eight hours would be critical. The heart attack damaged the heart muscles and it would be a miracle if he pulled through. Ethan's mother was beside herself and was sedated. Finally, the media was having a field day in front of the hospital as the elder Sullivan had been making a speech when he collapsed onstage. Although he wasn't involved in politics any longer, he was a well-known figure.

Julia did her best to sound supportive, but she was sure Ethan heard the distance in her voice. He asked what was wrong several times. She insisted nothing was wrong and distracted him by having Lilly FaceTime with him. Lilly asked for her daddy several times that day and was thrilled she got to talk to him. Lilly told Ethan she was sick and that only made him worry more. Julia reassured him it was nothing more than a cold, but she would take Lilly to her pediatrician tomorrow if she still had a fever.

This pattern repeated over the next three days. Ethan called at the end of every day and they exchanged information about their day. Daily, he sounded more exhausted and despondent. He told her his father was not improving and his mother was unable to cope with the reality her husband would most likely pass away. Ethan split his time between the hospital and the house, taking care of both parents.

Lilly developed a raging ear infection that kept them home for a few days. Each day Ethan spoke to Lilly and even though she was sick and in pain, Lilly always smiled for her daddy. She babbled and sang him songs that made him smile. Each night he ended the call by playing the how-much-do-I-love-my-angel game.

"How much do I love my angel baby? As deep as the…?" Ethan asked.

"The shee," Lilly said, the sea.

"As high as the…?"

"Sky."

On Saturday morning, as Julia prepared Lilly's breakfast, Ethan called. He never called in the morning and she knew his father must have died. Yesterday, Mr. Sullivan woke up briefly and told his son how much he loved him. Shortly after, he slipped into a coma and was placed on life support. Ethan said he wasn't expected to make it past a few hours. He was sad, but accepting of the situation.

Julia placed Lilly's breakfast in front of her and answered the call. "Hi, Ethan."

"Hi. Dad, he's … he's gone," he said, his voice breaking with emotion.

Julia sat at the kitchen table and closed her eyes as an overwhelming feeling of relief flowed through her. He was dead! She was free! She knew the call was coming and thought she was prepared to handle this conversation. She even practiced the words, so that she'd sound genuine. But now the words were lodged in her throat refusing to budge and she couldn't find her voice.

He was gone. It was done! The man that had Ella beaten half to death was gone. The man who threatened to continue to hurt them if she didn't break up with Ethan was gone. The man who separated her from the love of her life causing them both years of immense pain was gone, dead. It was over. Other than relief, she didn't feel anything, nothing at all. She was numb.

"Julia? Are you there? Did you hear me?"

"Ethan. Yes, I heard you."

She couldn't say the words, "I'm sorry." That would imply she was sorry the son of a bitch was dead.

She wasn't sorry and she couldn't lie. She was sorry for Ethan, however. She was sorry he lost a parent, even if the parent was a miserable excuse for a human being. That was the best she could produce, God help her.

In a flat, emotionless voice, Julia said, "I'm sorry for you, Ethan. I'm sorry for your pain. Is there anything I can do?"

Ethan was quiet for a long time and then he sighed. Even in his grief, it was evident he understood what she was and wasn't saying. She was sure he understood she wasn't sorry his father was dead. Julia understood she just added to Ethan's pain. She never wanted to hurt him. If she could, she would do anything to spare him a second more of additional pain. The problem was she didn't have it in her to rise above and if Ethan knew the truth, he wouldn't ask her to.

Chapter Sixteen

The next two weeks passed in a blur for Ethan. He arranged for and attended his father's funeral and wake and dealt with his mother's physical and emotional state. He tried to convince his mother to stay with him in New Jersey for a while, but when she heard the state of his house, she refused. Instead she agreed to stay with a favorite cousin in New Orleans for a few weeks so she wouldn't be by herself. After Ethan put his mother on a plane, he dealt with his father's affairs. That alone took a full week.

Being the only child meant he was the executor of his father's will and, thus, the entire burden fell on him. His mother knew nothing about the family's finances, the property they owned or even what bills needed to be paid. His father took care of every detail of their lives and his mother relied on him for everything. She enjoyed being taken care of and now it was up to Ethan to do that. He doubted she would ever live on her own. His gut told him her stay with her widowed cousin would most likely be permanent.

Although Ethan's relationship with Julia continued to deteriorate since the day he called to tell her his father died, he called daily if only to speak to Lilly. Each time he called, he and Julia said less and less to each other and he spent most of the time chatting with Lilly. He had no idea what to make of Julia's odd behavior and each day that passed he got angrier.

When she said, "I'm sorry for you, Ethan," he thought he might have misunderstood her meaning. But when she repeated it in that hollow, distant voice, he got the message. He couldn't believe his ears. This wasn't the loving, caring woman he knew. He deduced she still harbored some bad feelings about his parents and he even tried to understand, but this was too much. His father was dead and although there was no love lost between them, a decent person who understood the value of a human life would be sorry the man died. A person who loved him would understand this was his father, not a random stranger.

Ethan and his father had their differences. That was no secret. But no matter what those differences were, he still loved him. Ethan made the decision many years ago to accept his parents for who they were and to love them. He rarely fought with them about anything over the last decade. He knew they weren't going to be in his life forever and he decided the best course of action was to love them unconditionally.

Julia had a big heart. She wasn't a cold, unforgiving person and that's why her behavior puzzled and hurt him so much. If it were anyone else who treated him with such disregard, he would have cut them right out of his life. But he loved her and he chose to believe she had good reasons for behaving in this manner. Last night, however, when he called to tell her he would be home the next day and she replied, "Fine, Ethan," in a voice devoid of emotion, he lost his temper.

"Julia, for God's sake. Is that all you're going to say? We haven't seen each other in almost three weeks and have hardly said two words of any substance to each other in that time and that's all you can say?"

"I'm sorry. I don't know what you want me to say."

"Look, I know you didn't like my father and he was a bit tough on you when we were young, but don't you think you're taking it too far? The man is dead. Dead! If you can't put the past behind you now, when will you be able to? You disappoint me. You're not behaving in a rational manner. I'm asking you for the last time to tell me what the hell is going on."

When he finished yelling, there was only silence. She said nothing in explanation and nothing in her own defense. After a few minutes of exasperating silence, he was done. He reached his limit.

"Julia, you're not making this any easier. I think I deserve some kind of explanation, don't you? It's my father who died. If anyone should be acting out, it should be me, not you. Talk to me."

"I'm sorry, Ethan. I can't. Not now."

"Well, then when, damn it? When is a good time to behave like an adult and deal with whatever it is that is making you act like this?"

Silence.

"Fine, if silence is what you want. That's what you'll get. We obviously need some time apart to think things through. I'm not sure I know you at all anymore. I'm done. I can't fight for us by myself anymore. You've got to want us. You've got to be a willing participant in this relationship. A warrior willing to join me to save our relationship and you're not. You simply won't do the work. You won't fight and I'm tired of doing it all on my own. Do you understand what you're doing? What you're throwing away?"

This time he didn't need to strain to hear anything. He heard her crying and although he was mad as hell at her, the sound of her tears pulled at his heart.

With a trembling voice, she said, "Okay, Ethan. Goodbye. I'm sorry."

"What? Julia?"

But Julia was gone and all Ethan heard was dead air. She'd hung up.

Ethan didn't close his eyes that night. There was no point. His brain wouldn't shut off. He went for a run to clear his head, but nothing seemed clearer. After torturing himself for five miles, he gave up. He spent the rest of the night pacing and packing. After his temper fizzled out, he was left with the startling realization that in a span of a few weeks, he lost three people he loved.

His father was gone. He would never hear his voice again, never receive unwanted advice, and never have a chance to tell him about Julia. Then there were his girls. Julia and Lilly. How in the world had he allowed them to walk out of his life or, in truth, how could he have walked out of theirs? He was the one that opened the door and before he could walk out, Julia had, taking his baby girl with her. He'd made it easy. He'd all but pushed her. He felt lost and incredibly alone.

The next day on the flight home, Ethan replayed and dissected each conversation he and Julia had over the last few weeks trying to understand how everything had gone to shit. He couldn't believe he lost his temper and yelled at her. Yelling at Julia was never a good idea. She couldn't tolerate it and would shut down. She did fine with confrontation, but not raised voices and he yelled, actually yelled at her. He berated himself for losing his temper and doing what he swore he would never do.

Although Julia probably deserved to be yelled at and even shaken a bit, Ethan knew better. At this point though, he didn't know what to do. He thought of calling her before he left Indiana, but he figured they had enough of crazy telephone conversations. Their next conversation, and there sure as hell was going to be a next conversation, was going to be face-to-face. He needed to see her, plain and simple. Clarity would surely come once they talked things out and they were back to their normal routines.

Six hours later, he was home. He paid a small fortune for parking and drove home in the rush-hour traffic nightmare that could only be found in Newark, New Jersey at 5:30 p.m. Thank God for the handless telephone system in the truck. He checked in to work and let them know he would be in the next day. He also checked in on his mother. Like he predicted, she was already talking about extending her stay in New Orleans. He assured her he closed up the house, emptied the refrigerator, and forwarded all the bills to New Jersey so she didn't have to worry about anything.

By 9 p.m. he was wasted. He unpacked and went through the mail. Then he paid bills, returned calls from friends, and made an omelet for dinner. Finally, he sat drinking a beer, the only thing in the refrigerator, other than the eggs, that had survived the three weeks he spent away from the house. He thought about calling Julia, but considering the time and his exhaustion, he figured he better wait until the next day. He made his way to his room and crashed for the night, falling into a fitful sleep filled with the sound of Julia's sobs.

Over the next few days, Ethan worked like a dog trying to catch up on the backlog of paperwork piled on his desk in between seeing dozens of patients. Daily, he called Julia, but all his calls went to voicemail. Although he left message after message asking her to call him, he received no return calls. He tried texting, but didn't get any better results.

By the end of the week Ethan missed Julia and Lilly badly. He felt like a complete ass for losing his temper. He was worried about her and decided to go by her house after work just to see if she and Lilly were okay. He didn't want to walk in on her without notice, but she left him no choice. He managed to finish work at a decent hour for the first time since returning and by 7 p.m. he was in front of Julia's house. The problem was, it didn't look like anyone was home. His suspicions were confirmed a few minutes later when he looked through the front window and saw the house was dark.

Frustrated and concerned, he drove back home and decided enough was enough. He called Lexi. He hadn't done so earlier because he didn't want to get his friends caught in the middle, but now he was desperate. Lexi, under great duress, told him Julia took a week off work and left earlier in the week for a brief vacation. That was where her kindness and generosity ended, however, because she refused to tell him where exactly Julia was. Then she called him a bastard for making Julia cry and hung up.

Next, he tried Aimee, Christine, and Adam. He got nowhere with the women although Aimee assured him Julia was okay and agreed to tell Julia he was worried about her and Lilly and missed them both. Adam told him, although he knew where Julia was, Christine and the other women would make his balls into shishka-balls if he opened his mouth and gave him a hint. He did however confirm she would be back on Tuesday. That meant Ethan had to endure four more days of silence.

Ethan spent the next four days working, pacing, not eating, and rarely sleeping. He left Julia one final voice message telling her he was sorry things ended badly between them and he wanted to see her and Lilly when they returned. He said he wanted her to remember all couples fight and he loved her. Then he stopped calling and stopped texting, deciding to give her some peace.

Tuesday, Ethan left work a few hours early and went home. He showered and changed and then went to Julia's feeling unsure of himself. He wasn't sure what to expect, but he wasn't leaving without getting her to agree to at least speak with him again. They couldn't be over. They'd been through too much and survived too much to be over. Whatever this was, they'd work through it.

Ethan stood in front of Julia's door going through the speech he prepared in his head. He rang the doorbell and waited for her to answer. The muted sound of the television playing some children's show came through the door. This meant Lilly was still awake. He missed his baby girl and felt he let her down just as her jerk of a father had by disappearing out of her life. Hearing the lock being disengaged, he looked up as Julia opened the door.

The sight that greeted Ethan's eyes was both beautiful and concerning. As always, Julia's long lean frame, thick shiny blonde hair, and heart-shaped face took his breath away, but something was terribly wrong. Her eyes were dull and she had dark circles under her eyes. Her t-shirt and jeans hung loosely on her body, evidence she lost weight, a lot of weight.

"Jules, baby, what in the world…" he said in a shocked voice as he reached for her.

She flinched away before he could touch her and stared at him blankly with confused big green eyes. "Ethan what are you doing here?"

Before he could answer, Lilly's squeal of delight came from behind Julia. Lilly squeezed her little body between her mother and the door and wrapped herself around his legs.

"E! E! Daddy!"

At the sound of Lilly's sweet voice, a smile lit his face. He bent down and gathered his girl in his arms giving her a big hug. "Hi, angel baby. God I've missed my girl," he said as he stood carrying her in his arms and buried his face in her hair. Lilly wrapped her chubby arms around his neck and squeezed. The she gave him a loud wet kiss on his cheek.

"Have you been a good girl, sweetness?"

"Yesh!" Lilly answered.

"Well why does your mama look so tired then?" He met Julia's gaze, which had softened as she watched him and Lilly.

Lilly giggled and shrugged her shoulders. Then she wriggled around in his arms until he put her down. She grabbed one of his large hands with both of her tiny ones and tried to pull him through the front door. When he wouldn't budge, she said, "Pu-weese Daddy." That melted his heart and had an effect on Julia too. She stood aside and opened the door fully, gesturing him in.

Ethan spent the next hour playing with Lilly while Julia went down to the basement to do laundry and then upstairs to unpack. Finally, Lilly fell asleep in his arms while he read her a book. When he was sure she would stay asleep he carried her up to her room and tucked her in, like he'd done dozens of times before. He gave her a kiss on the forehead and breathed in her clean baby smell. Then he went downstairs where Julia puttered around in the kitchen.

While he played with Lilly, Julia had avoided any conversation with him. He looked up to see her watching him several times over the last hour with a wistful look on her face and each time she was caught, she looked away quickly. He was glad he had the chance to play with Lilly. It was good reconnecting with her. Children were so forgiving. He only wished adults were as wise.

Julia looked worn out, even ill. It was obvious she hadn't been eating or sleeping and the guilt he felt for causing her to spiral like this was immeasurable.

"Julia, please come sit and talk to me," he said to her from the family room.

At first she turned her head and stared at him without moving an inch and he didn't think she was going to come. But after a few seconds of indecision, she walked to the family room and took the farthest seat from him she could. He waited until she was seated to speak.

"I've been worried about you and Lilly. I've missed you guys."

She continued to look down, playing with the edge of her t-shirt. "We're fine. No need for you to worry about us."

"I don't think you're fine, not at all. What's going on, baby?"

"Stop, Ethan." Her eyes met his and they were filled with pain and sorrow. "Like I said, we're fine. It was a long drive back from Maine and I'm tired. That's all. Thanks for playing with Lilly and putting her down. I appreciate it, but I think it's time for you to go."

Ethan studied Julia and shook his head. She wasn't going to make this easy.

"Jules, please just listen. We have to talk. I'm sorry for the way our last conversation went. I was exhausted and stressed and I lost my temper. I'm sorry for yelling at you and hurting you. I have no idea what happened between us, but what we have is good, so good. We love each other. We can work through this."

She shook her head and her hand flew up searching for her necklace. That's when he knew they were in real trouble. She wasn't wearing the necklace! Her hand opened and closed, but there was nothing to hold on to. She'd given up on them. She told him she never took off the necklace because it reminded her he loved her. She didn't believe that anymore, didn't want to believe it, or didn't want to be reminded of him or what they have. She was throwing them away again.

"No. I can't do this anymore. I'm sorry. Love can't solve everything and isn't always enough. I'm sorry. Please, please go. You can see Lilly whenever you want, I wouldn't keep you from her or her from you. But,

I … we, can't do this anymore."

Ethan stood from the recliner and walked toward the couch where she sat. But she stood and rounded the couch before he could come near her. She didn't want him to touch her. He froze where he was. She was shutting him out like she did years ago. History was repeating itself, but this time he wasn't a teenager. There was no fucking way he was going to let her walk away from what they had. Not again and not without a fight.

"Julia, please sit down. Let's just talk. Whatever this is we can work it out. I don't even know what happened. We were doing great. We were happy and so good with each other. Don't give up on us."

"No, Ethan. No. We're not good with each other. Actually, I'm not good with anyone. Please, let me go. I can't do this. Please go, can't you see what this is costing me?" she asked, now openly sobbing.

"Baby, you once asked me not to give up on us and I haven't. Why have you? How can you?"

"I—I can't. You, you don't understand. You wouldn't understand. Please … please walk away. This hurts too much," she sobbed her words barely coherent.

He couldn't stand across the room anymore, not touching, not comforting her. He went to her and tried to gather her in his arms, but she wouldn't let him. She backed away from him, shaking her head. Then she went to the front door and opened it. She stood near the open door with her arms wrapped around herself. It broke his heart to see her in such pain.

"Please," she whispered, "just let me go. Do this for me."

He stood in front of her and looked at her tear-ravaged face for a long time, but she wouldn't meet his eyes. This wasn't working. She was too far gone and there would be no reaching her tonight. He had no idea where his Julia went, where he pushed her to. Ethan didn't want to cause her any more distress and he had no idea what else to do or what else to say to bring her back.

He hung his head and without a word walked out the front door. He waited while she closed and locked the door behind him. Her sobs echoed from the other side of the door. If he stayed much longer, he'd break down the door. He tore at his hair and stalked to his car, got in and started driving. He didn't want to leave Julia alone in that state, but he didn't have much of a choice. The more he stayed, the more upset she got. He did what he always did when they were teens and had a fight. He called Aimee.

Whether he was in the wrong or not, he always called Aimee and she always knew what to do. He could trust her and Julia trusted her. If anyone could get through to Julia, she could. He waited for Aimee to pick up and then said the only thing he needed to say. "Aimee, it's bad. Please, she needs you."

Aimee didn't ask for an explanation. But when he started talking, babbling really, she listened never interrupting him, never admonishing him, giving her opinion or saying the trite, "It'll be all right." Instead, she waited until he was done and said, "I'm on my way to her, Ethan. I'll take care of her tonight. Go home."

"Okay. Thank you."

"Ethan, don't give up. She needs you too. She's just scared."

"I know. I'm not giving up for forever, just for tonight. I'm no good to her tonight. She doesn't want me."

"No, you're wrong. She wants you and needs you more than you know. She always has and she always will. For tonight, go home."

Ethan hung up with Aimee and drove around aimlessly. Eventually, he found a local liquor store where he replenished his beer supply. Then he drove home feeling defeated.

Hours later he lay in bed after having consumed a large amount of beer, which he was sure he would be sorry for the next morning. He replayed his conversation with Julia, as was his habit these days, and came up with nothing, absolutely nothing. Then he replayed the last six weeks, trying to find hints of where it all went to hell. Still, his muddled brain came up with nothing. But that wasn't surprising considering the amount of alcohol he'd consumed.

There were a few thoughts he was able to string together. First, he and Julia were meant to be together. Each time they got close to making that a permanent arrangement, something came between them and their world was smashed to pieces. He didn't believe the nonsense Julia was spouting about her not being good for anyone. That wasn't true, but by the look of total devastation on her face, she actually believed it. Although he was the one that lost his temper and called a timeout, she was the one blaming herself for something. None of this mess made any sense to him whatsoever.

It was evident the past was coming back to bite them. Before he left for Indiana she was ready to talk to him and tell him what had her so spooked each time his parents were brought up in conversation. But those plans went to hell when his father had his heart attack. Now, she retreated to a place he couldn't reach her. A place so dark he wasn't confident, he would be able to reach her and pull her into the light.

Even in his inebriated state he pieced together whatever this was, it had to do with his parents. If he weren't so emotionally and physically wrecked when he was in Indiana, perhaps he would have put this together a little earlier and been more patient. But that couldn't be helped now. Now, he was going to have to find a way to win his girl back for the second time. This time he wouldn't let decades pass because without her, his life didn't have meaning.

Chapter Seventeen

Julia woke up well before the alarm went off on Wednesday morning. She lay in bed with swollen eyes and a beast of a headache from crying all night. She knew she must look like hell; she sure felt like it. The dark circles under her eyes attested to the fact she hadn't slept more than a few hours each night for the last few weeks and last night was no different, except she added uncontrollable sobbing to her repertoire of misery. She wondered if people died of a broken heart.

Aimee was a Godsend, well, an Ethan-send anyway. Twenty minutes after Ethan left, there was pounding on the front door followed by Aimee's shout to open the damn door. Of course, Ethan sent Aimee. The poor girl had been through it all with them and Julia wasn't surprised when she found her standing in the rain demanding to be let in. They stayed up half the night rehashing everything, but nothing seemed any clearer.

After Lexi's July 4th party, Julia had every intention of telling Ethan the whole story and was sure it was the right thing to do. Then his father fell sick and died and things went to hell. She couldn't help how she felt about Ethan's father and she couldn't fake it either. She actually tried that in the weeks leading up to the July 4th party, hoping she could spare Ethan the knowledge of his father's actions.

Although her ability to hide her feelings about his parents wasn't flawless, when Ethan's father died, her acting skills failed her and she just couldn't force the words Ethan needed to hear out of her mouth. She couldn't say she was sorry the man died and that made her a monster in Ethan's eyes. She wanted to defend herself, to come clean with the whole sordid mess, but the timing was all wrong. He was grieving and exhausted. She couldn't kick him when he was down.

After a while, though, she knew there was never going to be a good time. How do you tell someone who just buried a parent his father was not the man he thought he was? How do you say, "Your father was a thug, a monster, my worst nightmare and I'm glad he's gone?" The answer was, you don't.

Daily, she listened to Ethan talk about his father, all the people whose lives Mr. Sullivan touched and the impressive funeral Ethan was planning. Daily, she kept her mouth shut. Then came the conversations about his mother and how much she missed her beloved husband, and so on. Still, Julia kept her mouth shut, not uttering a single word against the dead although in her head she was screaming.

Their conversations became shorter and shorter and more and more strained until she couldn't listen anymore and he stopped talking to her anyway. She didn't know what to say to him to make things better. He'd given her the chance early on in their reunion to tell him what had driven them apart and she didn't tell him the truth. Now she was stuck, no other way to describe it. She couldn't travel back in time and she couldn't inch forward.

This is what secrets and lies led to. Ella was right. She warned Julia secrets have a way of getting out of hand if you held too tightly to them, insisted on keeping them, and refused to come clean. Eventually, you'd lie over and over again all the while wondering what on earth you were doing so. Secrets and lies were a living, breathing monsters feeding on a person's soul. Why hadn't she listened?

Julia spent the last few weeks thinking through every detail of the past and present and she couldn't see how telling Ethan the truth would lead to anything but heartache. He'd been estranged from his father and mother for years, but found his way back to them and forgave them. He didn't think they were perfect, but would he believe her if she told him the truth about his father? Because the truth was outrageous. It was the kind of stuff Lifetime movies were made of. She didn't know if he would believe her or not. What she did know was telling him at this point would be self-serving and she loved him too much for that.

At the end of the day Ethan was a good man and a good son who loved his parents despite their flaws. He had the ability to see past all the bad in people, accept them for who they were, and love them. Even though the Sullivan's didn't deserve a son as good as Ethan, he deserved the untarnished memories he had of a mother and father who loved him in their own way. Although their actions were reprehensible, they acted out of love to protect their son.

So where did that leave her? Alone and heartbroken. Asking Ethan to leave last night brought back memories of their last few weeks of high school when she convinced him she didn't want to see him anymore. She barely survived losing him the first time and she had no idea how or if she would be able to do it this time. At least last time she had his locket to wear and the promise written inside it to believe in. This time, she didn't.

After Ethan lost his temper on the phone with her and told her they needed some time apart, she knew it was over. She cried for hours and then walked woodenly up to her room and took off his locket. She opened the wings and read the inscription for the last time while wave after wave of white hot agony battered her body. Finally, she put the locket in its original royal-blue velvet box and placed it in the top drawer of her dresser. She didn't feel like she had a right to wear it any longer and she planned to return it to Ethan as soon as possible. It was too precious for her to keep.

Julia rubbed at her eyes and glanced at the bedside clock. It was time to get up and face the day. No matter how terrible she felt, she didn't have the luxury of lying in bed and wallowing in self-pity. She had a full day of work ahead. After work she had to meet Matt for coffee at the diner.

Matt phoned a couple of days ago out of the blue. He didn't ask to see Lilly or even ask how she was. Instead, he insisted on meeting Julia at the diner and was mysterious about the nature of their meeting. At first Julia refused and asked him to call Ms. Donaldson, but he was adamant about speaking with her alone and she was too tired to argue.

Julia had no idea what Matt was up to and she didn't have the energy to fight. For Lilly, though, she'd have to somehow find that energy by 4 p.m. At least she didn't have to worry about Lilly for the next few days. Aimee spent the night and insisted on staying with her for the next few days. Aimee had the rest of the week off and was going to spend it babysitting Lilly and Julia. She should have argued and insisted Aimee enjoy her days off, but Julia was grateful. Lilly loved Aimee and Julia needed an extra pair of hands right now. She was drained and was happy to have someone to lean on.

By the end of the day, Julia's energy level was at an all-time low. Still, she did her best to look strong and confident as she entered the diner to meet Matt. She worried about this meeting all day and for once she thanked Matt for giving her something to think about other than Ethan. She called Ms. Donaldson and let her know about the meeting with Matt. The no-nonsense attorney offered to be at the meeting, but Julia declined.

The diner was small and Julia spotted Matt in a corner booth and joined him. He looked polished, not a hair out of place. She, on the other hand, looked like a hot mess despite changing out of her scrubs and putting on some makeup to hide the paleness of her cheeks and the dark circles under her eyes.

"Hello, Matt."

"Julia. Would you like something to drink?"

"Coffee would be great. Thank you."

She waited for Matt to signal to the waitress and put in their order. When he turned his attention to her, she launched in. She wanted to deal with whatever he threw at her and get home to bed. Every bone in her body ached and she thought she might even be running a temperature.

"Matt, I'm sorry to be rude, but could you tell me what this is all about? I'm not feeling well and I've got to get home to Lilly—she's with Aimee."

"That's fine, Julia. There is no reason to prolong this anyway. I've come to a decision regarding Lilly. I've decided it's best for all involved if I give up my parental rights and give you sole custody."

Julia was stunned. She couldn't believe her ears. Did Matt just say he didn't want to be a father anymore? That he was disappearing out of his daughter's life permanently? She had no idea how to react. Should she be happy he wasn't challenging her for custody or should she be sad for Lilly? Isn't this what she wanted when she hired Ms. Donaldson? Now that it was happening, she second-guessed herself and Matt. They had to think about Lilly, not themselves. Is this what was best for Lilly?

"I'm not sure I understand. What do you mean you're giving up your parental rights? You don't want to see Lilly anymore? You don't want to be a father? I don't get it. How can you suddenly decide you don't want to be a father anymore?"

"Look, Julia, we both know I didn't want children. That wasn't a secret. You wanted Lilly. You had Lilly despite my protestations and you're raising her the way you deem fit. After our last encounter, I don't think it's in anyone's best interest to continue in this manner."

Julia's head pounded and her heart ached. This was really happening. Matt was erasing his daughter from his life. Lilly would grow up never knowing her father, always feeling she wasn't good enough. Just like Julia had. As she waited for the waitress to place their drinks on the table and leave, Julia wondered what the right thing to do for her daughter was. She met Matt's disengaged gaze. He delivered his message and was done.

Julia should accept this as a wonderful gift. Many would after everything she'd been through with Matt. But she couldn't let him walk out on his daughter so easily. Yes, he was inappropriate and even irrational last time they were in each other's presence, and yes, she hired an attorney to fight him for custody, but a part of her hoped he would come to his senses, discover he loved his daughter, and want to be a better parent. She wondered if he stopped to consider what was best for his child and not only for himself.

"Matt, I know you and Lilly have had a hard time connecting and she can be a handful at her age, but are you sure stepping out of her life is the best thing for her? We can't think of ourselves only. If I did that, I would agree with you and be overjoyed at the thought of having sole custody. But this isn't about you and me. This is about Lilly and how she will feel growing up without a father. One day she'll know you walked away from her, that you didn't want her. How do you think that will make her feel?"

Something she said penetrated Matt's stony façade because he dropped his eyes and rubbed his temple. After a few moments of silence, he looked up and she saw the pain evident in his gaze. It was the first time in a long time she was seeing something other than anger or indifference and it gave her some hope. Maybe there was a way to salvage the situation. Maybe she'd been too hasty and too judgmental. She had to put her feelings for Matt and Carla and all their messy past aside and think clearly for Lilly.

"Matt, listen to me for a second. We have a child. She is a wonderful blessing. I know what it feels like to grow up without a parent, to feel like you were never good enough for them. Despite our differences, I know you are a good person and wouldn't want your child to feel that way for the rest of her life. Maybe we've been going about this all wrong. Before you make a hasty decision, let's pause and think how we can do this better for you and Lilly. Maybe we should get some help. A counselor may be able to give us some strategies to help us all get through this difficult period."

"Julia, stop," Matt said in a defeated voice as he shook his head.

In a gesture that surprised Julia, Matt reached and held her hand as he looked at her, remorse written all over his face. She saw he was genuinely struggling. He dropped his mask of indifference and superiority and was revealing the person underneath, the person she rarely saw even when they were married.

"Julia, I'm sorry. For the last month I've thought about all of this and little else. Believe me when I say I have not come to this decision lightly. Despite what you might think, I'm not a monster. The truth is I don't have it in me to be anyone's father. I just can't. I cannot be the man you want me to be or the father Lilly needs. I'm not wired that way. I've tried to force myself to be something I'm not. It hasn't worked. I'm sorry to be a disappointment to you and to Lilly."

Matt squeezed Julia's hand and gave her a small smile before continuing.

"You're a wonderful mother and Lilly is a beautiful child. She is lucky to have you. With you as her mother she will grow into a strong, beautiful woman. You'll make sure she knows she is loved, of this I have no doubt."

They sat in silence for a few minutes, absorbing Matt's revelation and confession. This was the first time since she told him she was pregnant they talked like adults without anger and resentment at the forefront. In all the time they've known him, he rarely opened up to her. Julia was sorry they didn't have these kinds of conversations throughout their marriage. Perhaps if they did, things would have ended differently. Most likely they would have still divorced, but maybe they would have inflicted less pain on each other.

"I'm sorry, Matt. I'm sorry that you'll miss out on knowing and loving Lilly and she'll miss out on knowing and loving you. I can't pretend I fully understand, but if you don't think you can be the father she needs, then I appreciate you admitting it and stepping out of her life now rather than continuing in the manner we have been. I don't know what I'll say to her about you when she is older, but I'll cross that bridge when I get there. Thank you for talking with me so openly today. I wish we'd been able to talk like this earlier."

Matt released her hand and reached into the pocket of his jacket. He took out an envelope and handed it to Julia.

"This is for Lilly when she is old enough to understand," he said with a husky voice. "I'll leave it up to you to decide when and if you want to give it to her. It's unsealed. Feel free to read it. I tried to explain things as best as I could, but it's hard to explain something you feel but don't truly understand yourself. I hope one day she will understand that I loved her, in my own way, and because I loved her, I stepped out of her life."

Matt stood and threw some bills on the table. Then he handed Julia a business card.

"Goodbye, Julia. Have your attorney contact mine and they can get the paperwork done. You'll receive a check for all the back child support as well as a monthly check. I'm sorry I haven't done that earlier."

Julia stood and swayed slightly. Matt reached for her elbow to steady her.

"Hey, are you all right? You're pale."

Julie leaned against the booth. "Yes. I'm fine. I'm just coming down with a cold. Thank you. I don't know what to say. Take care of yourself, Matt, and if you change your mind or maybe want a picture or an update about Lilly every once in a while, just let me know."

Matt gave a small smile and shook his head. "Thanks for the offer, but a clean break is best. If you need me for anything, send a message through my attorney. Otherwise, I wish you both well."

Matt placed a chaste kiss on Julia's cheek, turned and left the diner.

Julia sat back in the booth. She stared at the envelope in her hand in disbelief. That was it. She was officially a single parent, or she would be in a few months. Although, she always was a single parent given the hands-off approach Matt took from day one, his decision to give up his parental rights and walk away from Lilly's life made it all too real. Julia never wanted this for Lilly. She wanted her to have more, to have better than she did and in many ways she already did and always would, if Julia had anything to do with it. But she wouldn't have her dad and one day Julia would have to give her this letter and explain to her why her father let her go.

Julia couldn't spare her daughter the pain that would come, but she would try to soften the blow by loving Lilly so much, she would never feel, not for a second, she wasn't wanted or loved. Still, there would be Father's Days, and father-and-daughter dances, birthdays, graduations and even, one day, a wedding. Lilly wouldn't have her father and would feel his absence acutely. Tears filled Julia's eyes and streamed down her face as she remembered missing her own father on such occasions. She reached for a napkin, wiped her face and blew her nose. She told herself to pull it together. There was nothing left to be done but to get home and get on with the business of putting her life back together. Lilly was counting on her.

The next day and a half passed in a blur. Julia went home from the diner, cried on Aimee's shoulder, and called her attorney. Then she went to bed and had nightmares all night. She woke up the next day feeling even worse than the night before, but dragged herself to work anyway. She couldn't afford to use any more sick days or vacation days.

Barely making it through the day, she went home at the end of her shift and went right to bed refusing to eat. Aimee looked anxiously at her and begged her to eat, but Julia couldn't stand the sight of food. She was grateful Aimee was there to take care of Lilly because for the first time in Lilly's life, Julia didn't have it in her. She could barely take care of herself, let alone a child.

By Friday morning, after taking one look at Julia, Aimee was beside herself with worry. When reasoning didn't work, she accelerated her campaign to get Julia to take better care of herself by threatening her. Her efforts were wasted on Julia who was operating in survival mode.

"Julia, you've got to stay home. You look wiped. You're running a temperature, you haven't eaten anything in days, and you look like you haven't slept in months. Please stay in bed and let me take care of you," Aimee pleaded.

"I know you're worried, but please don't be. I'm just tired. I'll be fine. This is nothing more than a virus. It'll pass."

"This isn't a little cold and we both know that. In the last few weeks you've taken one hit after another. On top of that you haven't been eating or sleeping. Your body is telling you it's had enough abuse and wants a rest. Please listen to it and me."

"Staying home is not going to help me. First, I can't take any more days off or I won't have any days to take if Lilly gets sick. Also, if I stay home Lilly will be all over me and will probably get sick. I have no patient care duties today. I'm sitting all day doing paperwork. I'll get rest at work."

"Okay, but I'm calling Ethan and telling him what's going on. I haven't told you, but he's called every day worried sick about you. I've been lying and telling him you're fine, but now you're leaving me no choice."

"I'm too tired to argue with you and don't call Ethan. What good would come out of that? Look, I have to get to work. I know you're only trying to help, but please let me handle this as I see fit. I know myself. This is what I need to do to get through. I'll see you later."

Julia barely made it to work on time. She parked and jumped out of her car. Her head spun and she swayed. She grabbed on to the car door for support, closed her eyes, and took in a deep breath. It was early

September and although it was still warm, she shivered like it was winter. She was sick and should have stayed home, but she would get through the day and then she would rest over the weekend. Her goal was to get herself so tired her brain would shut down and let her get some rest when she finally laid down.

The last couple of days had been difficult. Lexi, Christine, and Aimee had taken turns trying to talk her into changing her mind about Ethan. They saw and heard how miserable she was without him and begged her to give him a chance. Julia listened to her friends' talk, knowing they only wanted the best for her and hated to see her hurting, but nothing they said penetrated the wall she built around herself. She only wanted the pain to stop. She was tired of feeling, tired of thinking, and tired of crying. All she wanted was to sink into a deep sleep and not wake up until her heart learned its lesson and finally stopped hurting.

Halfway through the day, Julia stopped for lunch. Although she had no appetite she walked to the cafeteria for some hot tea. She took a couple of cold and flu tablets in the morning and they were wearing off. Her fever and body aches returned. Her supervisor took one look at her when she walked in and chastised her for coming in, but Julia smiled and told him she was fine. Now she wasn't so sure. The dizziness she experienced earlier happened again as she stood from her desk, and this time if a co-worker hadn't steadied her, she would have fallen. That's when she decided that perhaps some tea and crackers might help.

The hospital cafeteria was busy, the noise and lights hurt Julia's head. She purchased the tea and crackers and sat at a small table near the windows. She rested her head against the window and closed her eyes. She didn't know how long she sat there, but she must have drifted because the next thing she became aware of was someone gently touching her shoulder and calling her name.

"Julia? Come on, baby, wake up."

Julia opened her eyes, feeling disoriented. She blinked and looked up into Ethan's concerned face. She tried to sit up and doing so took too much effort. She shivered and her teeth shattered as a wicked cold chill ran through her body. Every single bone ached and every movement was agony. She gathered her last bit of energy and said, "Thanks for waking me. I must have drifted."

Ethan pulled a chair close to her and reached for her hand, his eyes filled with worry. "Jules, you're sick. You need to be in bed not at work. What in the world were you thinking coming to work in this shape?"

Julia's eyes filled with tears for no good reason. She was exhausted and felt too weak argue. She wasn't sure she could stand up without falling over. He was right, she had to get home and in bed, but she wasn't sure she could drive. She felt vulnerable and helpless. She looked at him as a single tear fell down her cheek.

"Damn it, Jules. Baby, don't cry. I'm sorry. Look, it's going to be okay. Everything is going to be fine. I promise. Let me help you. Please, just let me help you."

Julia was tired of fighting and tired of running away from Ethan. She wanted desperately to go home and home for her would always be in his arms. She nodded and whispered, "Okay, E. Take me home, please."

Chapter Eighteen

Ethan sat by Julia's bed, actually his bed, watching her sleep. Yesterday, when he saw the state his girl was in, sitting slumped in the cafeteria, his heart almost stopped. She was pale and fragile looking as she sat leaning against the window. She'd lost a ridiculous amount of weight. Her face was thin. The dark circles under her eyes were the only things that gave color to her features. For a few seconds he stood rooted to his spot. Then he acted. Enough was enough. He'd given her space and time, but no more. He couldn't let her just wither away to nothing.

About twenty minutes before he located Julia, Aimee called him and told him she was worried about her. Julia was supposed to call Aimee at noon and when she didn't, Aimee knew something was wrong. He was glad Julia gave in and allowed him to help her.

In truth, Julia was too damn sick to protest. He helped her up and supported her out of the cafeteria. He wanted to carry her, but she hated being the subject of gossip. So he did his best to get her out of the hospital and into his truck without raising too many eyebrows. At the truck, he seat-belted her and put the chair back so she could rest. She closed her eyes and fell asleep at once, without saying a single word.

As Ethan drove toward Julia's house, he thought better and headed toward his. He called the hospital first and informed her supervisor of the situation and then cancelled the rest of his patients for the day. Then he called Aimee and told her how sick Julia was and he was taking her to his house where he would take care of her. He didn't want to expose Aimee or Lilly any further to whatever virus she had. Aimee agreed with him and told him not to worry about Lilly.

By the time they arrived at the farmhouse, Julia was in a deep, fever-induced sleep. She was burning up. He parked, opened the door to the house, then went back to the truck and unbuckled her seatbelt. She never stirred. When he picked her up and carried her to the house she shivered and moaned in her sleep. As he walked to his room, she burrowed close to him and buried her face in the side of his neck while fisting his shirt in her hand. Taking a deep breath, she relaxed against him and whispered his name.

"Shh baby, I'm here. You're going to be okay. Hang on." He laid her in his bed, but as he came to straighten, she protested and held tighter to his shirt. "I'm not leaving. I just need to get some medicine in you. I promise I'm coming right back."

Julia opened her eyes and stared at him. Her gaze was glassy and unfocused and her eyes filled with tears again. "Don't leave, Eth. I'm sorry."

God, those eyes were going to kill him. The pain, confusion, and fear he saw there cut him. He sat on the side of the bed and took her in his arms as he smoothed back her hair.

"Jules, baby, I promise I'm not leaving. Not now, not ever again. Please baby, believe me. I'm going to take care of you. Just close your eyes and let me help you. I'm going to undress you, get some medicine in you, and then I promise to hold you for as long as you want."

After a few minutes, she relaxed against him. When Ethan was certain she drifted off, he laid her feverish body back against the pillow and got up. He undressed and covered her. Then he got some juice and medication to bring down her fever. He forced her to wake up long enough to swallow the medicine. Finally, he changed into sweatpants and a t-shirt and climbed in next to her. He gathered her small fevered body in his arms and held her as she trembled and moaned.

As she slept Julia mumbled and although he didn't understand much of what she was saying, it was obvious she was fighting her own personal demons. He continued his vigilance throughout the day and the night, waking her every four hours for juice and more medication. She never fully awakened that night and it wasn't until Saturday afternoon her fever broke and she became fully conscious. It was apparent she'd run herself into the ground until her body revolted. Now she had no choice but to rest and take better care of herself because if she didn't, her body would force her to.

Julia shifted and moaned. She opened her eyes and looked around the room until her gaze found Ethan's.

"Hi, beautiful. How do you feel?"

"Like I've been run over by a dump truck," she croaked. "Where am I? Where's Lilly?"

"You're at my place. Lilly's fine. I spoke to Aimee and they're having a picnic in the park and then meeting up with Lexi to go shopping. Today's Saturday around 1:30."

Julia was confused and frowned at him. "Saturday? How did I get here? The last thing I remember was talking to you in the cafeteria."

"You were pretty out of it. You had a high fever. I brought you here and force-fed you juice and Tylenol. I think you'll be fine. Your fever broke a few hours ago. Feel like a little soup?"

"Soup would be good. Thanks for taking care of me. I'm sorry to be so much trouble."

"You were no trouble at all, but you're in big trouble. I'm not happy you've not been taking care of yourself. Baby, you look like you've lost ten pounds and you haven't been sleeping either, have you? This madness has got to stop. We've got to stop torturing each other. We love each other too much for this."

Looking down, Julia mumbled, "I know. I'm sorry."

"Jules, no more apologies and no more running away. We've got to talk about things. Let's get you showered and fed and then we'll talk if you feel up to it. We've got all the time in the world."

Julia met his gaze and nodded. It was time.

While Ethan warmed some soup and changed the sheets on the bed, Julia showered and dressed in a one of his t-shirts and boxers. They were massive on her, but they were clean. By the time she was done, she was exhausted. He propped her up in bed with pillows and insisted on feeding her soup. After more juice and medication, she couldn't keep her eyes open. He tucked her into bed, kissed her on her forehead and instructed her to close her eyes and sleep. Without a fight, she did as she was told and drifted off.

As she slept, Ethan went out and bought a few groceries so he could cook them a light dinner. Then he stopped by her house and let himself in using the key she gave him months earlier. In her closet, he found a small overnight bag and packed some clothes and toiletries he thought she would need. He decided to search her dresser for underwear and the yoga pants she always wore when she was home. In the top dresser drawer, he stopped and stared down at the blue velvet jewelry box that contained the locket. Without even giving it a second thought, he reached for the box and placed it in the bag with all the other necessities he packed.

Ethan made it back to his house in plenty of time to cook a light pasta dish. He checked on Julia before he started cooking and found she was still sleeping. Leaving her overnight bag at the foot of the bed, he tiptoed out of the room and to the kitchen. As he finished making the salad, he tried to think of a way to broach the elephant in the room so Julia wouldn't close back up. They had to talk things out. He didn't want to lose her and he wouldn't let her decide the future for both of them without him having a say in things, not again.

"Hi."

Ethan hadn't heard Julia walk into the room. She'd changed into clean clothes and looked much better. She was still way too thin and the dark circles were still there, but she was regaining some of her energy.

"Hi yourself. How are you feeling?"

"Much better, thanks. What smells so good?"

"It's just some pasta with chicken. Hungry?"

"Surprisingly yes. I haven't had much of an appetite lately, but I'm starving now. What can I do to help?"

"Nothing. Just sit. Everything's ready."

He served them both and brought their plates to the table along with the salad and some lemonade. He ate and was pleased to see her appetite reappeared. She avoided his eyes and he ate in silence and waited her out. When she said she had enough, although she hardly made a dent in the small portion he gave her, he stood and started to clear the table.

"That was wonderful, thank you. Thanks for also getting my clothes. I'm sorry to have been such trouble. I feel much better though. You can take me home whenever you're ready."

So that was the way she was going to play this. Ignore the waltzing pink elephant and act as if they were nothing more than friends. Well, he wasn't falling for it. He knew without a doubt she loved him and the more he thought about her odd behavior, the more he concluded his girl was trying to protect him. The thing was, he could survive anything but losing her again, and she needed to know that.

"I'm glad you liked it and I'm glad you're feeling better, but you're kind of stuck here. Your car is still at the hospital and I'm not driving you back until we've talked things out. I'm not in a hurry and we can do this at your pace. I don't want to exhaust you, but we both can't go on like this. Look at me, Julia."

He waited until she raised her head and he was able to capture her eyes. He wanted to make sure he had her full attention for this next part.

"Julia, I love you. I know I was an ass when I was dealing with my father's death and I'm sorry. I think I know what you've been doing. I'm sorry I didn't see it earlier and I'm sorry I didn't push earlier, but it's clear to me now. You've been protecting me from something, something in the past. Baby, I love you for loving me enough to try to do that, but no more. I won't let you keep doing that if it means losing you."

Ethan stopped talking when she didn't say anything. Julia's eyes were big and filled with apprehension. He stood, went around the table and pulled her up. Before she could protest, he kissed and walked them both to the new overstuffed loveseat she'd helped him pick out a month ago. Sitting down, he pulled her into his lap and held her against him. Not only did this guarantee she couldn't get away, it also fed his need to feel her body against his. God, he missed her!

"Do you trust me, Jules?"

Without a second's hesitation, she answered, "Yes, of course I do."

He hugged her to him and smiled. "Good, baby. Here's what we're going to do. I'm going to sit here and hold you and when you're ready, you're going to tell me a story, one that you should've told me a long time ago.

Okay?"

Julia stiffened in his arms and the pulse in her neck hammered a mile a minute. He waited her out. He sat and stroked her hair and rubbed her back and every once in a while he gave her a kiss on her forehead, or cheek, or nose. After what seemed like an eternity, she began to speak in a small, sad voice.

Julia told him of some of the encounters she had with his mother when they were dating and how those cutting comments left her feeling cheap and never quite good enough for him. She never told him about some of the more vicious comments because she didn't want to be the cause of even more division between him and his family. She'd wanted his family to love her, to embrace her as Ella had him and when the opposite happened, she came close to breaking up with him for his own good several times. The problem was, she wasn't strong enough to do so—not until she was given no other choice.

No other choice. Those words and the terror he heard in her voice had his pulse racing. Why hadn't he done this earlier? Why hadn't he forced the issue earlier so he could help her carry the burden, so she didn't live with the fear he saw in her eyes from the second their eyes connected at Lexi's? Why did he walk away from her, from them, so many years ago? He'd blamed her for tearing them apart, but wasn't he equally to blame for not fighting for them harder? They had both been young, not children, but certainly not adults, but he was the man. He should have fought harder.

When Julia stopped talking and looked at him questioningly, Ethan gave her a soft kiss on the forehead and continued stroking her back.

"I'm with you, baby. I'm here and this time, I'm not going anywhere. No need to fear. I'll catch you."

Julia turned in his arms and searched his face, for what, he didn't know. She laid her hand against his cheek and he leaned into it.

"Ethan, twenty-years ago, I learned the definition of love and sacrifice the hard way. I walked away from you and everything we meant to each other, not because I didn't love you and suddenly wanted my freedom, but because I had no choice. I had to protect Ella and I had to protect you. My world narrowed and everyone and everything I held dear was threatened. You are the love of my life. I would give anything to shield you from the pain the truth will bring, but I see I can't shield you, not if we're going to be together. And Ethan—you're my whole life. I can't risk losing you again."

Ethan took Julia's face in his hands and kissed her tenderly, tasting the saltiness of her tears. He laid his forehead against hers and whispered, "That's never going to happen again. You're not going to lose me because I'm never letting you go, not again."

Julia's eyes locked with his for a few minutes and she must have found what she needed because she turned and settled against him with a heavy sigh. She picked up her story a few weeks before their high school graduation. She told him of his father's visits to the ice-cream parlor and his offer to fund her future. On some level Ethan was shocked, but on another level he could see his father pulling out all the stops to get his way. Still, he was certain there was more to the story.

He was right.

Julia trembled in his arms as she told him about the night of Ella's attack. She recalled waking up from a deep sleep to the sound of banging on the front door. It sounded like any minute the front door was going to cave in and to this day, this is the sound she startles awake to when she dreams of that horrible night. It's the sound she associates with her world, as she knew it, collapsing.

In a shaky, yet determined voice, Julia described the two policemen that came to the front door. She remembered every detail, from the color of their eyes to their approximate height and weight. Ethan recognized the two men because he'd seen them two days prior in his father's study and thought it was odd. When Julia told Ethan of the message the police officer gave her from his father as he dropped her off in front of the emergency room, Ethan's brain misfired and for a second he thought he might be having a stroke. His vision blurred, he stopped breathing, and he was fairly certain his heart skipped a beat or two or ten.

Julia was lost in the past, however, and didn't notice his distress. She continued the story without missing a beat, recalling the sheer terror that gripped her when she saw Ella lying in the hospital bed, broken and battered and how afraid and alone she felt. She told of the overwhelming guilt she felt for Ella's attack because she could have prevented it if she wasn't so weak and she'd done what his father directed. She recalled the terror she lived with every day for months even years after the attack, worried his father or his goons would show up again and this time kill her or Ella.

There was no one to turn to. No family or friends other than Aimee to rely on and no police to report his father to. In her eyes, Mayor Sullivan was all powerful, a force she couldn't conquer. She was by herself at the age of eighteen dealing with a problem most adults would have difficulty fathoming.

Although it caused her indescribable pain, Julia was relieved when Ethan finally gave up and left because she and Ella would be safe. Finally, Julia told him of the all-consuming depression that gripped her after losing him and how she even considered taking her own life on more than one occasion. If it weren't for Aimee, she probably would have. She was certain her life was over. It was almost two years before she could sleep the night through without waking up crying for him, years before she could breathe without pain slicing through her.

Ethan was sick. His head spun as his world shifted from what he thought he knew about his family to the terrible reality Julia was revealing. He believed every word Julia said. She had no reason to lie, but he couldn't assimilate all the facts, not yet. His elderly mother who proclaimed her love for her husband and son to anyone who'd listen was, in actuality, a ruthless bitch who tortured an innocent girl that wanted so much to please her. Worse, the father he'd just buried and was still mourning had been a monster.

Ethan knew his father had been a hard, uncompromising man, but the man Julia was describing was a not anyone he recognized and certainly not anyone he would've wanted to know let alone love and mourn. His father had terrorized Julia and Ella, hired people to threaten and hurt them. His father had preyed on two helpless women. Why? Because he could and because he would do anything to get his way. What kind of soulless deviants had given birth to him?

Growing up, Ethan and his parents hadn't agreed on much, but this was beyond anything Ethan could imagine. Ethan had learned to accept his father for who he was and he even admired him for some of the wonderful youth programs he put in place before he left politics. Ethan had forgiven him for the harshness by which he treated him when he was a young man, but this was unforgivable. The rage he felt now was overwhelming and it was a good thing his father was dead because if he'd still been alive, Ethan would not have been able to control his actions. His mind raced, his head pounded, and his stomach revolted.

"Ethan?"

"Hmm."

"Please say something. I'm sorry. I … It's okay. I'll go. I'll call Aimee and ask her to pick me up. I'm…" Julia started to pull away from him and out of his lap, her voice trembling and unsure.

Ethan was dazed, unable to put a string of words together to express what he was feeling, but he was alert enough to know what he needed from Julia right at this moment. He needed her, plain and simple. He needed to hold her and keep her safe as he should've done, as he failed to do. He needed to feel her in his arms. He tightened his hold on her and kept her firmly in his lap.

"Jules, sit still baby. It's okay. Just give me some time to digest all of this."

Julia immediately stilled. She sat in his lap and encircled him with her arms, hugging him to her. She laid her head against his chest. He sat lost in his thoughts remembering the days after Ella was attacked. He recalled how his parents acted when he told them of the attack. They didn't say much except the hospital was in a dangerous part of town and these things happened all the time. He remembered thinking they were wrong. The hospital was not in a particularly bad area and things like this never happened in their town. It had been a bizarre attack and was reported as such by the media.

Ethan's parents never acknowledged the fact he no longer mentioned Julia anymore. They acted like she never existed and even ignored his deep depression. When he told them he changed his mind and would be attending Duke, they said he made the right decision. That was it. At the time he didn't think anything of his parents' odd behavior. They weren't demonstrative or particularly warm people. He assumed they got what they wanted and wanted to keep the peace by not discussing anything controversial.

As Ethan sat deep in thought, time passed and the room darkened as the sun went down. Julia's breathing became steady and deep. In time, Ethan looked down and found she'd fallen asleep in his arms still holding him tightly to her. He stood and carried her to the bedroom. When he laid her in bed, she opened her eyes and sleepily gazed at him. She was exhausted, he could see that, but she was also afraid. Perhaps she was afraid he was angry for keeping this significant part of his life from him or that he blamed her somehow. If he knew Julia, and he did, it could be just about anything.

Julia carried the weight of the world on her shoulders. He needed to find the words to reassure and soothe her. She'd protected him for so long, but it was time he took over. Ethan wanted her to know the past no longer had any power over them. They brought the demons out into the light and in time, together, they would conquer them. Julia wasn't alone any longer. She and Lilly had him from now on. Together they would create a life filled with beauty. She would never feel so alone, so scared again that she would need to wrap her arms around herself because his arms would be there, holding her, shielding her, and loving her.

Ethan sat on the edge of the bed and brushed Julia's hair off her face. He needed time to work this shit out in his mind and once he did, he would find a way to lay the past to rest and put it behind him, behind them … somehow. She had years to come to terms with the past, but he'd known for approximately two and half hours.

"It's going to be okay, Jules. Go to sleep now. We'll talk more in the morning."

She searched his face. Reaching up, she cupped the side of his face with her hand and caressed his cheek with her thumb. "I love you, Ethan. I'm sorry sweetheart. I don't know what else to say. I didn't want to hurt you with this. I don't want to lose you. I love you."

He took the hand on his face in his and placed a kiss right in the center of her palm. "You're never going to lose me. I love you, baby. Nothing is going to change that. Now sleep. I'll be okay. We'll talk again in the morning."

Chapter Nineteen

It was almost 3 a.m. when Ethan slid into bed next to Julia. He reached for her and she went to him, molding herself to his side and laying her head on his chest. He didn't say anything. He didn't have to. He was hurting and she hurt for him. She kissed his chest and wrapped her arm around his abdomen and squeezed. Wordlessly, he squeezed her back. They slept wrapped in each other's arms the rest of the night.

As sunlight streamed through the curtains and directly into Julia's eyes, she wondered what this day would bring. She woke up a half hour earlier and couldn't lie still anymore. She wanted to get up, clean up, and check on Lilly and Aimee, but she didn't want to wake Ethan. She waited as long as she could, but then her bladder made the decision for her. She slid out of bed and moved as quietly as she could toward Ethan's newly-renovated bathroom.

The bathroom was beautifully updated to include a massive walk-in shower with multiple showerheads that she enjoyed briefly yesterday. As Julia brushed her teeth, she decided that a shower would do her good. She turned on the shower and as the water warmed and steam filled the room, she stripped out of her clothes and stepped under the steaming water.

Julia let the water massage her body from all angles. Although she felt better than she had the last few days, she was still a bit rundown. She closed her eyes, took deep breaths, and tried to get her muscles to relax as she thought about all that happened over the last few days. Matt walked out of Lilly's life and out of her life for good. She couldn't help but feel his loss, not for herself, but for Lilly. Then there was Ethan. The veil of secrets she'd held on to for so long was finally lifted and she could breathe.

Julia had done almost all the talking last night. It was a lot for anyone to take in and poor Ethan was overwhelmed. She wondered how he would feel about everything once he had time to digest it. Things always looked different in the morning. He was up most of the night pacing. This old house creaked with his every step. But at the end of the day, she was relieved it was all out in the open. No matter what the future brought, a huge weight was lifted off her shoulders and she felt lighter and freer than she had in a long time.

Cold air hit Julia's body and her eyes flew open to find Ethan with his beautifully sculpted, very naked body entering the shower. She took him in, her eyes devouring his sexy tousled hair, broad shoulders, muscular chest, flat abdomen, then continuing lower to follow his happy trail. When she saw his erection jutting out rigid and thick in front of him, she licked her lips.

She jumped when she felt his hand on her hip pulling her toward him. Their bodies collided skin on skin and it felt magnificent. She met his smoldering eyes and took in his soft smile before he took her mouth in a deep, wet, passionate kiss.

Julia sighed and melted against him. God, she needed this. They both needed this. They needed to connect on an intimate level again. It had been too long and she missed the feel of his hard body against hers and the reassuring sound of his heart beat. Her arms encircled his neck, pulling him even closer, unable to get enough of her man.

Ethan was a starved man. He feasted on her lips and then licked and nipped his way to her jaw, down her neck and to her breast, sucking hungrily on her nipple as one of his hands kneaded her other breast and rolled her nipple between his thumb and forefinger.

She held his head to her as he switched breasts and she arched into his mouth, loving the delicious sensations he was eliciting with his mouth. He walked her backward until her back hit the wall of the shower then lifted one of her legs to wrap around his waist as he continued his kiss. Her arms went around him and the fingernails of one hand dug into his back while the other hand kneaded his firm buttocks.

Ethan's hand found its way between them and he ran his fingers down her body to her center where he zeroed-in on her clit and rubbed it in circles with his thumb. Her eyes rolled to the back of her head as she felt the pressure build. Then he entered her with two fingers. She dropped her head back against the wall and let out a moan, calling his name as he pumped his fingers in and out of her fast and deep. He took her nipple in his mouth and bit down. That was it! An electric current ran down her spine and spread through every cell in her body. The pressure that built exploded and she let go crying out her release into the side of his neck as her body clamped down on his fingers.

When she floated back to Earth, her eyes opened and she gazed up at him with flushed cheeks and smiled. Her muscles were mush and she was deliciously sated.

"Good morning," she said against his lips.

"Morning baby. Hope you don't mind me sharing your shower."

"Nope. You can do that anytime you like."

"Glad to hear it because I plan to … a lot."

They took turns under the shower and she reveled in his touch when he ran the soap over her body and lathered his hands to massage it into every crevice. She returned the favor and when she felt his erection push against her belly, she decided it was time to return that favor as well.

Julia took charge and kissed Ethan, pouring all the love and passion she felt for him into that single kiss. She traced his lips with her tongue then kissed him deeper as her tongue explored every inch of his mouth. Her hands explored every inch of him, gliding over the muscles of his abdomen, chest, shoulders, back, and buttocks. When she made her way to his erection and firmly grasped him in her hand, it was his turn to moan. She smiled to herself, delighting in the knowledge she could give him such pleasure.

She ran the pad of her thumb over the tip of his erection, gathered the pre-cum that formed, and looked into his eyes as she brought her thumb to her mouth and sucked. He watched her with hooded eyes, enjoying the show.

"My turn. I want to taste you," she said with a sensuous smile as she turned off the shower, took his hand, and led him out.

Ethan grabbed a towel and wrapped her in it then grabbed another and hastily dried off as she led him to the bedroom. There she dropped her towel and dropped to her knees in front of him. She was nervous. They hadn't done this before and she wanted to please him. In all the time she was married to Matt, she only took him in her mouth a few times. She didn't enjoy it and although he got off, she was never sure if he enjoyed it either.

She raised her eyes up to Ethan and saw the love shining in his eyes as he stroked her hair away from her face then stroked her cheek. He was letting her lead and giving her time to do whatever she wanted at her own pace. She took him in her hands again, caressing the head of his erection with her thumb and enjoying its velvety soft texture. Bending down, she took him in her mouth and ran her tongue over the tip, tasting him.

She moaned as she took him deeper and rolled her tongue over him. God, she loved the way he tasted. She sucked and licked him up and down as her hand gripped him firmly and moved with her mouth. His hands slid through her hair as he guided her movements. When she took him even deeper and hollowed her cheeks sucking harder, he groaned and pumped into her mouth with abandon, finding his rhythm. Then she swallowed and he cried her name out, tensed and with a shudder came hard.

When his hand relaxed in her hair, she pulled away, giving him one final lick. The satisfied look on his face left no doubt he enjoyed himself and seeing that, she decided they'd be doing this a lot more.

"Come here, beautiful," he said as he pulled her to her feet and in his arms where he held her to him.

Julia buried her face in Ethan's neck and wrapped her arms around him, holding him to her. She gave a small yelp of surprise when her feet left the ground and Ethan carried her back to the bed. She asked him one time why he carried her everywhere and he said, "Because I can." She wasn't complaining. She loved being carried and held by her possessive caveman.

Ethan placed her on the bed and went to his dresser. He removed a clean t-shirt and a pair of boxers from the drawer. When he was dressed, he made his way to her, stopping at her bag on the floor.

He rummaged through her bag. In his hands he held a t-shirt, a clean pair of her panties, and the blue velvet jewelry box containing the locket. When she saw the box, her eyes filled with tears and she dropped her head. He didn't say a single word. Rather he let his eyes do the talking, eyes that were tender and overflowing with love for her it was impossible to miss. He brushed her tears away with his thumbs and placed a soft kiss to her lips. Then he dressed her, brushed out her wet hair, and took the locket out of its box, slipping it over her head.

"Oh Ethan, I…"

"Shh, baby. It's okay now. We're going to be okay. I love you."

"I know, Eth. I love you too, sweetheart."

Ethan arranged the pillows in the middle of the bed against the headboard. He got in and hauled Julia between his legs. She nestled against his chest and sighed. He held her for a long time stroking her hair and dropping kisses every now and then to the top of her head.

Julia felt the weight of the locket as it lay between her breast and she sighed happily. It had been painful taking it off and every day she spent without it she was lost. They still had a lot to talk about, but Ethan would start when he was ready. Unlike the stories he made up for her and Lilly, the story she told him was unfortunately not a fairytale. Julia had carried the truth and all its ugliness around with her for years. Now, Ethan had to face those demons.

"I'm sorry, Julia. Those words will never be good enough, but I want you to know. I'm sorry," Ethan said in a tortured voice.

Surprised, Julia turned around and straddled him. She took his face in her hands. "Eth, you didn't do anything. None of what happened was your fault. This had to do with your father, not you. I don't blame you. I never did and Ella never did. She didn't know anything about her attacker other than he was an African American male. He was never found."

Taking her hands away from his face, Ethan kissed them and held them to his chest. "I was supposed to protect you. Instead, because of me, and my family, you went through hell and you did it alone, carrying the weight of the world on your shoulders—trying to protect Ella and me at the same time. You're an incredible woman. I don't know what I've done to deserve you."

"Sweetheart, there is nothing you could have done to protect me. You were just as young as I was and your father was a force, a beast of a man. You couldn't have stopped him. In their own twisted way, he and your mother wanted the best for you and, in their eyes, I wasn't it. I wasn't the best. I wasn't even close."

"That's not true. You were the best for me. You are the best for me, the very best. They never took the opportunity to get to know you. There's no excuse for their behavior, no explanation good enough to ever justify what they did. I wish there was."

Julia saw the overwhelming sadness that lingered in Ethan's eyes. She wished she could say or do something to make this better, easier for him. She brushed his lips with hers and said, "Thank you sweetheart. You're the best for me as well, the only one for me. The past is just that, the past, and we have to learn to bury it if we're going to have a future. We can't let it rule us anymore."

Ethan held Julia to him and kissed the top of her head. "Thank God we found each other again. I understand why you didn't tell me about all this when we were young, but why didn't you tell me when we first got back together? I'm not angry, I just need to know."

There were so many ways to answer that question, but Julia guessed there was one thing she could say that would explain everything. There was one phrase that, by itself, provided all the explanation he needed.

"I love you, Ethan. I've loved you since the first time I saw you in biology class when I was just sixteen and I always will. In many ways it was torture keeping the truth from you, but it was easy loving you. When you love someone, you do what you have to in order to spare them pain. I never wanted you to know because I knew the truth would hurt you. Even though they were horrible to me, your parents loved you. I would never deny you the love of a parent. I wanted you to have something I never had … good, pure memories of loving parents. I thought I could keep the past buried and not let it affect our future, but I couldn't."

Julia dropped her head and rested her forehead against his chest. His arms began to rub her back in lazy, soothing circles. She stopped speaking for a minute, battling with herself on how to say what she needed to say. This was the time to tell him everything, to bring everything to the surface so they could bury the past and start fresh. She took a deep breath and continued in a trembling voice.

"Every time you spoke of your dad, the past came rushing back and I was gripped with sheer terror. I was afraid of how your parents would react once they found out I was back in your life. I know we are adults, but I was afraid your father would retaliate. Then he got sick and died and Ethan, sweetheart, I'm sorry, but I couldn't say what you needed to hear. I couldn't say I was sorry. I was relieved. I no longer had to live in fear. The person who'd hurt Ella, terrorized me, and torn us apart was gone. God help me, but I was relieved. I'm sorry Ethan, but that's the truth. It's how I felt and how I still feel."

Julia felt Ethan stiffen. She'd gone too far. She started to pull away from him, unable to look at him for fear of what she may see in his eyes and on his face. Ethan had stopped rubbing her back when she talked about his father's death and Julia didn't know what he was thinking. Perhaps he needed space to consider her words. She couldn't take it back and she wasn't sure she would, even if she could.

Julia scooted away from Ethan's warm body and was just about off the bed when two big arms wrapped around her waist and hauled her back so she was sitting once more between his legs with her back resting against his chest. Ethan dropped his head into her hair and inhaled deeply. He kissed the side of her neck as his arms tightened around her.

"Beautiful, I want you to listen to me. I get it now. It all makes sense. I wish I could go back and change the past in so many ways, but I can't. If I could, *I* would have protected you. *I* would have spared you all that pain because I love you and have loved you for as long as I can remember. It's going to take me a while to digest and deal with my father's actions. I want to know what part my mother played in all of this and figure out what to do. I'll work on it and I'll deal with it. Once that's done, I'll put it away for good because we have a lifetime ahead of us and we're not going to spend it reliving the past or giving the past power over us. Okay?"

"Yeah, Eth." Julia turned her head, tipped it up and caught his lips in a deep kiss filled with love and promise of the future. She straightened and straddled him once again and he gathered her close, hugging her to him.

"There's just one more thing, beautiful," he said into her hair. "I want you to promise me something and then I'll promise you something in return."

"Anything, sweetheart."

"Promise me that from now on, you'll never keep anything from me, not even to protect me. Let me share in your life, the bad with the good. I want to start a life with you and Lilly. You're the family I've always dreamed of having. We can't have secrets, though. Secrets are a destructive force in any relationship. We've had more than our share of drama and heartache all because of secrets."

"Okay, I promise. No more secrets."

"Good, baby." He brushed her lips with his. "Here's what I'm going to promise you, in return." Looking down, he reached for the locket and opened the angel wings to reveal the inscription.

"I promise with all my heart that I will love you and Lilly, forever. I promise that in my hands, your hearts will be safe. You can wear this locket every day if you want, but I'm going to make it so you don't need a reminder of my love. You're going to know it as the absolute truth every day when you wake up until the second you close your eyes and beyond into your dreams."

Ethan took her mouth in a deep kiss that left no doubt he meant every word. In his arms Julia found everything she ever wanted and everything she ever needed. Their love had survived twenty-two years of separation, and that was enough—enough loneliness and enough pain. They had their quota of misery and now it was time for happiness to come and stay a while, maybe even forever.

The End

www.norahbennett.com

NORAH BENNETT

EVERNIGHT PUBLISHING ®

www.evernightpublishing.com